SECRET OF THE LOST PLANET

By
DAVID WRIGHT O'BRIEN

Illustrated by
Julian S. Krupa

I0616680

ARMCHAIR FICTION
PO Box 4369, Medford, Oregon 97504

*For more information about Armchair Books and products, visit our
website at…*

www.armchairfiction.com

Or email us at…

armchairfiction@yahoo.com

THRUST INTO THE BOWELS OF A PLANET OF NO RETURN

All Wade Baron wanted to do is get back to Earth. He'd given three years of his life to government service and now it was time to go home. His fiancée would be waiting for him, and Wade practically glowed at the thought of their reunion. The image of her beautiful face was foremost in his mind. But there's nothing worse than a rude homecoming, and that's what Wade got when he stepped onto Terran soil after three years of charting asteroids out in the loneliest sector of the Solar System. First he was arrested as a traitor; then he was banished to the planet Cardo, home of the worst Penal Colony in the Galaxy. And all of this at the hands of the man Baron believed to be his best friend. It had to be a joke of some kind—but it wasn't; and soon Wade found himself on a spaceship headed for a planet where escape was impossible and death was a certainty.

FOR A COMPLETE SECOND NOVEL, TURN TO PAGE 77

CAST OF CHARACTERS

WADE BARON
He'd been stuck on a lonely planetoid for three years, charting asteroids. Going home to Earth would be great, or so he thought.

MATT MARKHAM
He was Wade's best friend, and he had promised to take good care of Nada while Wade was gone—<u>real</u> good care of her.

HANNES JARDON
In some ways he was probably the most brilliant scientist on Earth. So why did he end up on a deep space penal colony?

NADA WARREN
She was a real sweetheart of a young woman, totally loyal to the man she loved—even if he hadn't been around for three years.

CARSE JENKINS
He'd come to take Wade home— back to Earth after three years of government service. But why didn't he seem more chummy?

THE UNIFYER
This powerful leader of Earth's government didn't realize how close he was to losing his job—permanently!

CHAPTER ONE
A Close Shave

"THREE years," Wade Baron told himself happily as he stuffed the last of his space gear into the supply crates, "three long and lonely years on this God-forsaken rock in space. But I'm going back today!"

Wade whistled cheerfully and inspected his strong, clean-shaven jaw in the mirror above his bed. The three years he had lived alone on Planetoid Jaytwo, three years of solitude spent compiling charts for the Asteroid Survey Department, had enabled him to grow a beard as long as a fur coat. But now the beard was gone, for he'd shaved this morning. Shaved in honor of his start back to Earth.

He had even combed his lank black hair carefully, after doing a sketchy job of trimming it with his chart scissors. Combed his hair carefully while thinking of the girl who waited for him on Earth. The girl whom he would marry immediately upon his return, Nada Warren.

"Whoopee!" he chortled. "Damn, but it'll be fine to see Nada once more."

Now that the three lonely years were at an end. Wade was able to see that they had been worth it. Not only from the asteroid research he had been able to compile here on Jaytwo, but from the fact that his service here would be rewarded with a splendid post on Earth—at a fine salary that would enable Wade and Nada to live in luxury.

"Nada, an Earth position in the Survey Bureau, and plenty of dough on which to be happy! Wow...it's going to be great." Wade told the silent crates.

He sat down on the edge of his bed, after the last of the gear had been packed into the crates, and tried to picture his return. Nada would be at the Space Base, of course. She'd probably been marking the days to his return just as eagerly as he had. Nada would be there, of course.

Matt Markham, good old Matt, one of his closest pals, would more than likely be waiting there for him also. Matt was a grand guy. He'd been fine about seeing to it that Nada wouldn't be lonely during Wade's absence. The sort you could trust with the girl you were going to marry, that was Matt Markham.

Wade ground out his cigarette impatiently and rose to peer into the radio-receptor that had been installed in the corner of his tiny quarters. He saw nothing but the bleak expanse of little Jaytwo. It was hard to hold back his impatience. The Space Patrol ship, which was to pick him up and take him back to Earth, should be due pretty soon.

He lighted another cigarette and grinned.

"I'll probably go crazy at the sight of that patrol ship," he told himself. "More than likely want to kiss the pilot."

Even as he inhaled deeply from his cigarette, a faint humming started from the sound vibrator in the radio-receptor. In a single bound Wade was across the room, his hands trembling slightly as he tuned in the receptor to a higher volume. The humming grew into a louder and louder snarl. Peering into the view-sights, Wade felt his heart pound excitedly against his ribs, for there, approaching Jaytwo from the northerly end, was a Space Patrol Ship!

Then and there, in the solitary silence of the little room that had been his only home for three years, Wade Baron went into a dance reminiscent of the ancient movements of the Indian tribes that had inhabited Earth centuries before.

"Wow..." Wade repeated over and over again. "I'm acting like a fool, but I can't help it. Oh, Lord, I can't help it!" His eyes, glowing happily, were also a little moist around the crinkled corners.

LESS than fifteen minutes later, Wade was racing across the barren plain outside his cabin, rushing to greet the members of the Space Patrol Ship, which had just slipped to a graceful landing on Jaytwo. His long legs ate up the distance between his tiny shack and the spaceship, and even in the cumbersome clinging thickness of his space suit, he made speed.

Wade could see the percussion doors of the ship swinging open, could see the glass-helmeted heads of the crew peering forth, and he wanted to shout with joy at the sight of the lettering on the side of the craft. Huge, red, block letters that said, "Government Space Patrol." He wondered for a swift instant whether or not there would be anyone he knew in the crew. Any of his pals from the patrol service. He hoped so. But even if there weren't, just the sight of human beings was enough to send his heart leaping joyously.

He was almost able to make out the faces of the glass-helmeted patrolmen, but as yet he couldn't tell if he knew any of them. One of the crew—evidently the Flight Patrol Leader, for he was clad in a rich purple space suit—had already clambered to the rock terrain of Jaytwo. Wade could discern his features now, sharp and space-burned, like those of countless space pilots. This chap had a short pointed moustache and a deep scar across his brow.

Wade frowned. He couldn't remember any such person in the ranks of Patrol Pilots. But then, three years had passed, and the roster had undoubtedly changed a bit since the last time Wade had had contact with Earth.

The receptor mechanism on Wade's space suit hummed, an indication that the Flight Patrol Leader was speaking to him. Wade threw the reception switch wide, and the visitor's voice flooded into his helmet.

"Hello, there," said the Flight Patrol Leader, "you're Wade Baron, I imagine."

"Well," Wade grinned in answer, "I'm not Doctor Livingstone, old chap."

The Flight Patrol Leader, members of his crew following behind him, drew closer, so that Wade saw the answering grin flashing across his face.

"You sound glad to see us, Baron. My name is Jenkins, Carse Jenkins, Flight Patrol Leader for this ship. Have you your gear and equipment packed?"

Wade was finally alongside of him, taking the Flight Leader's outstretched gauntlet in a firm grip of greeting.

"Lord, Jenkins, I've had that gear packed and ready to go for the last three years!"

There was laughter from the lean Jenkins and a like response from the members of his crew. Good bunch, Wade thought; seem like fine chaps, all of them. The six or seven crewmembers passed Wade on their way to his tiny quarters to get his crates. Jenkins, still grinning, said, "They'll bring all your gear along, Baron. Come on into the ship with me, fellow, and we'll have a drink on your return."

"A swell idea," Wade answered. "The first swell idea I've heard in three years!"

CHAPTER TWO
Arrested For—What?

IN THE FLIGHT LEADER'S CABIN in the Space Patrol ship, Wade faced Carse Jenkins. Minus his space suit, the lean Jenkins looked slightly older than he had seemed to Wade at first sight. There was a gray tinge at his temples. But he was jovial, entertaining, Wade thought as he sipped his drink.

"And tell me," asked Wade, "how Matt Markham is getting along? Is he still with the Survey Bureau?"

Carse Jenkins looked at the glass he held in his thin strong fingers.

"No," he said after a moment. "Markham has been promoted."

Wade's enthusiasm was sincere.

"Great," he said, "that's swell to hear. Mark deserves all he gets. He's a smart chap. Always was. Knew what he wanted all along."

"Yes," Jenkins answered dryly. "Markham always knew what he wanted. But what's more important, he knew how to go about getting it."

Suddenly, and with no explanation as far as Wade could see, there was an embarrassed silence between himself and the Flight Patrol Leader. Perhaps it had been due to Jenkin's slightly peculiar response to the mention of Matt Markham. Wade couldn't tell. But he decided to get on to other subjects.

"It'll be great to get back," Wade said quickly, feeling slightly foolish at repeating a phrase he must have used at least two dozen times so far.

"You don't seem like a bad sort at all," Jenkins said quite unexpectedly. At the words, and the tone in which they were uttered, Wade looked up sharply at the mustached Flight Patrol Leader.

"What made you say that?" Wade asked bewilderedly.

Jenkins suddenly looked hard at the glass in his hands.

"You've been completely out of touch with things for three years, Baron. Changes can occur in three years, y'know."

Wade was frowning now. He didn't know what was responsible for the odd manner of Jenkins. Didn't know, but he was going to try to find out.

"I don't get it," he said sharply. "What are you driving at?"

Jenkins looked up from his glass. Unexpectedly he smiled, once again the affable host.

"Not a thing, fellow. Forget it."

Wade could see that any chance of getting to the bottom of the scarred, mustached Flight Patrol Leader's strange attitude was closed. So he gave it up, gratefully gulping the cooling liquid of his drink. What the hell, just getting back to Earth once more. Earth and Nada was enough to think of for the moment. Earth and Nada.

"EARTH and Nada," Wade told himself two days later as he gazed out the front vision plates of the Space Patrol ship. In another half hour they would be at Space Base in New York.

Just the thought of Nada. Nada, who was probably waiting down there at Space Base at this very moment, was enough to send the tingling of eagerness rushing once more through Wade Baron. He fished into his pockets and found a cigarette, lighting it with hands that trembled in excitement.

Five times already this morning Wade had been back and forth between the baggage compartments and the control room, checking his baggage and gear. He had dressed himself carefully, even had one of the crew trim his hair more carefully, and smoothed his garments every so often. No sense in returning to Nada looking like a space bum.

"Lord," Wade muttered to himself, "I wish this crate would get some speed on. Here I've gone three years without a sight of Nada, and now a mere half hour seems like a century," He grinned to himself. "It seems like the time will never pass."

But the half hour finally passed for Wade Baron. And he found himself waiting for the landing gangway to be dropped as the Space Patrol Ship nosed into berth at Space Base.

"Little old New York!" Wade marveled, as the towering city revealed itself to him on every side. Down below the ship he could see the crowds forming beneath the spot where they would moor. His heart pounded wildly in his chest, threatening to leap to his mouth, and peering down, he tried to imagine which of the tiny dots representing people was Nada.

It seemed like ten glacier periods later that Wade stepped out onto the landing gangway to take his first deep breath of Earth air in three years—and to search the crowd eagerly for sight of Nada. He looked, too, for some sign of big, blond Matt Markham, who would probably be there with Nada to meet him. It was going to be grand to see them!

Wade took three steps downward, then he heard his first greeting.

"Wade Baron?"

He looked up at the speaker, surprised to see that it was a huge fellow in the uniform of a government guard. Behind the towering government guard, Wade saw at least a dozen others waiting at the bottom of the gang landing, all of them wearing the crimson tunics of guards.

"Yes," said Wade bewilderedly, eyes still scanning the crowd in an effort to find Nada and Matt. "Yes, I'm Wade Baron. What do you want?"

The towering government guard reached forth his hand. Perplexedly, Wade extended his own hand, wondering at this strange greeting. A moment later, and Wade Baron's wonder had turned to icy horror, for the officer deftly snapped steel wristbands around Wade's outstretched hand!

"You're under arrest," said the huge guard, "by order of Government…"

TURNING swiftly, the big guard beckoned to the others at the bottom of the landing. In an instant, Wade was surrounded by a crimson uniformed cordon.

"Search him," the officer directed one of his platoon.

Before he could move, before his bewildered brain could find an answer to this ghastly mistake, hands held Wade helpless, while other hands ran through his clothing.

"Here," said one of the guards, pulling forth a sheaf of papers from the lining of Wade's tunic. "He had these hidden in there…"

Wade's eyes went wide at the sight of the papers. What they were, he had no idea. How they got there, he was equally unable to explain. Terror clutched at his heart with icy fingers, closing down until Wade felt he could scarcely breathe.

"What is this?" Wade cried wildly. "What in the hell is this all about? I demand to know!"

The large government guard had taken the papers, was scanning them swiftly.

"Our information was correct," he said grimly. "These papers are all the proof we need." He turned again to Wade. "Baron," he rasped, "the charge against you is treason against the government."

"Treason?" Horror was closing in on Wade. "What is this all about? I've done nothing I tell you. Nothing!"

Suddenly a red haze swept his mind, and he lashed out with his free hand, catching one of the guards in the mouth. In a split-second, bodies closed in on him, and he was buried beneath the bludgeoning blows of his captors.

In the short, unequal struggle that followed, Wade thought he saw the grim, unsmiling face of Flight Patrol Leader Carse Jenkins looking down on the scene from the cabin of the ship. Then he was being dragged down the landing gangway, still surrounded by the crimson cordon of police.

Despairingly, Wade called out wildly.

"Matt, Matt Markham! Damn you swine! Let me find Matt Markham. He'll rectify this outrage!"

The huge government guard laughed shortly, unpleasantly.

"I suppose Markham is a friend of yours?"

"You're damn right he is. He's somewhere in this crowd. Ask him about me, you fools. He'll identify me!" Wade was near hysteria, the hysteria of red, burning rage.

"You'll see *Commissioner* Markham soon enough," the guard said harshly. "You're being picked up on his orders."

CHAPTER THREE
Matt Markham—True Friend

IT WAS A CONFUSED, badly beaten, and terribly bewildered Wade Baron who sat hunched dejectedly on a cell cot in Government Prison Ten, several hours later.

In his mind, Wade was desperately turning over the events of the past hours, trying to put them together, trying to link them to an answer to his ghastly nightmare. The huge guard's remark, calling Matt Markham *Commissioner,* had been the most bewildering of all. And yet it fitted in perfectly with Carse Jenkins' statement that Matt had been promoted. But Commissioner...! Why, next to the supreme post of Unifyer, the Commissioner's position was the most important on Earth!

Even so, even if Matt had risen to a position of such importance in three years, what could explain the fact that all this was the result—if the guard could be believed—of Matt's orders?

"It must be a joke, a stunt on Matt's part," Wade mumbled in confusion. But the bitter futility of the remark was evident in the cuts and bruises about his body. That was no part of a joke. And Nada—where had Nada been?

Where was Nada now? Had she been in the crowd? Had she been waiting for him? She knew that he was to return today. If she had been in the crowd she would most certainly have seen what happened. Most certainly she would have followed him to the prison, straightened the mess out. Especially since Matt was now Commissioner. She would have gotten in touch with Matt immediately, had him take care of the ghastly error.

Error! The word flashed neon-like into Wade's mind. Error? Of course it was an error. But what about those papers, those papers that had been found on his person. Wade was certain that he had never seen them before, had no knowledge, even, of their existence. They must have been planted on him without his being aware of it.

"It *must* be a joke," Wade insisted desperately. "Probably Matt didn't tell those stupid thug guards that it was a joke. They probably took the thing seriously. He probably didn't know they'd push me around like they did. It'll all be straightened out. Of course it will. Of course it will..."

But Wade Baron argued against himself without conviction. The facts, as they stood, pointed inevitably to one conclusion. A conclusion that he tried desperately to push to the back of his mind. He wouldn't accept it; he couldn't accept it, until he had seen Matt Markham.

WADE'S thoughts were interrupted by the sound of heavy heels ringing down the corridor leading to his cell. He sat up sharply, just in time to see a platoon of four guards, all in crimson tunics, halt before the door of his cell. A fifth guard, their leader, inserted a key into the lock of the door, and it swung inward.

Standing, Wade spoke.

"What now?" There was bitterness in his voice. "Where to?"

The guard leader, a cold, impassive little man, answered unconcernedly.

"To the Planet Chambers. You're to be heard by the Commissioner and the Board."

A chill swept over Wade. Matt Markham was going to see him. What would the outcome be? Jest? Or—he still hated to face the idea—an incredible double-cross?

Then, guarded on all sides, Wade was led through the bleak gray corridors. Silent, damp, monotonous cell blocks on every side. The place sent a chill of apprehension shuddering along Wade's back. They came, at length, to a great steel door that Wade remembered passing when he was led into the prison.

There were other crimson tuniced guards outside the door, armed only with the small but very deadly light-lugers, pistols that could turn a human being to a cinder from the distance of five hundred yards. These other guards looked at Wade curiously, but without a trace of compassion on their faces.

The guard leader who had taken Wade from his cell spoke to the men before the great steel door.

"Tell them," he said, "that we have the prisoner awaiting their pleasure."

Moments later, after disappearing through the door, the guard who had entered the chamber reappeared.

"You are to enter," he announced. "The Commissioner is waiting."

Noiselessly, the huge steel door swung open. Surrounded once again by the cordon of guards, Wade was led inside, into one of the most enormous and richly colored rooms he had ever beheld. Vast and high ceilinged, the place was a cross between a mighty cathedral and an inordinately large courtroom.

Towering pillars of marble reached to the ceiling, and the rich red rugs beneath Wade's feet were as soft as thick velvet. Drapes of golden mesh formed a covering to the coldness of the marble walls. At the far end of the room was a huge dais, constructed of black oak and draped in red.

It was in the center of this dais, surrounded on either side by lower dignitaries, that Matt Markham, Commissioner Matt Markham, sat watching the approach of the prisoner.

To Wade, who had never had occasion to enter the Justice Chambers before, the place was bewildering, awe-inspiring, in its utter splendor. Seeing Markham, Wade tried to catch his eye, but his friend was gazing abstractedly at a sheaf of papers, and it wasn't until Wade was led directly before him—at the center of the dais—that he looked up.

"Matt!" Wade blurted. "Matt, I'm glad to see you, fellow. Get this mess straightened out immediately, won't you? A joke is a joke, and all that, but these chaps don't seem to know it," He was grinning embarrassedly at Markham, but the glance that his friend returned was cold, thoughtful.

"Wade Baron?" Matt Markham asked icily, his bushy blond eyebrows knitting in a frown.

Wade gulped. He looked wildly from one to the other of the lesser officials seated around Markham, hoping to find some sign of levity in their eyes. This had to be a joke. It had to be!

Wade's eyes flashed back to Markham, swiftly appraising his friend, noting the slight changes that three years had brought about in him. He was heavier, Markham was, and his face was lined with a sternness that Wade had never seen before. His blond hair was closely cropped, and his wide mouth was set in a rigid uncompromising line. His eyes, as they bored down on Wade, were gray and flinty in their hardness. Something inside of Wade, something akin to instinct, told him that there was no levity here. Markham was playing no joke. There would be no mercy, no friendship.

"Wade Baron?" Markham repeated again, impatiently.

Red flushed up from Wade's collar, sweeping hotly to his lean features, to the crown of his lank black hair. His hands were moist and shaking as rage took possession of him.

"Markham," he said as evenly as he could. "I don't know what in the hell this is all about. You'd know that. But something pretty rancid is going on here. I've done nothing. If this is your idea of humor—"

"You are charged with treason," Markham broke in coldly, and Wade sensed a hidden mockery behind those flinty eyes. "Treason against Government is a crime punishable by death. We..." he waved his hand slightly to indicate the other dignitaries, "...have debated on your case for the past three hours. The papers found in your possession were enough to damn you. Definite evidences of your alliance with the enemies of Government have been proven. What have you to say in your defense?"

"Defense?" Wade exploded. "Defense? Defense against what? Defense against something about which I know nothing? I've never seen those papers you speak of, except for that moment at the Space Base when they were supposed to have been found in my pockets. I haven't even the slightest idea of what they contain. If they indicate treason, I can't even tell you how, or in what fashion they do so. This thing is a ghastly fraud, a horrible frame-up, Markham. I don't know what it's all about. But I know my rights. I demand public trial, an Open Chamber hearing on this thing!"

Markham shook his head slowly, and his voice softened as he spoke.

"We were friends at one time, Wade Baron. Everyone in this Chamber knows as much. But my duty has always been my sacred bond. I cannot go back on it. There have been many changes in the past three years—three years during which you were under constant observation on Jaytwo. You thought you were alone, isolated on a deserted little planet. You thought that your dealings with the enemies of Government could be carried on in perfect secrecy from such an isolated base. But that is where you made your error. Your movements were constantly watched by us. Intelligence had you under constant surveillance."

Wade's interrupting laugh was bitter. "Watched, watched was I? Watched while I charted my asteroid surveys? Watched while I worked night and day in the service of Government?"

Markham shook his head.

"The evidence has been compiled and presented to the court. The most damning piece we have against you is contained in the documents found on your person when you returned to Earth. We have reached our verdict, Wade Baron."

THE rage had drained from Wade, leaving his throat dry and choked, his eyes blurred with tears of futility and bewilderment. Was the cold official sitting upon the huge dais Matt Markham? Matt Markham the friend he had eagerly waited to see? Matt Markham, who had taken care of Nada for him during those three years? What had happened? And Nada, where was she at this moment?

"As I said," Markham continued, "the punishment for treason is death."

A chill swept Wade's spine at the words. He tried to open his mouth, tried to find words to protest. But the very coldness around him told him that resistance would be futile, laughably futile. He was framed, solidly, definitely, and there wasn't a thing in the world he could do about it. He ran his hand across his face, trying to wipe away the nightmare surrounding him.

"However," Markham went on, "we have decided that, inasmuch as your previous service to Government has been more than exemplary, we will commute your sentence to life imprisonment. Life imprisonment in the government penal institution on the planet Cardo."

Wade raised his eyes hopelessly to Markham. Cardo! Death, he knew, would have been far better than Cardo. Markham knew it, too. Wade was certain. A frame-up, not a chance to demand trial, resulting in the living hell of the Cardo penal institution!

Softly, as if from a great distance, Wade heard his own voice speaking.

"Markham," he was saying, "Markham, I don't know the why or where—for of this. But I do know one thing. I'll get you, Markham. I'll get you if it's the last thing in the universe I ever do..."

There was a caustic relish in Matt Markham's voice as he replied.

"And, of course, as far as the world is concerned, Wade Baron, you are dead. Your relatives and ah, er, friends..." Wade knew he meant Nada Warren. "...will be informed of your death. It will save them the knowledge of the shame and disgrace you have brought upon them."

The world at that moment, collapsed utterly around Wade Baron. Numbly, helplessly, he stood there, gazing dry-eyed at the man who had conspired this ruin for him. The man who would, in another hour, inform Nada Warren that her fiancé, Wade Baron, was dead!

To all appearances, as Wade stood there powerless against the forces that had crushed him, he was beaten, impotent, drained of all emotion. But deep inside his chest a spark had ignited a glowing coal. A fiercely burning resolve that was deeper than hate, stronger than any anger.

"Markham," Wade repeated dully, "you'll pay for this. Pay for it with every last bit of searing agony I can bring your soul..."

"The prisoner is committed to Cardo for the remainder of his natural life," Commissioner Markham declared, and a gavel fell heavily on the thick oak of the dais.

CHAPTER FOUR
Cardo, World of Living Hell

FROM the porthole of the prison spaceship, Wade Baron, shackled hand and leg to twenty other prisoners, watched the planet Cardo grow in the distance. The past twenty-four hours had been burning torment to his soul. Hustled back to the cell from which he'd been taken, Wade was given a change of tunic to the gray prison garb, then speedily and secretly taken to Space Base where the prison spaceship was waiting to carry its cargo of condemned humanity to the penal planet.

When the guards had fixed the shackles on him, Wade had had to force himself to hold back the rage that swept him. It would have been futile to struggle. He knew that much. Others among the twenty-one convicts had tried it and were even now whimpering over the ghastly burns inflicted on them by the merciless guards. Burns that would remain open sores for many months to come.

Wade forced himself to endure the indignities heaped on him by the Guards, and spent his time in observation of his fellow convicts. He noted, with growing surprise, that there were only four of them, at the most, who looked or acted like men of criminal nature. The rest, like him, were clear-eyed, upstanding, with an air of decency about them. They looked like professional, medical, or businessmen.

Wade was puzzled. What had been the crimes of these men? Had they, like himself, been railroaded, framed? But Cardo—at least as recently as three years previously—had not been a political prison. It had been a Quarantine planet for the scum and riff-raff of the criminal world.

As for the names of the other prisoners, there was no way in which Wade could ascertain who they were, or had been. The huge block numbers on the front of the prison gray tunics were all there was to identify them. Wade's was 397. The white-headed old man beside him was 408. He was of special interest to Wade. There was an air of aristocracy, dignity, about him that commanded respect. He was short, with an inquisitive way of holding his head, and had a white moustache and goatee.

As soon as he could do so without the knowledge of the guards, Wade spoke to him. The old man was gazing forth at the approaching penal planet, his expression inscrutable, through a porthole near Wade.

"That's going to be some home, eh?" Wade remarked dryly.

The old man turned wordlessly, looking at Wade as though in appraisal. At length he spoke.

"Yes," he said, "a lovely home, indeed. Constructed to shield the universe from swine, it is now going to conceal the universe from you and me."

"My name..." Wade began. The old man interrupted, holding up his hand.

"What difference does a name mean to either of us now?" he observed dryly. "We are numbered, like cattle. But if you must stand on formality, my young friend, my name is Hannes Jardon."

Wade about to reply with his own identification, stopped short and gasped.

"Jardon?" Then, reddening, he blurted, "Not *Professor* Jardon?"

The old man smiled, nodded.

"Yes, Professor Jardon." Then, before Wade could speak again, "What is your name?"

Wade told him hurriedly, then went on to express his utter astonishment at the professor's identity.

"But *you*, Professor, one of the greatest minds in modern science, what, how, that is, why are you here? Why are you a prisoner shackled aboard this ship?"

The old man shrugged.

"Does it make any difference now? You might ask Commissioner Markham. I believe he mentioned something about treason."

Wade was about to voice his amazement when a guard approached.

"Break it up," the crimson tuniced captor snarled. Wade moved clumsily away, hampered by his shackles, and the old man did likewise nodding his head to indicate that they would talk later.

IT was much later before Wade saw old Professor Jardon again. Three months later to be exact. Three months spent in the damp dungeons of Cardo. Three months living in comparative solitude broken only by the twice-daily sloppy rations pushed into his stinking little cell by a guard.

The prison on Cardo was an immense affair. Countless winding corridors, endless lines of stinking dungeons. Dungeons in which a man had only to extend his hands to either side to touch both walls at once. Dungeons the blackness of which was never broken, save on the twice-daily ration visits of the guards. Men were not meant to serve out their sentences on Cardo. It hadn't been designed for that. It was a place where men vanished. No one returned from Cardo—alive.

All this Wade Baron had heard. And all this he now knew to be true. There were cells adjoining his, cells above him, cells beneath him. And from these, through the long endless hours, Wade could hear the ceaseless sobbing of his fellow unfortunates.

The sobbing invariably followed the visits of the guards, and the sickening sound of their heavy blows on defenseless flesh. Wade wondered more than once why he was left unmolested. But solitude, to Wade Baron, was not enough to break him. He had lived alone for three years. On Jaytwo there had been no voices save his own, no thoughts save those he conjured. Even hell can be bearable if a man can listen to his own thoughts.

And Wade Baron had learned to do just that. For he had much to think about after his first several days of solitude in his cell on Cardo. Wade had managed to push remorse to the back of his mind, knowing that it is remorse and remorse alone that licks a man. Wade wasn't licked. Didn't intend to be licked. For there was his score, his score with Matt Markham and the others who had done this to him.

Revenge, carefully planned, diabolically matured, was the one factor that kept Wade Baron living on. And bit by bit, Wade was arriving at a scheme, a possible way to freedom, and the fulfillment of that revenge.

A scheme that grew still more plausible after those first three months had passed, that took definite shape on his meeting with Professor Jardon.

For some unaccountable reasons of generosity, Wade and ten of the prisoners who had arrived on Cardo with him, were permitted a brief glimpse of light, a brief breath of air, in the exercise yards of the prison.

Jardon was among those ten. And, seeing him for the first time in three months, Wade paled, clenching his fists and biting his lip to hold back the exclamation of horror he felt rising to voice. The professor, wretchedly pale, terribly emaciated, was barely able to struggle along in the line of shuffling prisoners.

Twice he fell, and twice the brutal kicks of the guards brought him staggering once more to his feet. The men were unfettered, but shackles would have been unnecessary, such was their physical condition. Even Wade found walking difficult after the cramped confinement that had been his for the past three months. Looking at the ghastly pallor of his fellow prisoners, Wade realized that he, too, must look much the same.

"MOVE on there!" The command barked by one of the crimson-clad guards jerked Wade's attention from his fellow sufferers. He looked at the burly guard who had barked the order, and thought mentally of what he would give to have a light-luger in his hand for only a moment.

Then Professor Jardon fell for the third time.

"Get him up! Make that damned old goat stay erect!" Two of the guards crossed the exercise yard to where Jardon lay inertly on the ground. There was a series of sickening blows as their heavy boots thudded mercilessly into the old man's ribs.

Wade Baron could stand it no longer.

Somehow he was running, staggering, across the exercise yard to where the Professor lay.

"Blast your stinking hides!" he shouted. "Stand away from that poor devil!"

Wildly his hands tore at the guard closest to the inert old man, spun the fellow around. The blow that Wade smashed into the surprised fellow's face was feeble, but the unexpectedness of it caught the guard off balance, and he sprawled backwards.

In another instant, as Wade was dropping to his, knees beside Professor Jardon's beaten body, three guards hurled themselves on his back, flattening him to the ground beside the old man. Wade didn't have time to shield himself from the blows that rained on him a moment later, didn't have time to roll out of range of those punishing kicks. The merciful curtain of unconsciousness slipped over him as his tortured body could bear the pain no longer.

"Throw them in the same cell together," one of the crimson tuniced guards snapped, "and get those others back to their cells. We'll take care of them later."

CHAPTER FIVE
Professor Jardon's Secret

WADE BARON rose dazedly to one elbow, blinking back the pain that seared his aching head, and trying to focus his eyes in the stygian darkness that enveloped him. The damp musky smell that assailed his nostrils told him instantly that he was once again in one of the dungeons, possibly his own.

The sharp pain subsided to a dull throbbing above his eyes. Wade was able to see faintly through the aid of a murky light beam filtering into the cell from a narrow window close to the ceiling.

With the chill of the slimy cobble-stoned floor forcing him to shiver involuntarily, Wade managed to rise painfully to his feet. For a moment he stood there, swaying slightly, fighting to keep from toppling forward again. Then, the nausea in his stomach settling somewhat. Wade looked about.

Someone else was in the cell with him.

Someone was lying in a queerly twisted heap less than a yard from his feet. And as recollection came to him, Wade recognized Professor Jardon. Cursing softly between swollen lips, he stepped swiftly forward and bent ever the old man. In a moment he was cradling the scientist's bloody head in his lap, shaking him gently, trying to bring the old man back to consciousness.

"Professor," Wade whispered. "Professor, come around old fellow. They've gone…"

His only answer was a tremulous sigh, a soft moan.

Suddenly Wade gasped. His arms, in which the old man's head rested, were warm and moist. He didn't have to see the color of the substance to know it was blood that slowly oozed from a deep wound in the side of Professor Jardon's head. And as he tenderly touched his hand to the wound, Wade shuddered. The old fellow's skull had been crushed, just beneath the ear, by one of those brutal kicks!

Jardon's eyes flickered faintly. Then they opened, and he looked weakly, blankly, up at Wade.

"They, they shan't have them," he murmured.

Tears rolled down Wade Baron's cheeks, and he answered the old man softly.

"It's all right, Professor, no one will harm you."

The scientist opened his mouth to form words again, then his eyes lighted slightly in recognition.

"Oh, it is you, my young friend. You—you—" he was speaking with much difficulty, "shouldn't have endangered yourself for me."

Wild rage was flooding Wade Baron's mind. Rage at the beasts who had done this. Rage at the beast who had been responsible for this living hell. He bit his lip, choking back his emotion.

"Young man," the Professor was murmuring. "Listen to me, young man." He coughed hackingly, red saliva running from the corners of his mouth. "Listen to me," he repeated, his voice growing faint for a moment. "I'm dying, I fear."

Wade said nothing, merely biting deeper into his under lip until the blood ran salty in his mouth. Tears blurred his vision until he was barely able to see the face of the kindly old man.

"Someone must know," the scientist was saying. "I must pass my knowledge on to someone. Planet Twenty, they want Planet Twenty." His voice faltered once more, and he fought for breath, his frail chest heaving spasmodically.

Wade still held his tongue. There was nothing he could say, nothing he could do to help. The old man was dying.

Wade suspected that he was delirious. He tried to ease the scientist's head gently to a more comfortable position.

"YOUNG MAN," the scientist resumed in a voice a little more even, "you probably think me raving...delirious. Hear me, please. I am quite in possession of my faculties. There is not much time, hear me."

Voice choked, Wade managed to answer him. "Go ahead, Professor. I'm listening. Go ahead with what you have to tell me."

"They want Twenty. Planet Twenty. Markham wanted it. I wouldn't reveal its location. That's why I'm here." He broke off once more, his breath coming fainter. "Bend closer, young man," he faltered. "I've not long. Minutes precious..."

Wade bent his head to the old man's lips, brushing back the tears from his face as he did so.

"You will find the papers...papers giving the location of Twenty, in my tunic. Take them from my body. There is knowledge there, young man, and wealth and power that I would never allow to fall into the hands of Markham. My secret laboratories, no one else knows their location, others are long since dead." The old fellow's breath was beginning to rattle in his throat.

"Yes," Wade answered. "I'll take them, Professor."

"Use them, boy. You look clean, decent. Don't let them fall into other hands. Markham, Markham wants that knowledge to destroy the Unifyer, take control of Government." The old man's voice was barely audible now. "I pass the information on to you, use it boy. Destroy Markham. But if you fail, destroy the papers. Destroy them bef—"

Professor Jardon ended the sentence abruptly. As abruptly as Death took him from the arms of Wade Baron.

Gently, Wade lowered the old man to the damp cobblestones of the dungeon floor.

"Another item, Markham," Wade muttered softly, "another item for which you'll roast..."

Respectfully, then, Wade removed the shirt of his tunic. For an instant he hesitated as he held it above the old scientist. He bit his lip in indecision. The scientist might not have been raving. Gently, then, he placed his hands inside the tunic of Professor Jardon. Placed his hand beneath the tunic and stopped sharply at what it encountered, a sheaf of papers!

He withdrew the papers, placing them at his side, then gently placed his tunic shirt over the scientist's face. He remained kneeling there for a moment in silent tribute to the old man. Then, picking up the papers, Wade rose and walked over to where the murky beam of light filtered faintly in from the window near the ceiling.

There Wade, straining his eyes in the gloom, scrutinized the papers left by Professor Jardon. There were seven or eight electrotyped sheets, and one large parchment-like paper folded several times to the size of the others. Wade unfolded the parchment first.

It was a planetoid chart, a cosmic map. His eyes narrowed, then he gasped involuntarily. The charted planet sector was that in which his former habitat, Jaytwo, was located!

Running his thumb rapidly across the map, Wade located Jaytwo; located, also, the other planets in its vicinity that he had spent three years in charting. Then his thumb stopped at the far corner of the map. There was a planet charted there—a distant planet that—as far as Wade had previously known—was nonexistent!

Beneath the marking of this planet was scrawled the word, "Twenty."

Wade frowned. This, evidently, was the Planet Twenty that the old man had mentioned again and again in his last moments. But there couldn't be any such planet. He himself had charted that interspacial area for three years, charted it minutely and in infinite detail. It was impossible. But Jardon had mentioned a Planet Twenty, and this map showed it.

FOLDING the map, Wade stuffed it beneath his arm and turned his attention to the electrotyped sheets. The first of them, bearing Professor Jardon's signature, was titled, "Concerning Twenty."

Brows knitted, eyes straining in the faint illumination coming from the tiny window, Wade read the page. Then he reread it, excitedly. When he finally had done with it, he had scanned it a total of eight times.

The next sheet was titled, "Record of Twenty and its equipment. Details leading to Markham's discovery of its existence." This information, Wade saw at a glance, was contained in the remaining seven pages.

He slumped down to the floor, leaning his back against the damp wall, and gave himself over to the perusal of Jardon's manuscript.

It was a half hour later before Wade put aside the papers and rose once more. There was a burning restlessness in his movements as he paced rapidly back and forth in the narrow confines of the tiny cell. His mind was wrestling excitedly with the information set down in Professor Jardon's manuscript. Excitedly and incredulously, for the statements that were set carefully down in electrotype were the most astonishing revelations Wade had ever encountered.

"If I could be certain," Wade muttered, "that the old man was quite sane when he compiled that information. If I could be sure—" The implications left in his mind by those seven pages were staggering to the imagination.

Twenty, a planet previously unheard of, a planet containing untold treasure in scientific knowledge, containing incredible power. The story of that planet, Jardon's secret, of the old scientist's laboratories hidden there from the universe, all this had been contained on those electrotyped pages, the parchment map.

Wade looked at the silent figure lying on the floor, at the old man who had created this fabulous secret scientific hoard, created it and kept the secret sealed until now.

In the pages, too, was information that filled the gaps of Wade's knowledge of what had happened in the universe during his three years isolation on Jaytwo. Tersely, the old scientist had told of Matt Markham's rise to power in Government. Had told, too, of the Professor's realization that Markham had to be thwarted before it became too late.

Planet Twenty—that had been Jardon's solution to the rising menace of Matt Markham. With the aid of a few trusted fellow scientists, Professor Jardon had constructed his secret laboratories on the uncharted, unknown planet. Matt Markham, the pages stated, had suspected the plan of Jardon, had gotten some inkling of it. Jardon's aids had been mercilessly tortured to death in Markham's attempts to wring the secret from them. But they had died rather than turn the tremendous power of Twenty into the power-mad young politician's hands.

Until there was only Professor Jardon left with the knowledge of the secret.

Wade could see it all clearly now, and what he didn't know was supplied by the information contained in the documents the old man had passed on to him. The old scientist had been sent to Cardo to break him, to reduce him to a state wherein he would be willing to turn over his information to Markham. But the job had been done too well. And now Jardon was dead.

And the terse electrotyped pages supplied more information. They stated that Markham knew, had somehow found out, that the secret planet of Professor Jardon was somewhere within the cosmic area of Jaytwo. He had discovered that much, but had still been unable to get the exact location of the place, which, Wade realized, was where he entered into the scheme of his former friend, Markham.

Markham, knowing that Wade had spent three years in exhaustive research of that interplanetary range, and knowing that Wade was returning with extensive information about that cosmic range, figured that the surveys might lead him to Professor Jardon's secret Planet Twenty.

"I can see," Wade whispered bitterly to himself, "why Markham wanted me out of the way, why he wanted my asteroid survey reports." Even as he spoke, he knew also that Markham had another reason for wanting him out of the way. That reason was Nada Warren.

Markham's lust, Markham's greed for power, had been his reasons for framing Wade Baron. Even though Wade had once been his closest friend. The picture of that scene in the Justice Chambers flashed back to Wade Baron, then. He saw himself facing Markham. He heard his own voice saying huskily, "I'll get you Markham..."

There in the darkness and stench of the tiny cell, standing above the body of the brutally murdered Jardon, Wade Baron reasserted his vow.

"It's still a bet," he told the silence. "I'm going to get you, Markham. I'll get you if it's the last thing I do..."

CHAPTER SIX
A Break for liberty

FOR THREE HOURS Wade kept silent vigil beside the body of Professor Jardon, and during those hours his mind explored the possibilities of escape.

The murky half-light, which seeped into the cell from the high barred window near the ceiling, had almost vanished, making the gloom of the tiny cell deeper. Frantically, Wade searched for some idea, some method by which he could escape.

The guards, he knew, were due to arrive at any moment. It was imperative, consequently, that he prepare himself to strike for freedom then. His opportunity would never be better. They would be thrown into confusion when they found Jardon dead. It might give Wade a chance to make his break.

For the knowledge from those documents would never be of aid unless he could gain freedom. He had stuffed the papers deep into the side of his space boots, which he still wore.

Once he was free, once he had gained Planet Twenty— Wade had plans after that.

Wade slunk like a panther, back and forth in the narrow confines of the tiny cell, accepting ideas only to reject them again as implausible, unworkable. Time was an essential. At any moment he might hear the tramp of guards marching down the silent cell corridors.

His lean features twisted in desperate concentration. Wade ran his hand through his lank black hair, across the short beard—which in three months had grown considerably—and looked up toward the ceiling.

The tiny aperture, barred and high from the floor, which served as the only window, provided no chance for escape. It was much too narrow to permit Wade to wriggle through, even to slide half a shoulder into. He discarded the thought. Discarded the thought and then returned to it.

Brow wrinkled in contemplation, Wade studied the window. He looked, then, at the still body of Professor Jardon. Restlessly his eyes scanned the barred opening once again.

"It might," he muttered softly. "It might work."

Rapidly, then, he tore long strips from the tunic shirt that he had placed over Jardon's face. Working swiftly, lest the guards approach before he was ready, Wade twisted the strips into a long cord. He jerked it several times to test its strength, was satisfied that it would hold. Long enough anyway.

Then, improvised rope in his hands, Wade sat down on the damp cobble-stoned floor of his cell to wait for the sounds of approaching guards. Silently, desperately, he was praying that it would work.

Later, perhaps a half hour, perhaps an hour, the faint sound of heels clacking down the corridor outside the cell came to Wade's ears. He leaped to his feet, straining his ears. He had to make certain. Couldn't take a chance.

"The guards," he grunted in satisfaction a moment later. Then, swiftly, Wade Baron went to work. A lot hinged on the reaction of the guards when they'd find Jardon dead by the door.

His makeshift rope was through the bars of the tiny window. Through the bars while Wade, finding foothold in the irregular surface of the damp wall, clambered toward the opening until he could hang from it by one hand.

The sounds of the approaching footsteps were growing much louder, and sweat broke out on Wade's forehead as he worked desperately with his free hand—fastening a noose.

It was ready, and Wade managed to swing his head through it, after tying the other end of the improvised rope to one of the bars. He still clung, with his remaining strength, to the bar by means of his free hand. A lot was going to depend on timing. He couldn't wait too long and couldn't be too hasty in letting himself drop into the strangling bonds of the noose.

For Wade Baron intended to hang himself.

THE sound of the footsteps was less than twenty feet from the cell door now. Twenty feet, coming closer. Wade prayed that the guards would cut him down in time. The strangulation would black out consciousness—it would be better than feigning it—and seem similar to death. But it couldn't kill him, if the guards acted in time. Wade had to chance that.

The death of the scientist, and the consternation of the guards at it, would make Wade's pseudo-suicide seem real enough when they saw him dangling from the bars.

Keys were clicking around the lock of the cell door. Voices muffled by the intervening door, were grumbling. Wade released his grip on the bars. Released his grip and felt the strangling cord cutting in on his throat, cutting off his breath.

Spots were dancing before his eyes, and he could feel the veins bulging out on his forehead. The keys were still clicking tantalizingly in the door. Through the wave of horrible darkness that was pressing in on him, Wade had time to pray that they would enter the cell in time, would cut him down before his trick turned into horrible reality.

The spots were bigger and blacker, flashing sparks mingling with them. Voices swam dizzily in Wade's brain. As if in a nightmare, he could feel his hands reaching up to his neck, clawingly, desperately. Then Wade Baron knew no more.

The noose had closed out consciousness...

"Throw 'em in the corner. Dead ones. Stiff cremation tomorrow morning." The voices buzzed fuzzily in Wade Baron's mind, and he felt hands lifting his apparently lifeless body high, a few steps, then a sickening drop as he struck stone pavement.

Some instinct enabled Wade to keep from moving, keep from crying out, although his mind was still hazy, still dazed. He lay there, scarcely breathing, hearing the voices, hearing footsteps sounding by his body.

"Going to catch hell," he heard the voices clearer now. "The old man wasn't supposed to have been liquidated, just pushed around a bit. Doesn't make any difference about the other, though. Just as good dead." Recollection of what had happened was returning to Wade. "I'd hate to have been the one who kicked the old man's skull in."

It had worked. The air on his cheek told Wade that he was in some sort of a clearing. He'd been cut down in time, taken for dead, and dragged outside with old Professor Jardon's body!

He held his breath, certain that the excited hammering of his heart could be heard by anyone within a yard of him.

The voices were moving away.

"Pick 'em up in the morning. There are other stiffs to bring up. Six more passed off in their cells today. Cremation for the bunch tomorrow."

Eyes shut fast, Wade waited until the last echo of the footsteps died away on the pavement. He didn't move then, however, for he couldn't be certain that all had gone. He wondered if it were dark enough to risk opening his eyes, then remembered that twilight was descending into the gloomy cell when the guards were approaching. It must be dark, he reasoned, for his eyes would have sensed any light, even though shut.

Nevertheless, Wade waited for what seemed to be an endless century until he was certain that there were no more sounds. Then he opened his eyes a hairbreadth of an inch. Darkness surrounded him.

Moving his head slowly to one side, accustoming his eyes to the darkness as he did so, Wade could see that he was in a large court, open to the sky. A large pavemented court in which at least fifteen or twenty bodies lay lifelessly together. Lifelessly with the exception of one—Wade.

Still Wade acted with infinite caution, moving laboriously, slowly, inch by inch, until he was in a better position to view the court. It was deserted save for the corpses.

CAUTIOUSLY, Wade rose to his feet. Looking at the bodies lying around him, he was forced to shudder. Some of them had obviously been here at least a week. Evidently the cremation spoken of by the guard took place at spaced intervals, possibly every two weeks.

The freshness of the air did not entirely drive off the stench of dead flesh. Wade's jaw shut grimly. So far so good. But this was a momentary sort of freedom. He couldn't stay here.

He was free of the cell. But now he had to find some manner of escaping Cardo itself. Slipping into the even inkier blackness along a wall beside him, Wade proceeded cautiously toward a gate, which was visible at the far end of the court.

Now and again he would pause, listening, craning his neck to peer through the darkness ahead. Then, assured that the way was safe, he would move forward several yards more. In this fashion he finally reached the gate to the courtyard.

There was no one at the gate. Dead men need no guards. With a soft sigh of relief, Wade slipped through the portal. He forced back an exclamation of joyous surprise, as his eyes swept the terrain ahead of him.

Off in the distance was the towering black bulk of Cardo prison—which meant that the guards had taken him outside of its confinement completely! Evidently the convicts who died inside its walls were removed to this court where they were left until cremation.

Wade judged the prison to be more than a mile away, and lying on the far side of it, he knew, was the landing base for the prison spaceships.

The government guards and wardens who served on Cardo Planet were quartered less than a quarter of a mile from the space landing platforms, Wade recalled, remembering a descriptive map of the planet that he had studied in connection with a survey some years before.

Between Wade and the space platforms lay the prison, with guards stationed in watchtowers, and the Resident Service quarters. If he could slip past these... His jaw hardened. He *had* to!

Wade Baron started toward the prison, across the open terrain. Suddenly he stopped short. The chance of his being seen by a Guard was too great. He dropped to the ground instantly on this realization. His fingers, as he pushed himself slowly across the barren stretch, kept slipping in the peculiar clay substance from which Cardo was formed. He paused, breathing heavily, the confinement of months in the cramped cell telling heavily on his strength.

He wondered if his gray tunic could be discerned from the watchtowers, and as he wondered he was seized with an idea.

Five minutes later, Wade had smeared himself from head to foot with the black slime clay—perfect camouflage.

Inching once more along the open terrain, Wade stopped suddenly, his veins turning to ice.

"Watch!" The word came from somewhere behind him, accompanied by the *sluck sluck* sound of boots moving toward the place where he lay. His heart began a furious tattoo of terror in his chest, and he buried his face deep in the slime clay.

"All well. Watch!" another voice answered through the darkness. But the boots moved closer, closer. Wade thought he could hear other steps retreating, fading away.

There was an almost imperceptible knoll to Wade's left, and he prayed that it might conceal him from the approaching sentry. From the sound of the sentry's steps, Wade judged him to be less than ten yards away by now.

Five yards. Wade held his breath.

There was a startled gasp, and simultaneously Wade knew that he had been observed and the guard was investigating. He cursed inwardly, body tensing, as the steps slucked directly toward him. He knew that he would never be hidden, once the sentry drew within a few feet of him. So he did the only thing left to him under the circumstances. He waited until he heard the tread of the boots almost directly beside him.

Then Wade Baron rose from the slime, black, terrifying, gaunt. Rose from the slime and launched himself in a swift dive at the guard who stood frozen in open-mouthed horror less than three feet away!

CHAPTER SEVEN
A Way to Escape?

To WADE'S ADVANTAGE were the surprise and confusion of the guard. Whatever he had expected to find, when his attention was drawn to the object in the black slime, he certainly wasn't prepared for an incredibly wild attack by an escaped convict.

A hoarse cry catching in his throat, the guard went down beneath the weight of Wade's body. Wade's fingers had found the jugular vein, worked along the neck to the windpipe, and he squeezed without compassion, without mercy—savagely.

The cry choked off into a weak gurgle, and minutes later, Wade felt the helpless struggling of the fellow cease, felt the body go limp beneath him.

Wade's hand flashed to the side of the guard's body, found the holster, and pulled forth a light-luger. He rolled off the inert, unresisting form of his victim, lying silent on his stomach for an instant, looking wildly about to see if the struggle had been noticed.

It hadn't.

Light-luger clutched in his hand, Wade started to inch ahead once more. Started, then stopped. Quickly, he inched back to the body of the guard, an idea born. Stripping off his tunic trousers, Wade used the inside of the garment to partially scrape the slime from his body. Then he went swiftly to work on the guard.

Five minutes later, still slightly dirtied by the remnants of the black slime, Wade Baron rose. He was clad in the crimson tunic of a Government guard. In the darkness, from a distance, he looked like any patrolling sentry.

Wade walked rapidly, now, and with confidence. From the watchtower he would never be taken for anything but a sentry. That was all he needed, to get past the prison. Past the prison and onto the space landing platforms.

He passed beneath the first watchtower some three minutes later. Passed beneath unchallenged. The same held true of the other three watchtowers. Five more minutes, and Cardo Prison was behind him.

Down a gently sloping hill lay the Resident Service quarters, a series of alumno-chrome structures as modern as the prison was medieval. From the glowing fluero-domes on the tops of the buildings, Wade knew that many of the guards and wardens were resting for the night.

He hoped, with a brief fervor, that they were resting soundly. For going through that small village was going to be his most difficult task by far. The streets, through which he would be forced to pass, were all illuminated. Not brilliantly, but enough to give him away should he be seen by any restless guards.

Wade steeled himself. The streets were deserted, but he couldn't be certain that they were going to remain that way. His hand slipped to his side, and he patted his holstered light-luger for reassurance.

"This should help," he muttered, "if anything goes wrong…"

On the other side of the little village were the space landing platforms. In gaining those platforms lay his only chance of gaining freedom. Wade stepped into the first of the streets, walking swiftly, but not at a pace that would cause undue suspicion. He was conscious of the appearance he presented under light.

Clay slime still matted his beard and hands and face, and although he was clad in the Guard crimson, he knew that one look at his face would betray him.

WADE made the first block unmolested, unnoticed, and breathed a short sigh of relief. There were two blocks left to cover. Two blocks left to the landing platforms. Already Wade could make out the platforms in the distance. Huge space hangars, squatting frog-like along the edges of the platform, seemed empty-jawed in the darkness.

On the landing runways were at least a dozen spacecraft, set in mooring for immediate take-off. Wade could see this by the outlines of shadow on the platforms, even though the platforms themselves were cloaked in darkness.

He was in the middle of the second block when it happened.

The sound of a door swinging open made him turn. Turn to face a man emerging from a building less than five feet off the street beacon he was passing. The fellow, Wade saw instantly from his flashing tunic, was a sentry, a guard!

The fellow, a burly man with massive shoulders, had just strapped on his holster when he sighted Wade. His mouth opened, as if to voice a greeting, at the sight of Wade's crimson tunic. Then his startled glance shot to Wade's face, took in the matted beard.

Wade's light-luger was in his hand at the same moment that the guard drew his. Simultaneously, white flashes spat from both guns, the peculiarly loud whine of the shots breaking the silence.

Wade had thrown himself forward even as he squeezed the trigger, taking his fall into consideration as he aimed. The guard hadn't thought as speedily. An expression of horrified pain split his wide features, and his light-luger clattered to the pavement as he crumpled face forward after it. The acrid stench of burning flesh filled the air immediately, but Wade didn't need it to know he'd scored a hit.

Scored a hit and roused the other houses with the sounds of the shots. Wade didn't wait. He set out at a dead run for the landing platforms. Somehow they seemed miles away, and Wade, zigzagging wildly down the center of the street to destroy the aim of the guards whom he knew would be in pursuit, knew that luck and luck alone would enable him to reach the platforms alive.

Flashing light-lugers were already whining behind him, and Wade knew that luck wouldn't play partner long enough for him to reach the platform. Shouts from the street from which he had just fled told him that the guards were pouring out after him. Soon, he knew, he'd be brought down by a staring light blast.

One block remained. One block between Wade and comparative safety. But even as he turned down its lighted pavements, he knew it would be too much. His light-luger was still in his hand, and he resisted a crazy impulse to turn and fight it out with his pursuers. His breath was tearing in his throat, rasping, choking him.

Flashing spurts from the light-lugers of his pursuers whined around his ears, and Wade knew that he'd be lucky to make fifteen steps more before one of those shots brought him down.

An then, to his right, he saw the glimmer of a neon conductor pole, a thin, column-like tube placed back three or four feet from the street edge. Wade aimed as accurately as his stumbling run would permit, his mind subconsciously registering the fact that the street lighting depended upon the power from this tube. Aimed and squeezed hard on the trigger of his light-luger. It was a direct hit.

The neon conductor tube shattered explosively, and the streets were thrown into utter darkness in the next instant.

Breathing a choked prayer of thanks, Wade darted sharply to the right, lurching onward to the space landing platforms. He gained the first platform two minutes later. He could hear the confused shouting of his pursuers ringing in the darkness behind him.

Wade clambered onto the second landing platform, heading for a row of small space fighter ships. If there was one ready…

There was, and Wade climbed inside its cabin just as he heard the footsteps of his pursuers clattering onto the first platform. Wade made his way to the control board and struggled into the pilot's seat an instant later, and he threw the rocket throttle wide. His heart caught somewhere in his throat as he listened for the answering response. If the ship wasn't charged—it was!

The deafening detonations of the rocket explosions belched sweet music in Wade Baron's ears, and orange streaks of flame splashed across the platform from the rear and side rockets of the tiny space fighter.

Wade released the gravity brake. Released the brake and felt the angry power of the rockets hurl him back against his seat as the ship hurtled upward toward space—and freedom!

CHAPTER EIGHT
Planet Twenty

PROFESSOR JARDON'S Cosmic Map in his chart panel, Wade Baron sat at the controls of the tiny space fighter more than thirty hours later.

There had been no pursuit from the guards on Cardo. The darkness, the confusion, had evidently made them give up the idea of following Wade. A radiograph, Wade knew, had more than likely been issued to the Space Patrols, warning them of his escape. But Wade, taking an obtuse course, stayed away from the space lanes.

And now, according to the interplanetary range chart of Professor Jardon, Wade knew that he was less than three hours away from the old scientist's fabulous Planet Twenty.

The strain was telling on Wade Baron, and his eyes were red and puffed from fatigue, his muscles screaming their demand for rest. But he clamped his jaw tighter, shaking the veil of weariness from his mind. He had to carry on. Once he reached Planet Twenty, there would be a chance for badly needed rest. But not until then.

"Not until then. Not until then. Not until then." The voice was a drone in Wade's ears, buzzing, humming, sleep provoking. With a start, he sat bolt upright. He realized that the voice was his own, that he had almost fallen asleep at the controls. Looking at his panel he gasped. The time register told him that two hours had passed! His gaze shot swiftly forward to the visa-scope, and he threw back on his space brake violently, slackening speed.

He was rushing down on Planet Twenty!

It was less than a quarter of an hour later that Wade eased the space fighter gently along the smooth terrain of Twenty, slipping to a landing; then less than three minutes later he clambered out of the spaceship.

Wade had donned space-gear over his crimson Guard tunic, for he knew the atmospheric conditions of such a small planet would make such protection necessary.

Standing there, Wade gazed openmouthed at the gleaming silver domes of a village-like cluster of buildings a quarter of a mile in the distance.

"Jardon's science structures," Wade breathed. His mind was still grappling with the realization that here was a planet about which no one—save himself—had any knowledge.

He moved forward then, toward the science structure village, a hundred questions in his mind. Questions concerning the power that lay within those silver-domed buildings. The power at which Jardon had only hinted.

Wade found himself on the streets of the strange, silent village a short time later. On all sides of him were the silver domed structures that—on closer inspection—resembled great dynamo turbines.

There was a tall, box-like building of chrome alloy directly in the center of the village, and Wade made his way toward this. It was, he was fairly certain, the central laboratory about which Jardon had spoken in the electrotyped documents.

The documents had stated that there, in the central laboratory, would be contained the information key to Planet Twenty and its treasures of scientific power.

The deserted streets seemed ghost-like, ominous, to Wade. And he recalled again that men had died, that Jardon had given his life, rather than reveal the secrets of these silent avenues.

WADE had taken forth the electrotyped documents as he climbed the steps leading to the door of the central laboratory. There were directions on these pages, directions that would lead him to the power he sought. Halting momentarily before the chrome alloy door, Wade flipped swiftly through these papers until he found the page concerning the laboratories.

"In the fourth room in the center of the laboratory, a room marked ZR2, will be found the necessary information," Wade read.

He marched through the door, his space boots ringing hollowly along the aluminum floored corridors of the vast hall in which he found himself. A hall that was lined on either side by a series of doors numbered in the fashion of the one he sought.

Wade pushed back his curiosity concerning these other rooms. He knew that the scientific wonders of Planet Twenty were not confined merely to the power he was after, but the rest could wait. His mission was clear. First of all, to satisfy Jardon's dying wish and his own revenge, Matt Markham would have to be taken care of.

"Ah, there it is." Wade paused before a door on his right. "ZR2…"

He pushed in through the door and found himself in a small room, utterly barren save for an oblong chest of a peculiar metal, which stood in the center of the place.

Wade frowned as he walked over to the chest. He bent over, inspecting its odd construction. He tried the lid, and it swung open, revealing a small, blued-metal box resting on a sheaf of papers.

Lifting the box from the chest, Wade saw that it was equipped with a double set of leather thongs, running along on either side of it. They looked as though they might be meant for a man to slip his arms through, like the straps of a knapsack.

Wade placed the metal box on the floor and pulled the papers from the chest. His brows creased bewilderedly at the title on the first of the papers.

Slowly, then, he began to read, now and again bending to inspect the small metal box and the series of dials on its flat surface. When he had finished the papers, Wade picked up the metallic box, slipping his arms through it, so that it hung suspended from his shoulders, dialed side facing outward. He had only to reach his hand to his chest to adjust the mechanism.

For a moment Wade stood there, continuing to study the papers that he had taken from the chest. Then he crossed the tiny room to the door, stepping once more into the corridor. He still held the papers in his hands as he moved down the long hallway toward the door by which he had entered the central laboratories.

Moments later, and Wade Baron found himself again in the silent streets of the science structure village. He moved along slowly, stopping every so often to inspect the turbine-like domed buildings.

"No wonder Markham wanted this information," he muttered in awe. "Good God, the havoc that could be wrought through it is more than incredible!"

Utter exhaustion was claiming the mind and body of Wade Baron, and he knew that he must rest before he collapsed there in the deserted ominous streets of Planet Twenty.

But after he was rested enough, once the fatigue was conquered, Wade had plans. Plans that involved Earth, and Matt Markham, and the reclaiming of Nada Warren—before it became too late to act. Before Markham had time to act.

Wade's red-rimmed eyes were utterly lackluster from his weariness. But a fierce determination blazed in his soul.

He would need rest; he knew that. But it was a selfless rest he sought as he retraced his steps to the tiny space fighter on the outskirts of the science structure village. A selfless rest that would strengthen him enough to carryon from where Professor Jardon had left off, to settle a long-awaited score with Matt Markham, and to rid Earth of the menace of Markham's greed.

Even as he unstrapped Jardon's precious secret from his shoulders, placing it carefully in a compartment near the instrument panel of the space fighter, Wade knew that he would have to force himself to sleep. For the burning eagerness to get on with his mission, to get back to Earth, was a ceaseless throb in his temples.

Wade stretched out on the cushions of the control seats in the tiny spacecraft, deliberately closing his eyes, letting the blissful blanket of coma slip about his mind. Minutes later, Baron slept...

IT WAS A REFRESHED, refurbished, newly resolved Wade Baron who sat behind the controls of the space fighter some twelve hours later. Planet Twenty—its secrets and strength symbolized by the small metallic box lying next to Wade—had faded back in the distance. Ahead lay Earth. Earth and Matt Markham.

Grimly, Wade pictured Markham's confusion and horror at the sight of the man he had thought condemned to a living death, pictured the swift and deadly justice that would come to Markham from Jardon's secret.

"I don't think," Wade muttered, "that Matt will have any welcome banners out for my arrival." Then he thought of Nada Warren, and the tiny muscles at the corner of his jaw tightened in a brief prayer. A prayer that he would arrive in time to prevent Markham from getting Nada. For Nada, thanks to Markham, thought Wade Baron was dead. Wade could vision Markham's phony condolences to Nada. Condolences that might make Nada turn to Markham for solace.

Hours slipped by as Wade drove the tiny craft mercilessly through space. In his mind he was forming a plan. It was obvious that he didn't dare land at Space Base in New York, for Government guards would seize him before he could reach Markham.

But there was a long unused and now deserted space-landing base at Long Island. Wade decided to land at this point. From there he could make his way to Markham's palace at Government headquarters. For a while Wade had contemplated going directly to the Unifyer. He could place his information, information pointing to Markham's treachery before the Unifyer and leave the rest to the Government Leader.

This was the logical thing to do, if it weren't for the fact that Wade knew Markham had undoubtedly placed men in key positions close to the Unifyer. Men who would prevent any such information from reaching the highest official in Government.

Besides, Wade had a driving desire to see this through alone. In addition to the other scores that were to be settled with Markham, there was his own personal accounting to be demanded. Wade didn't want to relinquish this pleasure of revenge.

So Wade slipped to a landing, many hours later, at the long deserted space-landing base at Long Island. He noticed, as he braked his tiny spacecraft into mooring at a rusty catch-tower, that there was no one about the place, which was what he had hoped for.

Divesting himself of his space gear, Wade once more slid his arms through the knapsack-like harness attached to the metallic little box. When it was resting securely against his chest, he made several careful adjustments on the dialed front.

Moments later, and Wade stood alone on the deserted landing platforms.

"Now," he said to the silence surrounding him, "for a personal accounting with Matt Markham!"

CHAPTER NINE
Face to Face

GOVERNMENT HEADQUARTERS in New York, located in the mile-high Unification Building, centered in the heart of the metropolis, buzzed with a suppressed excitement. On the top floor of the towering structure were the personal offices of Government Commissioner Matt Markham.

Behind an elaborate chrome alloy desk, attired in the brilliantly crimson tunic of his military rank, sat Matt Markham, Commissioner. Blond and beefy, his face an inscrutable mask dominated by the coldness of his eyes, Markham faced three guard officers who stood at attention before him.

"This," Markham declared matter-of-factly, "is the day of reckoning. Our men, men loyal to your Commissioner and our Cause, have all received their instructions. To you three belongs the burden of this task." He looked at them for a moment of dramatic silence, then continued.

"Our plans have been carefully, exactingly made. There should be no flaw in the mechanism. Each and every man knows his exact duty. Each and every man knows our appointed zero hour, at which time he is to perform that task." He stopped again for an instant. "You men represent the inner guard. It is your duty to see that the armed forces of Government fall behind us in this plan."

A short, dapper little guard officer spoke.

"That will be taken care of, Commissioner. Everything will go through as scheduled. The rank and file of the guards, of course, knows nothing of what is to happen. But the officers are so strategically placed that there should not be the slightest hitch in the plan. The men will follow the officers in control. We have seen to it that only officers loyal to our Cause will be alive when the zero hour arrives."

Markham smiled.

"Splendid, then. Our friend the Unifyer should be quite unpleasantly surprised within the next few hours…"

A thickset guard officer, heavily pockmarked, bared his lips in a jagged-toothed smile.

"The old fool will never know what happened to him."

"Neither," added Markham, "will the people."

Markham nodded, then, indicating the meeting was at an end.

"The next time I see you, gentlemen, it will be in the luxurious suite of the Unifyer. Good day…and good luck!" He gripped the hand of each briefly. Then they turned and left the room.

The pockmarked officer paused at the door.

"Good day, *Unifyer!*" he smiled.

Commissioner Markham smiled in return, and when the officers had gone he leaned back in his chair, a curious expression on his face, the lust of power in his cold eyes.

In just two more hours, Markham told himself, he would have complete control of Government. The neon board on his desk flashed a deep purple, and Markham leaned forward, flicking the switch.

"Yes?" he said into the board receptor.

"Miss Nada Warren to see you, Commissioner," a voice answered in reply.

Markham's grin of self-satisfaction deepened.

"Send her in."

SEVERAL moments later Nada Warren entered the elaborate suite. Her ash-blond hair, falling to the shoulders of her black, close-fitting tunic, her delicately chiseled features, soft red mouth, and warm brown eyes, served to produce the usual sensations on Markham. Behind the cold glitter of his gaze, his mind was inflamed with the dancing sparks of desire.

"Nada…" Markham rose from behind his desk and stepped forward to meet the girl in the center of the room. He took her hands in his, and the touch of them served to make his beefy face flush deeper.

"Matt," Nada was speaking, "I've just come from the Patrol officers."

Markham's eyes narrowed.

"I told you, Nada, you must get reconciled to the fact. Any further search for poor Wade is useless. He's gone, Nada. Dead. I've checked the Patrol offices myself, every day for the last three months. If there was anything to indicate that Wade was still alive, they surely would have known."

Nada Warren seemed to crumble inside at the words.

"I…I suppose you're right, Matt. But I can't help clinging to some hope. You know how I feel about it."

Matt Markham forced himself to soften his tone.

"Sure, Nada. I know how you feel, poor kid. I feel the same about Wade myself. But we must accept the fact that he'll never return. Lost in a space wreck, poor devil. He's gone, Nada, and we must face it, the two of us."

Nada Warren turned tear-stained eyes to the man who held her hands in his.

"Matt," she said brokenly, "you've been splendid. I shall never be able to repay you for what you've done, for the consolation you've been to me."

Matt Markham was thinking: *Yes you will, Nada, you'll be able to repay me. You're going to repay me, Nada, and sooner than you think.*

Markham said, "I don't expect any repayment from you, Nada. Wade meant much to me, too, don't forget it." He dropped her hands. "Sit down, Nada, and relax a bit. I've something I must tell you."

Nada Warren took a seat beside the huge chromarble desk.

Matt Markham brought forth a platnoid cigarette case, offered a cigarette to Nada, took one for himself. When he had lighted them both, he returned to his seat behind the chromarble desk.

"Funny," he said, blowing a cloud of blue toward the ceiling, "how many ancient customs have clung, in spite of civilization. We still smoke, for example, just as those in centuries before us."

But as Markham spoke he wasn't concerned with the words he uttered. He was thinking: *Yes, many things are the same in spite of progress, Nada. The desire of a man for a woman. My desire for you. Civilization's progress hasn't been able to change things as basic as that. I want you, Nada, and I'll have you. I'll have power, too, beyond all reckoning, within this hour. Within this hour my men will strike. You don't know about that, Nada. But it doesn't really matter.*

MARKHAM'S thoughts made him glance abruptly at his watch. Less than an hour. In less than an hour the revolt would be under way. He cleared his throat, shifting his gaze to Nada Warren, knowing that the words he spoke would have to be carefully chosen.

"We've learned to have much in common, Nada," he began.

Nada Warren nodded.

"Yes, Matt. I guess we've been thrown together pretty much these past three years."

Markham smiled. This was taking the trend he wanted.

"The two of us have been through much," he continued. Then, abruptly, "What do you think of me, Nada?"

Nada Warren was slightly startled by the question.

"Why," she said slowly, "I think that you're splendid, Matt. You mean a great deal to me—as a friend and companion. You know that, Matt."

Markham pursed his lips thoughtfully. This would have to be well acted. Nada was no fool.

"Nada," he said, in an excellent imitation of painful hesitancy, "I don't know if I should tell you this." He paused abruptly. "No forget it Nada," his expression was one of remorse, "forget I ever tried to tell you."

Nada Warren frowned.

"What, Matt? What is it you're trying to say?"

Playing his role to the hilt, Markham shook his head sorrowfully.

"No, Nada, please forget it. I can't say it. I wouldn't be fair to the memory of Wade."

"Matt," Nada Warren's voice was soft. "Matt, please tell me what you're trying to say. Please."

Markham forced himself to keep his voice calm, with just the proper amount of torment in its undertones.

"I'd never say this, Nada, if Wade were still alive."

The girl remained silent, gazing at him in perplexity.

"Nada," Markham burst forth, "you've come to mean more than anything in the universe to me."

"I...I don't understand, Matt," the girl replied. "We've had much in common; you've been grand. I think you're fine. But for anything—"

Markham rose, face flushed.

"Nada," he said huskily, "you have to listen to me. I want you, girl. I can make you happy. I can make you forget the tragedy of Wade's death. You think a lot of me, Nada. You said so. You'd make my life utterly complete..."

Nada Warren rose from her chair.

"Matt!" she said, and Markham could feel the shock in her voice, the bewilderment.

"Nada," Markham said desperately, "I'd never had told you, if Wade were still alive, believe me, Nada. Please believe me..."

Nada Warren's face had gone white, strained.

"Please, Matt. Please... You don't know what you're saying."

Markham moved to where the girl was standing, reaching out, and taking her hands roughly in his.

"Please, Matt..." The bewilderment in Nada Warren's voice, bewilderment and growing alarm, was lost on Markham. He pulled the girl toward him.

Nada freed herself in a quick twisting motion, retreating a few steps.

"Matt...don't...please. Don't!"

Markham's eyes glittered coldly, while cursing himself inwardly for his poor timing. But the die had been cast. It was up to him to force the thing through.

"I just want to give you happiness, Nada, that's all. I love you, Nada. I always have. Now that Wade is gone, can't you, won't you consider me?" His voice was hoarse, pleading.

"Matt, you're forgetting yourself!" The alarm had gone from Nada Warren's voice, to be replaced by icy frigidity. She fixed Markham with a cool level gaze, her eyes meeting his.

"Nada!" Markham's voice was strangled with passion and he moved toward her a second time.

His eyes, the lust he couldn't conceal behind them, made Nada gasp in terror.

"Matt! No...no!"

"I'll have you, Nada. Just as I'll have the world at my feet within the hour. I'll have the world to offer you. Riches, power, anything you want will be yours..." Markham had abandoned sham, abandoned pretension. His face was shining in unholy triumph, greed.

NADA WARREN had backed to the huge windows to the side of Markham's desk. Windows as wide as the other three walls. She felt their cool surface against her palms. Her heart was pounding wildly in terror, as she read the truth in his eyes. Her hand went to her red mouth.

"Matt..." she whispered hoarsely, *"you killed Wade!"*

Markham's soft laugh was cruel.

"So you've figured it out, eh?" His voice became sharper. "Don't be a fool, Nada. I'll control the universe within this hour. I'll give you anything you want. I'll have you whether you say yes or no."

"You're mad!" Nada's voice was vibrant with horror and loathing for the man who advanced menacingly toward her.

Despairingly, Nada was aware that the window behind her was too thick, too solid, to smash her way through it, through it to the streets a mile below.

"Don't come any closer," she choked, "stay where you are!"

"I want you, Nada," Markham leered, moving cat-like toward her. "I want you, and I'm going to have you..."

"No Markham. No, I don't think you are."

Nada's glance shot to the far corner of the room, cloaked in heavy draperies. Markham halted, puzzled, bewilderedly, in his tracks. He turned automatically to face the intruder.

Nada Warren's voice came to him as he turned.

"Wade!" Nada gasped hysterically. "Wade!"

Wade Baron, mud-caked and bearded, gaunt and unsmiling, clad in a tattered crimson tunic, stood facing them! A small metallic box was strapped to his chest, and he held a light-luger unwaveringly in his right hand.

"Your draperies," Wade said with ominous softness, "provide an excellent listening post. You should have them removed, *friend* Matt…"

CHAPTER TEN
The Flame of Revolt

"BARON!" Markham's cry was choked, strangling. "Wade Baron!"

"You seem surprised, Markham." Wade said with the same deadly softness to his voice. "Didn't you expect any visitors? Or was it that you didn't expect any ghosts as visitors? For I am a ghost, Markham. A man you sent to Hell. Remember?" Wade was moving slowly toward him.

"No…" Markham's voice was a trembling moan. "You're dead, on Cardo. They told me you died there." His hands shot convulsively to his jaw.

"Look into my eyes," Wade said quietly, menacingly, "look into my eyes and tell me what you see there. A soul? No, Markham, you killed that thing they call a soul."

Nada Warren crumpled beneath the strain, falling forward in a faint.

Markham's hand flashed to his side, but Wade was quicker. He was across the room in a bound, smashing the side of his light-luger against Markham's unprotected cheek. The weapon for which Markham had grabbed thudded to the thick rugs, and he stumbled backward, holding his hand to the gash inflicted by Wade's blow.

"Don't get any ideas, Markham. I want to talk to you, before I take care of you for once and for all," Wade grated.

"How did you get in here?" Markham bleated.

"That's unimportant. Take a seat behind that desk," snapped Wade, indicating his command with a movement of his light-luger.

Wade was beside Nada Warren, now, the hate in his eyes softening for a brief instant as he bent over her body. His light-luger, however, was still trained unwaveringly on Markham.

"Water," Wade indicated the decanter on Markham's desk. Hand shaking, eyes fixed in horror on Wade's light-luger, Markham complied. In a moment Wade was forcing the liquid down Nada's throat. She was whimpering softly, and he held her tenderly in his arms.

"Nada," he whispered. "Nada…"

The girl sat up, dazed, shaking. She looked at Wade, at Markham, still frozen in terror behind his desk.

"Wade!" she sobbed, burying her head in his chest.

Wade helped Nada to her feet, light-luger never leaving Markham's body for an instant.

"Go over there, dear," Wade said, pointing to the far corner of the room. Mechanically, Nada moved away, and Wade turned on Markham.

"Markham," Wade said with quiet menace, "we'll forget the things I've sworn to make you pay for—for the moment. I have a message for you. A message from another soul you ruined, Professor Jardon…"

Markham sat looking rigidly at Wade's pistol, wordless, hypnotized. A faint murmuring, a rumbling, drifted into the room from the huge windows by his sides.

"I've learned enough to fill the gaps during my absence from Earth, Markham. Jardon told me. A kindly, decent, splendid old man. The man you had kicked to death. Remember? He told me of your greed, your madness for power, and the way in which you intended to seize that power. I swore to him that I would prevent it, Markham. And I shall!"

Suddenly, as if coming out of a coma Markham leaned forward. The mention of Jardon, the reminder of his scheme, had changed him instantly.

"Baron," Markham said with returning confidence, "you're too late for your Girl Guide heroics. In another ten or twenty minutes I'll be supreme here on Earth, supreme in the councils of universal Government!"

Then his head cocked to one side, as the murmuring coming through the window grew sharper, louder. "Baron!" Markham rose from behind his desk, face flushed in triumph. "Hear that noise drifting up here from the streets?"

The sounds were stronger, a strange confused mixture of staccato roaring. Wade, listening, paled slightly.

"That's the little coup you intended to stop, Baron!" Markham snarled with savage triumph. "It's started. No one is going to stop it, Baron. It means that in another hour I'll be Unifyer. My men are moving across the metropolis at this instant, sweeping on toward the Government quarters of the Unifyer. The army is behind them."

WADE stood rooted, facing Markham, doubt and anxiety mingled on his features.

"Harm me, Baron," Markham continued, "and it will be hell for you, hell for Nada, too..."

Wade had moved now, moved swiftly to the great window. He peered out, out down into the streets a mile below. It seemed as if thousand tiny ants swarmed excitedly, angrily around the streets. He knew, then, that Markham wasn't bluffing, that the hour of revolt was at hand!

Markham was laughing, now, laughing harshly.

"Go ahead, Boy Scout. Stop it. Stop it if you can!"

Wade was still facing Markham, light-luger trained on his enemy's body. His hand shot quickly to his chest, to a tiny dial on the lower right side of the metallic box strapped there.

"I'll turn it over to Jardon, to the hell he made for this emergency. The secret which you sought to wring from him," Wade said evenly.

Markham's laughter was redoubled. "A little metal box, excellent!" His soft body shook with mirth. "Capital, Baron. A splendidly stupid bluff."

"Wait..." Wade said, "perhaps you'll change your mind." His voice was level but his mind was chanting a desperate prayer, a prayer that beseeched his Creator to let the dream of the old man, Jardon's secret, not fail him.

Wade's gaze flashed momentarily to the great window, through which was pouring the increased volume of roarings from the street below. In the sky, he could see tiny red dots, doubtless space fighters controlling the revolt from the air. Wade knew that it was these space fighters of Markham's that would decide the fate of the battle. The Unifyer's loyal troops might crush an uprising on the ground but not while the insurgents controlled the air. Wade knew that Markham's space fighters must be conquered...destroyed before the revolt could be put down.

His hands flew to the metal box strapped to his chest, made swift adjustments. If Jardon's plan worked...

At that instant, as Nada screamed warning, Markham launched himself on Wade.

Wade had only time to half-wheel, as the heavy body of the other drove into him. He felt himself going down. The light-luger was still in his hand, and he brought it down heavily on the top of Markham's skull. Again, and again, until at last Markham went inert beneath the blows. Wade pushed him aside and rose to his feet, cheek torn from Markham's clawing hands.

He glanced quickly again through the great window. The huge clouds of scarlet-coated fighting ships were thundering in on the defenseless city, sending their streams of death blasting into the ranks of the Unifyer's troops.

A grim smile touched his lips as he felt a sudden throbbing hum emanating from the metallic box strapped to his chest. From across the uncharted expanses of space, from the silver-domed dynamos on Planet Twenty, power was flowing to him.

He waited anxiously, while precious seconds ticked away, while Markham's hordes of ships spewed destruction on the city, until suddenly an orange glow gleamed from a crystal indicator set on top of the metallic box.

Wade's jaw hardened. This was the moment. He moved closer to the window overlooking the vast panoramic view of the holocaust that raged below.

HIS fingers touched the master switch; the switch ominously and cryptically marked, RELEASE. For a frozen atom of eternity he breathed a silent prayer and then his lean fingers shoved it home.

The humming stopped for a split second; then it crescendoed into a shrill whining roar of power. Wade felt the metallic box on his chest quiver as untold, unimaginable power poured into it.

For an instant the volume of power grew—and then— from the tiny inch-wide opening in the face of the metallic box a myriad of silver pellets began to pour.

Like angry wasps they flashed toward the window, smashing through it with savagely destructive power. Wade watched tensely as the silver pellets continued to blast from the metallic box and roar into the atmosphere, swiftly gathering into white clouds above the scarlet-coated space fighters.

A savage exultation filled him. This was Jordan's secret. Electron bullets! Electron bullets powered by the mighty dynamos on Planet Twenty and possessing a destructive force beyond the imagination.

The stream of electron bullets had stopped now and Wade's fingers flew to the rheostats that controlled the flight of the silver streaks of death that had blazed from the metallic box. He made calculations desperately, adjusted the rheostat with trembling fingers that steadied suddenly, became sure, deft. It was as if somehow Old Jordan the scientist was beside him, cautioning him, advising him, even in death.

The silver hordes of electron bullets were plummeting downward now, diving into the closely packed scarlet-coated space fleet of Markham.

Tiny streaks of death and destruction! For every hit they scored a spaceship exploded with ear shattering detonations. Under Wade's miraculously inspired guidance the silver wasps of death flashed through the ranks of Markham's fighters, looping and circling, leaving in their hissing wakes a trail of tremendous explosions and carnage. The ships that hadn't been hit rocked and swayed, tossed about helplessly by the mighty blasts that followed the destruction of their fellow crafts.

Wade's mouth set in a mirthless smile as he watched the destruction of Markham's crimson tube-ships. The remnants of the once-mighty fleet of space fighters were turning now, turning frenziedly and streaking away from the scene of battle.

The struggling in the streets, Wade could see, was slackening as the traitors turned their eyes to the heavens and saw what was left of their most powerful ally driven from the sky.

GRUNTING in grim satisfaction Wade swung the silver streams of electron bullets into the fray below. Again and again he sent hissing streaks of death flashing through the barricades outside the palace, mercilessly decimating the crimsoned ranks of the traitors.

Under this onslaught Markham's men broke at last, running madly, hysterically for shelter. It was then that the Unifyer's personal battalion, wearing the gold and purple tunics of the Home Guards, poured forth from behind the barricades they had set up to defend the palace.

It was then that Wade felt assured that the backbone of Markham's coup was shattered, and that the Home Guards would swiftly be able to restore order in the streets.

Every nerve, every fiber in Wade Baron's mind and body screamed tautly from the strain he had endured. His entire being was flooded with a vast and infinite weariness. The battle had raged only an hour, but in that hour Wade had been forced to project his command to every quarter of the hostilities. It had been a staggering, incredibly taxing job, but he had managed it. Managed it, and now watched the revolt turn into a route, as the Home Guard broke the remaining resistance among the shattered ranks of Markham's followers.

Wade, with the gesture of an ancient warrior sheathing a battle sword, flicked the dial that would end the wasps of death back to the silver-domed dynamos of Planet Twenty.

He felt no personal triumph, for it had been Jardon who had conceived this, whose staggering knowledge had given birth and actuality to this tool by which democracy had been preserved.

Wade ran a hand wearily across his browned lean features, through his lank, matted black hair.

His ears rang loudly from the sudden hush brought about by the cessation of the loud explosions. All was silent, save for the muted noises drifting ever more faintly up from the streets.

Suddenly Wade wheeled rapidly, thinking of Nada, of Matt Markham whom he had left unconscious on the floor. Wheeled, and turned ghastly white in sudden fear.

Both Nada and Markham were gone!

CHAPTER ELEVEN
Markham's Last Ace

WILDLY, Wade's gaze swept across the room. There wasn't a sign of the girl he loved or the man he hated. Despairingly, cursing himself for a fool, Wade realized that Markham had probably dashed for escape after coming out of the semi-conscious state in which he had left him. Dashed for escape, taking Nada Warren with him.

Wade realized that the deafening noises of battle would have drowned any cries made by Nada, even had they penetrated his tremendous concentration at that time. He realized this and cursed again, starting toward the door.

There was no sign of them as Wade dashed through the outer offices of Markham's suite. There was no sign of them as Wade raced into the corridor. The elevator tubes, by which passengers were taken to the various floors of the towering Government Building, were, Wade found an instant later, not in operation. Naturally, at the start of the revolt everything else had ceased, and the operators had deserted their posts, probably leaving the tubes at the first floor of the building.

Which left only the emergency shaft passage out of the building. Wade started for this, certain that Markham, too, had been forced to use it. It was at the far end of the corridor, an opening to long successive flights of stairs that led eventually to the bottom of the gigantic building.

Wade was starting down the first of these stair-flights, when a muffled sound came faintly to his ears, bringing him to an abrupt halt. He waited there on the stairs, listening for a repetition of the sound, his heart hammering wildly at the realization of what it meant. The sound, seeming like a choked cry, had come from above, from the opening onto the roofs above. The roofs that, Wade remembered quickly, were used as space landing platforms by the building employees and officials.

The sound came again, and Wade knew it for what it was—a sob from Nada Warren!

In an instant Wade had turned on the stairs, and was dashing wildly upward once more, past the top floor, onward to the roofs, toward the vast landing platforms up there.

Even as he struggled gasping up the last flight, the flight leading directly out onto the roofs, Wade heard a grunted curse that could only have come from the throat of Matt Markham!

Seconds later, Wade burst out onto the roofs, onto the broad aluminoid space landing platforms. Burst onto the roofs and caught sight of Nada and Markham!

In that split-second, while time hung motionless, suspended, the tableau stamped itself indelibly on Wade's brain. There was a spacecraft there, in front of which Matt Markham struggled frantically with the wildly clawing Nada Warren. An object in Nada's hand—the wrist of which Markham held savagely—made Wade's glance shoot swiftly to the atomic motor of the spaceship. It was cracked, useless, from a series of sharp blows. Blows that could only have come from the metal space landing bar that Nada held.

What had happened was now clear to Wade. Crystal clear. The spaceship was the only one on the roof. Markham had contemplated making his escape in it. But Nada had somehow gotten the metal bar, opened the motor cowl, and rendered the ship useless.

All this stamped itself on Wade's mind in the instant he stood there after emerging onto the roof. Then, snarling savagely at the sight of Markham brutally twisting the bar from the grasp of Nada, Wade went into action.

MARKHAM hadn't seen him emerge on the roof, had his back half-turned to Wade as he approached. But Nada, spying Wade, cried out sharply, and Markham wheeled just in time to catch a vicious smash on the side of the jaw. The blow drove him back and to the side, so that he sprawled on his knees beside the spaceship.

Nada Warren had dropped the bar, and it slid to within an inch of Markham's hand. Wade, diving face forward for it, was too late. Groggily, Markham seized it and drove it in a smashing blow toward Wade's skull. It missed its mark, landing sickeningly, paralyzingly on Wade's shoulder, bone cracking beneath the impact.

Wade felt searing flashes of pain drive through his shoulder. Nevertheless he managed to roll free from a second blow and rise to his feet. Markham, too, was now standing, facing him, the bar held menacingly in his hand.

The fury of madness was in Markham's eyes, the blazing hatred of revenge in Wade's, as the adversaries faced one another.

"Wade!" Nada Warren's scream split the air, as Markham hurled the bar savagely at Wade's head. Hurled it savagely and cursed hoarsely as it snicked past Baron's head by inches.

Wade could feel that the arm that had taken Markham's first blow was useless, and automatically his right hand shot to his belt, pulling forth his light-luger.

Deliberately, Wade centered the gun on Markham's head, was sliding his finger to the trigger. Then, he lowered the luger, threw it far to one side of the platform, beyond the reach of either of them.

"To hell with it, Markham," Wade grated. "I could burn your damned brains out with that gun. But I'd prefer to beat them out. Beat them out, slowly, just to see them splatter the platform!"

Markham who had paled at the sight of the light-luger, then gasped in amazement as Wade tossed it aside, grinned ghoulishly. His eyes darting to Wade's injured arm. He knew that these odds would be better than ever for him. And he moved forward toward Wade with an animal-like growl.

In the next instant he drove in a flying tackle, catching Wade below the knees, smashing him to the platform beneath his crushing weight.

Kicking desperately, Wade rolled free, his good fist smashing twice into Markham's unprotected face. Smashing twice, to be followed by a driving blow from his elbow as he rose.

But Markham was on his feet also, and coming after Wade again, endeavoring to drive in toward him from the side he knew to be injured. Twice, Wade lashed out with his uninjured hand, sending Markham reeling back from the sledge-like force of the blows.

Their struggle had carried them more than twenty yards from the spaceship, and now they were less than the same distance from the edge of the landing platform, from the sheer drop one mile to the streets below.

Wade was unaware of it, but Markham was cunningly forcing the struggle in that direction, forcing Wade back toward the lip of the platform, back toward that sheer drop to death.

AGAIN Markham carried the fight, butting in toward Wade with his bullhead lowered, arms lashing clumsily, yet tellingly against Wade's ribs and face. And again Wade managed to slip most of the blows, to send several more thudding into Markham's soft midriff.

But the struggle was horribly unequal.

Markham had the odds, and he was playing them to the hilt. He knew that he had merely to keep his eyes on Wade's uninjured arm. For from there, and there only, could Wade do damage.

Wade was further impaired by the presence of the metallic control box. Still strapped to his chest. Its straps confined even his uninjured arm, making quick movement difficult. Steadily, therefore, he was forced to yield ground to the dogged charges of Markham.

Perspiration clouded his vision, and his matted lank hair slipped constantly over his eyes. But Wade fought on with a desperate fury born of stark revenge, lashing, lashing, backing step by step, as Markham kept coming in.

Wade was less than ten yards from the edge of platform when another rush from Markham made him retreat a step as he drove his fist into his adversary's now bloody face. It was then that he slipped.

He felt himself falling forward, but was powerless to stop, and he felt Markham's huge bulk hurtling down on him as the platform rushed up. Another instant and Markham landed on his chest, driving every last breath of air sickeningly from his lungs. Groggily Wade tried to roll out from underneath him, fighting for breath as he did so.

To Wade's amazement Markham had risen to his feet, was weaving blindly, holding his hands to his eyes, his face pouring blood. And in that instant, Wade realized that Markham's face must have struck full force against Jardon's metal box on his chest and been badly lacerated by the stunning impact.

Somehow, Wade struggled to his feet, blinking back the sweat from his eyes, the sight of the weaving Markham dancing fuzzily in his vision. He started out after that vision, a scream shrilling in his ears as the vision of Markham suddenly vanished!

Someone was holding him, wiping the blood and sweat from his face, sobbing, crying his name. The fog cleared and he saw Nada.

"Over the edge," Nada was sobbing hysterically. "He was blinded with blood, and staggered over the edge of the platform! You started to follow him, but I stopped you in time! Oh Wade, Wade!"

NADA WARREN was waiting outside the chambers of the Unifyer when Wade emerged the following day. Her face, glowing with possessive pride and happiness, shone especially brightly at the sight of Wade's clean-shaven lean features, carefully combed black hair, and smiling wide mouth.

"You look a little different, Wade," she said, taking his arm as they moved toward the door together. "So differently that I'll bet you impressed the Unifyer into handing over an odd planet or two!"

Wade paused there in the hall, beside the main door where the Home Guards in purple and gold stood stoically at attention, and put his hands on Nada's shoulders.

"Look, honey," he said, drawing her closer, "we don't want any planets today. Or tomorrow, either, for that matter of fact. All we want is what I asked for, and got, that soft berth in the survey department of Government. A soft base on Earth, good old terra—whatcha-m'call-it, hub?"

"Terra firma, honey," Nada replied, "terra firma!"

Wade looked pained.

"If you're going to start picking on me already, we might as well get married pronto. Make the persecution legal, huh?"

Nada Warren disregarded the stolidly watching sentries, disregarded everything, in fact, except her answer to Wade Baron's question…

THE END

If you've enjoyed this book, you will not want to miss these terrific titles…

ARMCHAIR SCI-FI & HORROR DOUBLE NOVELS, $12.95 each

D-141 **ALL HEROES ARE HATED** by Milton Lesser
AND THE STARS REMAIN by Bryan Berry

D-142 **LAST CALL FOR DOOMSDAY** by Edmond Hamilton
HUNTRESS OF AKKAN by Robert Moore Williams

D-143 **THE MOON PIRATES** by Neil R. Jones
CALLISTO AT WAR by Harl Vincent

D-144 **THUNDER IN THE DAWN** by Henry Kuttner
THE UNCANNY EXPERIMENTS OF DR. VARSAG by David V. Reed

D-145 **A PATTERN FOR MONSTERS** by Randall Garrett
STAR SURGEON by Alan E Nourse

D-146 **THE ATOM CURTAIN** by Nick Boddie Williams
WARLOCK OF SHARRADOR by Gardner F. Fox

D-147 **SECRET OF THE LOST PLANET** by David Wright O'Brien
TELEVISION HILL by George McLociard

D-148 **INTO THE GREEN PRISM** by A Hyatt Verrill
WANDERERS OF THE WOLF-MOON by Nelson S. Bond

D-149 **MINIONS OF THE TIGER** by Chester S. Geier
FOUNDING FATHER by J. F. Bone

D-150 **THE INVISIBLE MAN** by H. G. Wells
THE ISLAND OF DR. MOREAU by H. G. Wells

ARMCHAIR SCIENCE FICTION CLASSICS, $12.95 each

C-61 **THE SHAVER MYSTERY, Book Six**
by Richard. S. Shaver

C-62 **CADUCEUS WILD**
by Ward Moore & Robert Bradford

ARMCHAIR MYSTERY-CRIME DOUBLE NOVELS, $12.95 each

B-1 **THE DEADLY PICK-UP** by Milton Ozaki
KILLER TAKE ALL by James O. Causey

B-2 **THE VIOLENT ONES** by E. Howard Hunt
HIGH HEEL HOMICIDE by Frederick C. Davis

B-3 **FURY ON SUNDAY** by Richard Matheson
THE AGONY COLUMN by Earl Derr Biggers

IT WAS AN INVENTION OF STAGGERING POTENTIAL!

George McLociard's "Television Hill" is one of the most unusual novels ever to grace the pages of Amazing Stories during the 1930s. McLociard fashioned what is essentially two stories within one novel. It begins as a tale of great scientific achievement—a true "hard science" story if there ever was one. It describes in great detail the building of a revolutionary television device, a device so fantastic in nature that it allowed its creators to peer into even the most secret chambers of mankind. Nothing could be concealed from its prying eyes—nothing. Such scientific achievements are not without peril, though, and the second half of this fantastic tale sends the reader down one of the wildest paths of scientific intrigue ever concocted. It is a tale of conflict, utter suspense, and betrayal. The final eight chapters of "Television Hill" are filled with so much excitement that they will literally keep you on the edge of your seat.

CAST OF CHARACTERS

TOM McMANUS
He was a filmmaker at heart, brought in to shoot some footage for two eccentric scientists—but it proved to be far more than that.

CYRUS KING
It was his dream, his vision: a television device that did far more than show pictures, a device so fantastic that it was…dangerous.

BOB WENTWORTH
Television Hill had been Cyrus King's brainchild, but it couldn't have come near so far scientifically without the help of this genius.

DIANNE KING
She was the daughter of one of the world's brainiest men, and she was smarter than she was beautiful—perhaps too smart.

ALEXANDER CHALMERS
Another great scientific mind, implicitly trusted, and one of the main go-to guys at Television Hill.

SMYTHE
As the chief engineer at Television Hill, he was shocked when he discovered evidence of sabotage.

RAY HEINEN
He was just a young kid. But he was also a great driver and had the fastest car this side of Chicago!

TELEVISION HILL

By
GEORGE McLOCIARD

Illustrated by
H. W. Wesso

ARMCHAIR FICTION
PO Box 4369, Medford, Oregon 97504

For more information about Armchair Books and products, visit our website at…

www.armchairfiction.com

Or email us at…

armchairfiction@yahoo.com

CHAPTER ONE

THE moon, a huge disc of yellow-red glowing low in the clear, star-studded heavens, was slowly climbing over the distant eastern horizon, bathing the world in an ever-strengthening soft, revealing illumination. From the heavy growths of pine on the hill and the tall poplars of the winding river valley came the ever-present sigh of the south wind. Extending my feet to the veranda rail, I relaxed with a contented sigh, deeply enjoying the momentary snatch of actual peace of mind and rest coming so pleasantly on this cool mid-summer evening.

"Well, McManus, judging from the way you sit there, it would appear that you were rapidly becoming acclimatized to this place."

My glance went to the slightly indistinct form of a tall man seated on the wide rail, his back resting against the nearest of the supporting pillars.

"Considering the events of this afternoon, and the fact that in time things will be made more and more interesting, there's no reason why I shouldn't take to it," I returned, settling deeper into the comfortable wicker chair.

"Mighty glad to hear that." The faint point of light from his cigar flared out brightly as he struck off the ash.

"This certainly is a quiet piece of country—after being cooped up in tumultuous Chicago all winter and spring," I half-mused, hoping to keep the ball of conversation rolling.

"Yes, it is," he agreed and was silent for some time, lost in reveries, apparently.

"Indeed," he exclaimed suddenly, "it is a quiet place—or so it seems."

I pondered, in a somewhat lethargic state, why be had uttered the last words so softly and why they struck me as being fraught with so much meaning.

"Lonely? Perhaps," he added at length. "That largely depends on how you look at life. Some of us humans are always lonely—even in the big cities."

"The desire to be alone grips all of us at times," I led on, determined to work the thread of conversation to the thing that was uppermost in my mind—the reason why I had been so mysteriously summoned here from Chicago, and why I had been forced to sign so many unusual documents. "Often I have dreamed of discovering a locale similar to this one and have actually spent days searching for it in the lake region around the Wisconsin State line. To tell the truth, Wentworth, the drive south from Rockford along the wide, tree-lined river was simply one thrill of amazement and joy after another, as the majestic, old-world beauty swept past. I had often heard about the beauties of the Rock River Valley but did not realize it was as close to Chicago as it is."

Wentworth remained silent for some time. "Indeed, it is a beautiful strip of scenery and is comparatively little known—or was, until the new concrete road was laid several years ago. When King and I first came out here, there was a narrow gravel road paralleling the river's edge, practically impassable in winter and in bad weather."

As the moon rose higher, the light strengthened and the darkened landscape surrounding us grew more distinct; the river glittered through the openings in the trees, while the thick woods on the rolling slopes to the west took on the strange, unearthly, stereoscopic abruptness only seen in full moonlight.

Wentworth began speaking in his slow meditative manner, and I aroused myself to listen. His first words excited my full attention.

"McManus, it seems as though now would be an appropriate time to acquaint you with some of the work and history we—King, his men and I—have made. You arrived too late this afternoon to make it worthwhile to take you on an explanatory trip through the plant or to begin to tell you why we appear to be so mysterious in our dealings with you. Besides, I was pressed for time.

"It's a long story and one that, no doubt, will be exceedingly interesting to you, but I'm afraid that some of the detailing will have to be skimmed over in order to cover as much of the ground as possible. As you have willingly agreed in your contract with us, all information and knowledge of the special research work being carried on by us—whether King or I tell you or you pick it up yourself—is to be kept strictly confidential, and none of your discoveries are to be told to another party— not even to one of our own men—without King's or my consideration and permission. There is a reason for this unusual request—a reason you will readily understand when you have heard my story."

Wentworth stepped into the cottage, returning with a box of cigars, which he placed within easy reach on the smoking stand. His deliberate motions, as he drew up his chair, suggested that the story was to be a lengthy one. The sputtering flame as he lit a fresh cigar highlighted the forceful lines of his rugged features and after a long contemplative puff he began:

*　　*　　*

"IT was in the fall of 1923 that King came to me with a wild tale of an experiment he and his son had conducted in their home laboratory. Cyrus King had been interested in things scientific from his early youth and upon the completion of a postgraduate course at Chicago, had turned to teaching, spending twenty-five years at the University of Illinois. In 1922 an explosion, causing more damage to his reputation than bodily harm, forced him into retirement. However, he still retained his love for spectacular experimentation and continued research work at his home assisted by his only son, Jim, who gave promise of becoming a wizard in the newer fields of electro-chemistry. About this time there was a rumor of a successful attempt on the part of the Government in the unusual feat of plating rubber on metals. The processes, for apparent reasons, were kept secret. King, his innate curiosity aroused, determined to duplicate the stunt—if he could.

"Cyrus King is a mild-mannered, keen-thinking, and at the same time, bull-tempered scientist of the rare type who deem failure but an incentive to even greater efforts. And failure was the only result he obtained, although he and Jim kept up a continual siege at their goal through the entire winter and spring, trying everything and anything in their power, just to see where they had slipped.

"Then, for some reason we have never been able to ascertain, Jim began to experiment with silver and rubber colloidal solutions. King stormed at this display of his son's inconsistency, but the lad, with a knowing grin, kept right on with his 'fooling', as he termed it.

"I was called away to Brazil in early summer and returning in November was met by King who sorrowfully informed me of Jim's marriage and departure to the east, where he was then employed in an experimental electric plant. He was anxious for me to make a special visit to his home as soon as possible and spoke in an indefinite manner of 'a great stunt done by my boy, Jim.'

" 'Bob,' he said, as he led the way to the laboratory, when I had finally managed to call several evenings later, 'that lad of mine is a wonder; he's started something so big and so wonderful that, as yet, I cannot begin to believe he accomplished it unassisted.'

"King then pointed to a queer arrangement of flat glass plates, rubber and bakelite boxes, porcelain jars and crocks, and much interweaving tubing; all being enclosed in a tunnel-like shelter of black-painted wood. There were many powerful lamps grouped at one end of the tunnel while the other expanded funnel-like, to take a ground glass sheet some two feet square. I did not even try to guess what it might have been, although it was obvious, from its type of construction, that it was not even remotely associated with rubber plating.

"King did not make any explanations but turned out all the lights save one ruby lamp nearby. As he threw several switches, the lamps within the enclosure blazed out, while pumps began to throb under the table. King thrust his hand through the side door—in front of the lamps—and on that glass screen there appeared, momentarily, a perfect, though somewhat elongated, reproduction of his hand in black and white—in the order of a negative print—reversed in tint—you know.

"Not the least impressed, for I judged the machine to be some sort of a projection device. I asked what there was to get excited about. King turned on the lights and said, 'You are familiar, Wentworth, with the action that goes on when you take a photograph. You place a sensitized celluloid sheet, on which has been deposited silver compounds, behind a focusing medium in a lightproof shelter and expose your film for the fraction of a second necessary to take the actinic rays reflected by the object, of which you wish to keep a visual record. Then this exposed film is run through various baths and finally printed on substantial paper.

" 'Well, in this machine, Jim and I have been able to combine *all* the chemical changes involved in photography up to the final positive printing—the latter a problem yet unsolved. We can throw on this screen moving reproductions of whatever we place in the *receiving end.* The actual chemical processes only take minute fractions of time, and since my son has hit upon a liquid just as sensitive as the usual celluloid-backed film, and one that can change from the *exposed* to the *unexposed* state by electrical impulse and pump action in the space of a fiftieth of a second— well, we can make use of this startling characteristic in the only logical and satisfactory means of screening a moving image sent or transmitted by wire or wireless!'

"What do you mean? I had asked him, for his talk was not clear to me then, knowing very little as I did about our present 'radio.'

" 'Simply this,' he told me. 'I have gone far enough into this experiment to see the tremendous possibilities a liquid film holds in screening television images, compared with the precisely ground and delicate revolving glass discs Mister C. Francis Jenkins is now using.'

"This model, King thought, was sufficient to prove all his claims, wild as they were. Then he went on to tell of how he had previously spent over two months' careful inquiry covering the field wherein photography was used, his efforts being directed to learn where such an unusual film could be put to practical use. He knew, from its inception, that it would play an important part in projecting an enlarged image on a screen from moving objects placed before the negative plates—if the rest of the complicated mechanism necessary were perfected to the desired requirements. But then he had not known where it could be applied.

"After much thought King had acted upon his son's suggestion and called in a group of engineers versed in various lines and bluntly put the problem up to them. One of them brought up television by recounting his experiences along that line. King saw the point instantly and had only awaited my return to start further work.

"During the years King had been teaching, I had been engaged in steel construction work—The Wentworth Engineering Corporation of Illinois. Perhaps you can remember seeing some of my skyscrapers in the loop. I had started off in this game in my early twenties, aided by my Dad, who turned over a considerable part of his estate to my venture, mortgaging me with the condition that I make our name known over the world. King and I had met during college and though we were often separated by continents due to my roamings, our friendship had continued to grow until now, when he has something really big. He has enlisted my help to push this idea. At first I laughed at him, holding that I knew so little of the extremely intricate and technical sciences bound to be involved; but he would have none of my excuses and continued, through all that evening, outlining his plans. They interested me—to say the least, and before I realized it, I was as wrought up about the thing as he was.

"You recall, McManus, what thrilling visions the word 'Television' conjured up several years ago. Radio—then widely mistermed 'wireless'—was barely creeping out of the five dollar a tube stage—and the mere mention of television carried us into the misty future of twenty to fifty years. Jenkins was the only active experimenter in the field, and the meager news he suffered the world to know, was eagerly headlined by the radio magazines and other similar publications.

"But to go on, King rented an upper floor of a factory building near North Avenue and the Chicago River, and after much advertising and search, finally selected five men to aid him. He spared no expense, but threw his life-accumulated savings into the maws of his unproductive brainchild. His men, fired with the enthusiasm of a gigantic project, worked ten and often sixteen hours a day. Success, it seemed, was destined to be his fate, for everything ran smoothly along without a single serious hitch, and in late 1924 he was able to screen an entire photoplay sent by wire from one end of the laboratory to the other. It was wired television and King could have realized millions had he placed his machine on the market then."

"I'm not stretching the truth, McManus, when I state that King, in that year 1924, had progressed further along in television in regard to oscillators, synchronizing devices, transmitters, receivers, and all the rest of the necessary special lamps than the experimental world has gone, playing with radio today!

"His force had increased to eleven men, all so wrapped up in their work that suggestions and improvements came so rapidly they could scarcely keep abreast of them. There was one fellow, Smythe, our present chief-engineer, who occupied en entire room in which he had duplicates of all the various types of tubes and oscillators then known and used. It was in this room that all sorts of utterly senseless and apparently foolish experiments were carried on in the endeavor to find a better photoelectric cell and kino lamps. King spent most of his time in here during the next year, leaving to the other men the lesser problems of ironing out the rough spots in scanning discs, shutters, lenses, pumps, and film liquids.

"Often I had asked King when he would announce his timely invention to the world.

" 'Not yet, Wentworth—not yet,' he would say. 'Don't you realize we have barely touched upon the real possibilities surrounding this mighty discovery? I was puzzled at his unexpressed demand for secrecy and would shrug my shoulders at the suppressed smile that lingered in his eyes, even through trying difficulties. His fortune dwindled rapidly as expensive machinery was hauled into the old factory building.

"One night, early in June 1925, I paid my usual semiweekly call to find the entire two floors, which he now occupied, in a state of general excitement. Everyone was running around hectically, shouting meaningless instructions to each other as they made adjustments to the dynamos, motor-generators, switches, and the numerous other queer contraptions littering the floors and hanging from the ceilings, spread over benches and stands. Cables, encased in thick rubber coverings, snaked over the floors, crawling around timbers and obstructions, through manholes cut between the floors, and even out the windows to the fire escapes. Fine wires and insulated copper and glass tubing were streaking in all directions, making, in all, such an incomprehensible maze of machinery that I just stood and gasped my amazement, although I had seen some of these preparations a day or two previously.

"King met me with a grin. 'Well, Wentworth,' he greeted as he shook my hand with more enthusiasm than I had ever known him to show before. 'The world is ours!'

" 'What, er—the world is ours?' I repeated, frowning at the absurd expression.

" 'Yes, Old Pal, the world can never again hide any of her secrets in darkened places, nor can mere distances hinder man's knowledge of what is happening on the other side of the globe!'

" 'What the Sam Blazes is the matter with you?' I had muttered, grasping his shoulders and giving him a look that would have startled anyone else. He seemed tired, but his body was tensely vibrant with some great joy.

" 'Get it, Bob? We've hit the real thing! We have Television! The real stuff! Right now we are looking upon the lakeshore. Come on—take a look.'

"I followed him into the light-proof room where stood the glass screen on which he had a year before projected his movie play, and was surprised to find a shadowy, semi-half tone reproduction of the Lake Shore Drive off North Avenue. It was at times so clear, that I could recognize the features of the people wandering up and down the beach walk, and I wondered much at the misty flow of black streaks, odd shapes, triangles, and other queer forms cutting into the picture at close intervals. Then I became aware of the scene moving southward as King made adjustments with a controller similar to that on a trolley car.

" 'What,' I exclaimed, 'Since when did you shift your transmitter to a truck?'

" 'Now,' said King softly, a slow smile breaking over his face. 'This is the reason of my secrecy—why I did not wish to reveal any details of our discovery—and leads to my long awaited surprise for you. The transmitter is on the *roof* of this building!'

"I stared at him for a long time, realizing instantly just what his words meant. The world was ours! Still, I couldn't believe it! 'You mean to say you can see anywhere you please—without the transmitter being itself on the spot you are screening?'

"He nodded, 'Surely. That is why I say we have the world in our hands.'

" 'Television—sight from afar,' I mused. 'What! It's not possible! Why, look at the difficulties and the unthought of conditions positively prohibiting such a thing. How can you do it? You can't do it!'

"With a smile at the expression of doubt, which must have been engraved on my face, King said, 'Remember, that is just what the world said of the airplane twenty-five years ago—and then the learned critics proved it impossible by intricate and exact mathematics. But human-like they neglected to take into account another important factor in their calculations—the factor of PROGRESS. They based their near-sighted convictions on the designs and weights of the machines then flying, never daring to think for a moment that motors could be so developed as to enable horsepower to be drawn from a pound of motor, nor did they dream of metals three times lighter than steel yet of the same tensile strength. There you are. Impossible? We have since gone from those crude contraptions, barely supporting one man in the air less than a minute, to the marvelous giants of today, soaring aloft for hours and transporting hundreds of men. Progress! It is that and nothing else! What may be apparently beyond the power of human intelligence to conquer today, may be so ridiculously simple tomorrow that you feel like kicking yourself about the streets for not thinking of it before!'

" 'If you were standing on the Lake Shore, Wentworth, wouldn't those people look as though they were conscious of some weird machine set upon the beach following their movements? Notice, they do not even glance in this direction with that stare you see so often in newsreels.'

"I admitted the truth, but was about to suggest he might be pulling off some colossal practical joke at my expense, when he cut in. 'Now, watch closely, we're going to sweep up the Drive.'

"I'M not going to spoil the new and thrilling treat you will experience tomorrow night, when you see the perfected television machine in operation; so I will not go any further in detail on that point, nor tell you what King and I did in the ensuing months with the extremely crude apparatus. Crude as it was—it was a world wonder, and the men spent hours with us as we roved on the Televise rays within our restricted range of three miles.

"King was elated with his success, and I was almost crazy with interest. Truly, then, was I convinced that the world was ours. King spoke of increased power, of better transmitters, and of the necessary seclusion. Our two strange searchlights, atop the factory roof and their attendant violet-red beams when in operation were beginning to draw comments and questions. Therefore, I told King to go ahead, make his plans, pick out his ground, and order machinery, and I would bear all the expense from then on.

"King and his men, now a select group of forty—a wizard every single one of them—after a month's survey of the entire middle west, decided that the present locality was the most favorable as regards the central point from which to cover the entire area of North America, along with adequate transportation facilities, instant communication, and of course, seclusion. Then with plans and instructions, I had my construction gang erect the structures to house the machinery. As the winter of 1926 passed on, this hill, once a heavy woods, became a beehive of industry. After much fuss with State officials and the well-meaning War Department, we were permitted to throw a single span bridge across the river to the old State road, which you know is on the west bank of the river. A village of a hundred homes was laid out and built down the river about a half mile from here. It is a model town, complete with paved streets, lighting, sewage disposal plant, well water, and is the home of the men employed here. The first unit to be completed was the powerhouse; of a size to furnish a city of a hundred thousand with light and power; its tall exhaust stack rising behind the hill caused much discussion throughout the community. Next came the projection house, and if you strain your eyes a bit in this moonlight, to the southeast you can make out the darker shadows of the two water towers rising above the trees. They overlook the three-story building wherein much of our work is done today.

"In the meantime, this cottage had been built, and a twelve-foot steel mesh fence was erected around the entire plant area, which covers, in all, some seven hundred acres. A series of secondary fences, where needed, with radio-capacity detection devices, were connected with the office alarm system and the lookout stations.

"On we went about our work constantly and quietly, hiding our plans and identity under the corporate title of 'King-Wentworth Experimental Radio Engineering,' and thereby put an end to embarrassing questioning by State officials by declaring we were about to attempt radio-beam transmission. It was no lie—we certainly were."

"McManus, you know how such things go. When one is working toward a new goal, how swiftly he stumbles upon other interesting things associated with his quest. That is what happened here at Television Hill, as we have come to call this place. During the years 1926 and 1927 we did very little in expansion of the apparatus we had designed, but spent much time on improving what equipment we had been using and becoming acquainted with the machinery we were installing. New ideas and developments confronted us daily. We were not in the position occupied by the radio manufacturers (with whom we kept constant pace) as much of our amplifying apparatus was based on radio-principles and we did not have a market on which to dump the half-completed and untried efforts of our plant. Our only aim was *perfection;* and our worry—how to keep going. That worry increased with the passage of months and at length I was forced to return to my own business and expand in order to keep up with the heavy drain the experiment was making on my resources. I never had a single doubt but that we'd come out the winners, whether or not we achieved the pinnacle of perfection King was striving for.

"King had made startling discoveries in liquid film projectors, had gone more thoroughly into the investigation of all forms of the so-called rays than anyone else to our knowledge; had whipped the cathode and other associated rays and used them in our research work; had been able to generate infra-red rays in the attempt to improve the Baird System of Fog

Television, or Noctovision. I believe it's rightly named, to the extent that we were able to char woodwork two thousand feet away; had played with radio waves, both the extreme long and short; had designed radio tubes and power-oscillators and ballast control valves to fit the unusual demands of our apparatus; and through it all had gathered such a mass of material and notes that when accounts of his experiments are published, much of the theoretical electrical formulae and other standards will have to be revised.

"Do you know, McManus, that King is about ten years ahead of the whole electrical game? Why, rabid fiction writers, with all their fantastic pipe dreams, could never begin to hope to duplicate in wild rhetorical description some of the astounding achievements we have found possible!

"I think the most spectacular incident I ever witnessed happened here last spring. King's men had found a new type of high frequency oscillator with some characteristics warranting further investigation. A large model was built and set on top of the then wooded Television Hill. In appearance you would have taken it for a crude sixteen-foot mortar mounted in the manner of the usual rifle. From the mouth of this strange gun was shot a beam of positive electricity, riding on a rod of ionized air, somewhere in the neighborhood of twenty million volts. It was directed at a tall tree some three miles north of here. There was a puff—a sheet of dull flame, and the green tree had been torn asunder almost instantly. That is a fact that can be verified by just walking down to the village and asking anyone you meet. All our men were witnesses that day."

Wentworth stood up and stretched himself. Reaching into his pocket, he drew forth his pipe and tobacco, filled the pipe, while I watched every move, and lit it. My cigar had gone out long before and the end was soggy from unconscious chewing. Then, too, I realized I was perched on the edge of the chair as close to him as I could have gotten, so engrossed had I been in his story. From the parlor came the melodious boom of the Telechron, announcing the hour of ten.

"Well," Wentworth again settled into his chair. "So things proceeded. The years have fled like months and today, at the end of seven years of relentless work, King has finally admitted he has reached his goal. He has brought his means (and the only means, by the way) of television up to the point where his theories and practices are comparable to the heights now reached by radio engineering. The basic principles are there—there is little room now for radical change—only minor improvements and refinements can be made.

"Today King and I are, to the world, poor men. I have disposed of my business, my home, and spend all my time here watching King and aiding him in my little way. Nevertheless, we are the world's most-to-be-feared men. We have three transmitters. One here; Television Hill. One seventy-five miles northwards at New Glarus, Wisconsin. And the last the same distance from these two mentioned stations—at Lake Geneva, Wisconsin. An equilateral triangle of such immense dimensions and untold power as the world has never known.

"We could, at a moment's notice, demand whatever we might from any of a half hundred shady individuals in Chicago alone, on whom we could get inside dope the press would fight to print. But blackmail is not our object. Television is to be the revealing light of the world—tearing away all the concealed mystery and unfounded superstitious fear holding back the progress of mankind—not to be its all-seeing oppressor and tyrant.

"No, McManus, we hope our machine will never be used for that terrible leeching. King and I have come to be cognizant of the awful potentialities lying dormant in this invention, should it ever get into the wrong hands. And we have taken steps to prevent such a thing from happening—if possible. We have made detailed plans of all our equipment, of the chemicals, of the constructional data, and of our other discoveries on a special paper that will change color when once exposed to any form of light, and sent them in sealed tubes to the War Department.

They have instructions to build duplicate machines should any emergency arise calling for their use.

"We alone know what terrific forces we have stumbled upon in bringing this modern miracle into being, and well we know that once our secret is made known to the world, we will never be secure from determined efforts to wrest the system from us."

"From this hill, King and I could rule the Earth with hand and eye, for we have sole possession of a machine by means of which we can follow any movement on the surface, or under the surface, within the range of our power. *There is no such thing as solid walls to television!* Everything from here to New York could be laid on our screen as though the walls of the house and buildings were made of glass. We could at will, give a complete X-ray examination of any person or object anywhere in a radius of seven thousand miles!"

"That is *TELEVISION!*

"And, then, McManus," Wentworth's voice lowered as he leaned closer, "to climax that—the rays—the carrier beam of the projectors, are potential weapons, by which we can strike as well as see. Cathode rays with all their reputed destructiveness are a mere child's play-toy compared to the awful beam issuing from the mouths of our projectors— But never you fear, McManus! We have those rays under control so that no harm comes when we are in operation other than a pleasant tingling sensation felt by those persons directly in the focus of the transmitters and only such delicate instruments as millimeters, galvanometers, and radio receivers give evidence of their presence.

CHAPTER TWO

"THAT, McManus, is the reason why such an intimate and disturbingly personal search was made into your past history before you were sent here. We *must* be able to trust our employees to go among their friends and relations without revealing that they are involved in something, the revelation of which; would undoubtedly imperil the lives of millions. It is no guess to say it might be the pardonable cause of a war! In that light we have sworn in a select group of the War Department upon their solemn oath to do their best to keep all stories concerning us under surveillance, and to contradict all press rumors.

"WE have brought you here to aid us in our latest work—that of supervising the taking and development of miles of motion picture film we are to shoot shortly. We are going into the newsreel game, not because we want to, but because we have decided it is the only way we can rebuild our depleted treasury in order to carry on further development. Our extensive plans call upon us to cover the entire globe with our trio-system of stations within the next ten years.

"We have figured that it would be logical to introduce television to the unsuspecting world by slow stages, mainly through the medium of newsreel productions, rather than to explode the news suddenly. It will, no doubt, take years to do that, by that time we will be able to withstand any forcible attempts to take it from us.

"We are now working on the plans for an immense machine, whose stations will be thousands of miles apart and which will be so powerful that we will be able to penetrate the Heaviside layer and this, in turn, will allow us to see and talk with the nearer planets.

"That, McManus, is what *TELEVISION* really is…"

Wentworth yawned and knocked the ashes out of his pipe.

"Well, I guess that will do for one evening—sleep it off—in the morning I'll make you acquainted with the plant. We have a few planes here and we might hop over to the two other transmitters and look over the sights," He yawned again, and then laughed," Gosh, I'm all tired out from talking." He arose, gazing a moment at the face of the moon, now almost directly south. Turning in my direction he said, "It's pretty late, so, if you'll pardon me, I'll say goodnight."

At my well-wishing words he turned and went into the cottage.

FOR a long time I sat there smoking, my thoughts ranging between doubt and conjecture. Television? It didn't seem possible! Although my line was principally film development and printing, I had taken a passing interest in other things allied to photography and projection that I felt might come my way in some future time. Television had always engaged my curiosity and I was aware of the obstacles met within the eastern laboratories. I had seen some of the slapped-together machines presenting poor substitutes of silhouette pictures, and had marveled at them. But to find a man like Wentworth—an ordinary-appearing fellow, a builder in steel, who appeared to have spent most of his life in the open—stating he had played an important part in the development of a perfect Television machine! Well, it was just too astounding to believe! Still, his lengthy story had been filled with the constant reminder that their work was not an overnight discovery; that it was one continuous striving for a definite goal. It was just such tireless, determined labor on the part of Edison that had brought the incandescent lamp to the world, years before it had been expected. And if Edison was able to perform such an unparalleled feat with absolutely no foundation for his work, why could not King accomplish the less amazing task of building a television outfit—backed, as he was, by twenty-five years of close relationship with the most spectacular rise of mechanical and electrical progress ever seen on the face of this globe?

I was getting muddled. A walk, I decided, would clear my head. Then I could sleep. Rounding the cottage, I picked out a narrow gravel path leading to the top of the hill and passed into sudden enveloping darkness as I entered the fringe of trees. It was cool—a pleasant place despite the absence of light. Finally, after much stumbling about I came upon a clearing running in a wide swath apparently around the hill. Ahead I made out the delicate reflections returned by a closely woven twelve-foot wire fence set in the center of the clearing and it, too, appeared to encircle the hill. Surprised, I turned my eyes up toward the crest to see the reason for the added precaution.

Through the filigree of steel I made out some sort of a widespread construction on the hilltop, the details of which could not be readily distinguished in the moonlight. It appeared to be in the nature of a long gun with massive verticals supporting a gigantic searchlight. Figuring I'd see more of it to one side, I started to walk around the fence.

Suddenly a terrifying shock struck my taut nerves; the night quiet was torn by the rising, blood-curdling shriek of a siren. Alarmed, I stopped dead and listened. It ceased after a lengthy period of lowering its whining burr and from somewhere in the trees came a powerful beam of light, fingering in a questing manner over the well-kept grass, towards me. Bathed in the blinding glare I heard a voice, loud, directed, and metallic as from a mechanical reproducer, "Is that you, Mr. McManus?"

"Yes," I shouted into the treetops, very much startled and wondering if I were the cause of all this uproar.

"Sorry, Mr. McManus," resumed the metallic voice, signifying my shout had been heard, "but no one is allowed near the fences after nightfall. Usually we shoot first then investigate when we discover prowlers along *that* fence. Better get back to the cottage."

The light snapped out and I watched the glowing point of the filament until it, too, faded into the night. When my eyes had accustomed themselves to the darkness, I hurried down the path and a few minutes later was trying to calm a wildly thumping heart on the steps of the cottage.

Then I was ready to admit, whatever truth there was in Wentworth's story, there was certainly enough circumstantial evidence pointing to his veracity.

THE next morning Wentworth grinned at me over the breakfast table. Got caught looking through the hilltop fence last night, eh?"

I felt my face flush with humiliation and managed a dry, unconvincing laugh. "Yes, I didn't think you had this place garrisoned with sharpshooters sitting in hidden lookouts!"

"Well—we have to have some sort of protection. There's no telling what may happen in the night. With those concealed stations and our radio-capacity guarded fences, we think we are fairly safe from unwanted intruders. The only way to get in here after dusk is by passing the two guards at the bridge, or by dropping by chute from a plane or dirigible; neither of which is very practical. The only thing that really could dislodge us now from our position would be long distance bombardment by heavy rifles; but so long as one projector stands in operating condition, we will make our presence exceedingly uncomfortable for the attackers." He grinned and winked meaningly.

I ate in silence, wondering if this machine were not some sort of a Frankenstein monster, whose penetrating eyes were already permitting it to grasp long tentacles of horrible power throughout the world, tearing away all conceptions of personal right and seclusion and sullenly awaiting the moment to thrash out all life within its range.

Breakfast over, Wentworth led the way down the hill to the many stalled garage in which were housed the private cars for their owners' use. My own mud spattered coupe stood out conspicuously alongside the other five glittering machines. Wentworth, after a glance around, singled out a new flivver roadster.

"Might as well drive as walk," he said laughingly as we swung out of the doors and up the drive away from the river. Directly east, through the closely growing poplars and pines, he guided the purring machine up the winding cinder road, and on rounding a sharp left turn, the solid looking three-story building whose western shadow had not as yet allowed the early morning damp to disperse from the trees came into view. A tall steel stack swept upwards of a hundred feet in the air, a faint curl of smoke trailing from its lip.

"THIS is the power plant," explained Wentworth as we came to a stop beside the two-storied steel corrugated roll doors. "There isn't much to see here except the generators and the transformer room. We burn oil in the engines and the heating plant and have a very devil of a time getting the stuff, especially during the winter months, as all of it has to be hauled by tank truck from Oregon. We haven't been able to induce the Northwestern to run a spur here on account of the nature of the land and the objections from land-owners; so we are forced to tank two months supply in a reservoir up the hill a bit."

As he was talking, we had entered a small office whose slate walls were studded with meters and switches.

Seated at the only desk and engaged in a telephone conversation was a thin, sandy haired, squint-eyed, spectacled man of fifty. He gave us a pleasant welcoming smile and, reaching into a drawer, withdrew a large red-lined graphed sheet which he handed to Wentworth with, "Here you are, Bob."

Wentworth studied the sheet while the man continued his talk. Finished, he arose.

"Fine, Alex," nodded Wentworth. "That's just the dope I've been anxious to get. By the way, here's a newcomer to our ranks: Mr. Thomas McManus, who is to take charge of the Newsreel Division. McManus, this is Alexander Chalmers, the best Swedish stationary engineer in the States."

Chalmers' wrinkled face broke into a grin. "Better watch your step—that Englishman has a bad habit of stretching the truth." He shook my hand heartily. "Coming in to look at my toys?" he invited, stepping to the door.

At the threshold I paused, looked, and gave vent to my feelings in one long, low whistle of surprise.

Toys? Man alive! Those generators!

There were six of them. Gigantic majesties of iron and copper, hunching their rounded shoulders high into the vast vault of the lengthy building. Back and above each dynamo towered the square and angular piles of the mighty Diesel engines. Three tiers of balconies, guardrails, and steel rod stairways traversed and crawled over their inspiring hulks. Never before in my life had I ever seen anything to compare with them in their very shocking display of power, and I say this backed by ten years of work in motion picture studios, where reproductions of monster sets depicting man's greatest works were common. Standing on that cross-ribbed, rubber-covered floor, the early morning sun slanting through the many-paneled, two-story windows, glittering off the polished brass and chrome-plated instruments and rods, highlighting the cool morocco green and flaming red paint of the motor assemblies, I experienced a thrill in looking upon man's handiwork that went singing down into the depths of my soul.

Man, the creator, becomes a mere wondering creature, a speechless servant to the might that was expressed in these colossal productions of his brain.

Only a single sound broke the cool, ringing silence of the building—the pulsing whine of one generator assembly at the northern end. Men in overalls were leisurely climbing about with tools, making adjustments, wiping dust and oiling bearings.

Wentworth's inquiry, "Amazed at this stuff?" brought me back to earth. His full face reflected his enjoyment at my open-mouthed expression.

"A—little," I admitted drawing a deep breath. "I didn't think it was like this. They certainly are wonderful. Just imagine the power all of them generate! What make are they and how in the world did you get them here?"

"They are special jobs turned out for us by the Cliff-Clemzon Electric Company of South Carolina., the new giant in the electrical world, and are capable of delivering eight thousand kilowatts at two thousand volts apiece. The Diesels come from Germany and are said to develop around ten thousand horsepower. A story could be told on how we transported these giants in parts and sections by rail and barge and freighter to Davenport and there placed them on barges for the eighty-mile tow up the Rock River to our landing stage from which we hauled and rolled the tons of iron up this hill here. Those were the days of *real* work! Some husky-looking jobs, eh?"

"I'll say," I agreed heartily, trying to imagine sixty thousand horsepower gathered under one roof!

"Yet, this is only the beginning of the story, McManus. Suppose we take a look at the transformer section—where the two thousand volts are stepped up to forty-five and seventy thousand?" He led the way through the length of the building, past the long line of six towering generator assemblies, and entered a small red-painted steel door.

Now I was on my guard and did not reveal my surprise when I gazed into the chamber, which must have been forty or more feet high and of the full width of the building. Centered on the concrete floor, with rubber-covered walks was an expansive platform supported on thick five-foot insulating columns. Upon this stage rose crisscrossing steel framing of I-beams and heavy strap screening, upon which were hung the transformers. Two rows of ten, they were twelve feet in height and between and over their corrugated bulks were runways and balconies of glass flooring and rubber railings. Almost numberless smaller transformers were suspended all over the steel work and the interweaving maze of right-angled cooling pipes and the heavily insulated wiring beyond comprehension. I felt as Wentworth must have felt the night he first saw King's television machine spread out in the old factory building. Overhead streaked the high-tension wires, perched on top of three-foot insulators, to the out-jutting balcony in the north wall. The illumination came from skylights only, the whole chamber falling into a cool, restful silence. I spied the shuttered grating of a huge ventilator opening on the west wall, and decided it must get pretty warm in here when the apparatus was in action.

I turned to Wentworth, a thousand questions ready to pop from my lips.

He cut me short with a depreciating wave of his hand. "This is nothing; you haven't seen anything yet worth mentioning. I'd like to show you about the sub-building, which is partly under this floor, and extending to the east as a one-story building by the time it goes a hundred feet down the hill. In that building we have an immense battery of storage cells from which we draw our reserve current when necessity demands.

"McManus, some day you might learn the reason for this tremendous reserve of power!"

"But tell me, Wentworth," I asked, "do you actually need all this—all this power for television?"

"Yes, McManus, we do. Our system calls for it—every volt and ampere. Kind of disturbing, eh? Matter of fact, it spoils the efforts of our fiction writers who have so nicely made use of vest-pocket television apparatus in their amazing stories. Take it from me, McManus, we will never see the day of a really portable television machine of our type; it's far too delicate and complicated to warrant even thinking about it."

"I don't know why I should feel like apologizing for it, but I have read quite a bit of those stories known as pseudo-scientific and scientific fiction," I said, grinning, "and have often regretted that they always run in the same channel; the hero, a bulbous-headed mechanical-minded recluse, discovers the secret in a happy thought and straightaway builds the entire machine in a few weeks, or even days, if it is to be instrumental in saving the much-destroyed world, or someone dear to him, and fares forth alone to subdue his enemies. Some have had television screens by which they traveled on light waves and looked upon incidents known to have occurred in ages past. But they all end up the same way; the inventor either dies with the destruction of his machine in a great spectacular consuming climax, or destroys it himself for the good of mankind."

Wentworth had listened with a smile overspreading his good-natured features. "Fiction," he chuckled, "tantalizing, impossible fiction, interesting and amusing to the scientific minded. I read it too. Life may be full of funny tricks but, thank the Lord, it's a whole lot nicer and more reasonable than some of the insane tommyrot printed in the name of literature." He turned, leading the way back through the generator house and out beside the flivver.

"YOU were going to take a look at our projector last night, eh?" he drawled as he settled into the seat and started the car. Grinning, he turned toward the rear of the powerhouse, over the place where the battery house lay partly concealed, and took a winding road upward. A few hundred feet on our way we passed four oil storage tanks and seeing them I could not resist remarking that the powerhouse would be out of luck should they ever explode. Wentworth's sudden glance and instantaneous burst of laughter caused me to wince at the senseless break I had made! He gunned the light car unmercifully and a cloud of dust rose from our wheels as we swung in and about the tree-lined path. Arrived at the high wire fence, the gate was rolled open—apparently by motor drive under control of a sentry somewhere in the vicinity. Again that strange machine, projector I should say, caught my eyes by its very vastness, and now in the revealing light of the sun, I could make out the details of its crude metallic construction.

Inside of the encircling wire fence the entire top of the hill had been leveled off to a perfect plane on which, about fifty feet from the enclosure, ran a circular two rail track over three hundred feet in diameter. Between the rails, of conventional gauge, was a gear rack whose teeth were so fine that, at first glance, I thought it was the third rail.

Walking along this carefully concreted ballasted roadway we approached the outer end of the projector assembly resting on a mighty ten-wheeled carriage riding the track. Under this truck could be seen the gear enclosures, guarding the mechanism engaged with the rack. The truck itself formed the sole outer supporting member of the sturdily built triangular truss, bridge-like in appearance, leaping over the intervening space of a hundred and fifty feet to the central pivot. This pivot, I learned as we traversed the boardwalk, slung alongside the truss, was made up of a concealed bearing of massive proportions. Around the bearing a foundation slab of concrete had been laid six feet deep resting on pine piling covering a circular area of a twenty-foot radius. Imbedded in the top of this slab was another set of tracks on which rolled the many-wheeled, heavy, steel, fifty foot circular flooring. To this flooring the lower ends of the truss were riveted and from this pivot-carriage rose two sixty-foot, three-legged towers. These vertical members were circular in section and almost three feet in diameter, hollow, and filled with concrete. They were elaborately braced for stress and strains. And, slung between these towers, was the projector—an affair of thick sheet steel plating—crudely wrought and angular—as large as an ordinary sized house. Above our heads swept the fifty-foot vertical gear quadrant driven through a slot cut in the rambling shack under the projector on the carriage floor.

There it was, silhouetted against the blue of the morning sky like some impossible creation of a giant; so strange and uncouth, I could scarcely believe it was the work of man!

"WELL, what do you think of this?" chuckled Wentworth, when I looked at him again.

"I—er. Really, Wentworth, I don't know what to say! It stuns me by its very size. I've been trying to put my impressions in words but all I can think of is *immense, monster,* and *wonderful.* Tell me something about its inner workings."

"Indeed I will." He took a pack of cigarettes, offered it to me, and we lit up.

"The nature of the rays we use in this machine requires us to shield the oscillators and the tube with quite a bit of lead. In fact, the projector housing alone weighs seventy tons; sixty tons of lead and steel being required to house the electrical outfit, weighing only ten tons complete. That's the reason why this display of strength comes in. Then there is one important factor that I honestly believe very few, if any, engineers working in this field know. And that is *control*.

"Do you realize that in the operation of this machine—television—we must split hundreds of seconds of arc in order to follow a moving object even a few miles away?

"I'll go into this in detail, for I see by your puzzled expression you don't understand me. Suppose we attached a beam one thousand miles long, one end of which is pivoted and the other free to swing in a complete circle—a radius-arm in other words to a motor car traveling at a rate of speed enabling it to traverse sixty miles in an hour. How much movement could you expect at the pivot of your projector?"

I dwelled upon this a moment, scratching a little diagram with a match on the wood railing. "Oh," I exclaimed as sudden realization dawned upon me. "Why, it would scarcely revolve at all!"

"Exactly," he declared. Taking his pencil, he placed a dot on my sketch a short space from the pivot. "Now, suppose you travel along this beam—say a hundred and fifty feet and figure out how much travel there would be at that point?"

I thought it over a few minutes, seeing it was nothing more than a problem of simple proportion, made the necessary changes of units, and figured it out on the back of an envelope. "Nine feet," I told him.

"Yes, nine feet—and at six thousand miles distance your hundred and fifty foot beam would only move eighteen inches in an hour!"

"Now, do you see the reason for the three-hundred foot diameter track? Objects don't move sixty miles an hour all the time, neither do they always travel concentrically with our radius. See that vertical gear quadrant? We must move the projector vertically just as precisely if not more precisely—as we do for the horizontal movements. We have to trace 'motion' no matter which direction it's going or how slow it's going, and the only way to do it with accuracy is to use immense means of control. Sometimes we move this one hundred and forty ton assembly so slowly that only an eighth of an inch of the rack is traversed in an hour."

"Couldn't you use the floating system that has been adopted in the big telescopes?" I queried.

"Could—yes. But why go to the trouble of balancing that awkward projector when this system is a whole lot simpler?"

For a time I stood regarding the details of the construction while thoughts raced. So that was it! The truss was geared to the rack and formed the long lever turning the projector whose face would be under such perfect control that very little trouble would be felt when following a distant object. What! Why those scatter-brained writers! The nerve, the audacity, and the ignorance of those fools in supposing they could expect to see things with a device no bigger than an ordinary searchlight and mounted in the same identical manner. Why, it was plainly evident, here was the biggest handicap to successful television in the entire mechanical design! And how spectacular and vivid a description could be put into words if some competent technical writer saw this projector as it stood on Television Hill!

Wentworth was speaking, breaking the train of my thoughts: "So, you see, McManus, the problems in television were not so much electrical as they were mechanical. When you begin to learn of how some of our equipment has been carried to the superlative peak of mechanical ingenuity by the clear thinking of our engineers, you will see to what degree of preciseness the human brain can conquer a supposedly impossible task. I know you will be driven almost to the wall of despair in your effort to find adequate words with which to picture your impressions, but, if you pass the next year here and do not change your opinion of man's limitations—well, I'd say you were not human." He laughed.

"I'd like to take you up that ladder to the projector now, but we won't have time. We have planned to run a working test tonight—the first since June, and I have to make a run around to the other two transmitters to make sure all is in readiness."

I was in such a mental muddle, trying to connect all the things I had seen and heard, attempting to put them in order so as to form some sort of a theory of how television was accomplished, that I paid no attention to where Wentworth drove after we had left the hill. He pulled to a sudden stop on a concrete drive skirting a steel building bearing the unmistakable markings of an airplane hangar. We were at the river's edge and the hangar faced the water, while back of us rose the sharp slopes of the tree-covered banks. A short distance to the south could be seen the white sides and red roofs of the workmen's homes Wentworth had spoken of last night.

An explosion of sharp detonations cut off an explanation Wentworth was about to make. With a humorous shrug, he motioned me to follow as he entered the side door.

CHAPTER THREE

IT was a conventional aviation structure in every respect. Two standard cabin monoplanes of metal construction, and equipped with pontoons were quartered in one corner, wings folded back, while on the concrete ramp leading into the river water was a huge orange painted Sikorsky amphibian, its two motors bellowing a chest-throbbing roar.

A mechanic stepped up to Wentworth and I heard his shouted words: "We just started to warm up—be ready in a few minutes."

Speech was impossible in the thunder amplified by the steel walls of the hangar. After a time Wentworth tapped my shoulder, pointing to a portable stairway swung out of the overhead hatchway of the plane. Once inside he went forward into the pilot's compartment and after a mouth-to-ear conversation with the pilot, returned and seated himself in the chair ahead of me.

In my position I could see over the right stub wing and look up at the vibrating motor. The men were motioned away; the motors roared anew, a blue trail of smoke flooding from the exhaust pipe. Easily we rolled down the ramp and settled in the river. A metallic thud announced the withdrawal of the landing wheels into their streamlined compartments and, heading into the south wind, the unleashed Wasps took up their deep-throated, reverberating song of power in earnest—the flame-tipped blue exhaust gas streaking rearward into the swirling ripples raised by the air-stream. The cabin floor tilted up slightly as we began to plane over the surface, the hull vibrating under the pull of the motors until the windows rattled in their frames. Rising in a spreading white feather on both sides of the cabin, drenching the motors in a mist torn to flying shreds by the spinning discs of the propellers, was the spray. Suddenly the veil of spray receded and was gone.

We were flying!

The water was dropping away from us in annoying and slightly unpleasant jerks. The booming motor-music of the Wasps grew deeper and steadier as we seemingly moved slower and slower along the river course, until the plane itself seemed rigidly fixed in the skies, while the earth drifted past like some mighty curtain. I confess flying was a new sensation to me, and I gloried in every new discovery, thoroughly disgusted with myself for ever backing out of the many chances I had had.

The trees, I would have sworn, were tiny masses of sponge hugging the surface, and of their height nothing could be judged except for the dark shadows they cast. The countryside, wonderfully beautiful in a crazy quilt of horizontal, vertical, and diagonal lines of every imaginable color, was a sight so strange and unearthly that the eye was held in rapt attention. From the air the world was beautiful!

Farmhouses and their attendant buildings were miniature replicas of model-like unrealism. Incredulous it was that men and women lived and worked in them!

Away to the south was the tiny village, Dixon, a silver thread snaking through and out past it.

The plane tilted suddenly, cutting off my view of the ground and throwing the cabin in shadow as the sunlight shifted from the left windows around the front of the ship and swung to the roof of the cabin on my side. Leveling out, the plane began to retrace our aerial path over the river, now a curving polished streak apparently no wider than eight inches.

Below the right motor I saw a bird's eye view of Television Hill. The projector, with its circular track, was at this height a monster clock whose hands pointed due south. A tiny toy block with a stub pencil standing close by, almost hidden in the trees, was the powerhouse, while a longer building on the southern slope of the hill, and about a thousand feet to the east of the cottage was the projection-house, for atop it were the two water towers Wentworth had drawn my attention to last night. Almost below us, now, were the homes of the workmen.

Wentworth pointed out a power-line-tower system stretching far into the north. They began directly at the powerhouse.

"Ours," he shouted. "They go up to the Wisconsin line— then split. One branch goes to New Glarus and the other to Lake Geneva. A forty-five thousand volt system. The towers carry all of our lines—power, phone, control, and so on."

Near Oregon, Illinois, the towers lined toward the north and we left them, bearing toward Rockford, over which we soon passed, following the Rock River to Beloit. From there it was a cross-country flight until the deep blue depths of Lake Geneva appeared. A wide, booming circle over the town and we headed toward the surface, dropping swiftly. I watched a bug of an ambitious speedboat make a humorous attempt to keep up with us. The far-carrying beat note of the skipping launch became audible as the Wasp went idle, and I sensed, all the more, the slipping, uneven, and uncomfortable slide downward. There was a century long moment as we poised a few feet above the water; a slither of spray wetting the stub wings; a hollow rebound; a heavier splash, and we were skimming over the surface, the thundering motors pulling us toward a concrete ramp similar to the one we had left on the Rock River. The wheels were shipped and we emerged upon the landing.

"WELL, how did you like the ride?" asked Wentworth as he hurried me up a narrow stairway.

"How else can one describe his first air flight than to say...wonderful!"

At that he turned with a rare and perplexing smile on his lips. "Wonderful? That is all you have been muttering since you came here! But you haven't seen anything yet. Wait until tonight and we'll see what other descriptive adjectives you can muster."

"THIS projector is back in the country quite a bit and rather inaccessible to a plane; so we'll have to motor there. This shore property once belonged to my Dad. I'm sorry to say I've been forced to parcel it out to real-estate sharks to keep Television Hill going." At a garage we found a small sedan with waiting chauffeur. He took us down the highway a bit to a deserted and little traveled dirt road circling about through the tiny ravines and steep hills famous to this region. The trees were thick on all sides and frequently we passed glaring signs warning against trespassing on this private ground. We climbed a steep grade and near the top we were halted by a wire fence of the type I had made such startling acquaintance with at Television Hill.

Several cottages and the brick structure housing the transformer group were the only constructions inside the barrier. The driver played his horn and the gates opened in that mysterious manner by electric control.

At the cottage we were met by John Somerset, the manager of the station, and his daughter Eloise. Wentworth, as soon as introductions were over, started right in with an incomprehensible discussion in which figured many code numbers and shop terms of such a highly technical nature that I gave up the attempt to follow them and retreated to the porch, smoking and looking at the fantastic bulk of the projector. What must those astonished persons think who happened to get a glimpse of that monster affair spread out over the hilltop? It was plainly visible for miles in any direction from the surrounding hills and surely someone at some time must have become curious enough to make inquiries about it. Whatever King and Wentworth told these curious ones must have been satisfactory for I had never heard a single rumor of a television apparatus being built in the country, much less in my own home State!

On the far end of the porch was a hooded searchlight and near it—a steel tripod. Yes, a machine gun rest!

The girl came to the door and smiled as I nodded. "Were you looking at our defenses?" she asked.

I admitted I had been doing so, somewhat perturbed by her frank scrutiny of my person.

"Those are more for effect than for anything else," she confided, closing the screen door and seating herself on the porch step. "Do you see that little triangular house perched high on the right tower?"

At the Television Hill projector I had first noticed this tiny building set atop the tower and had wondered about it, seeing that the only means of access was to climb up the sixty-foot vertical ladder fastened to the tripod.

"In there a man is always on watch—day and night. He's got half a dozen machine guns in his armored castle and those searchlights hung from the tower platforms can make the hill as bright as day."

During the next hour I learned much about Television Hill and its people from the well-informed Eloise, whose knowledge of the mechanical side of the plant was amazing. She and I were well on the way to being good friends when Wentworth appeared.

"Ready, Eloise?" asked her father.

Wentworth explained. "She's coming back with us to Television Hill. King is bringing his daughter, Diane, with him. The girls were great school chums; so they'll be all-up-in-the-air to see each other again."

"Yes, Diane must have much to tell, having been in Europe for the last five years," admitted Somerset, lighting his cigarette. "But say, Bob, you didn't make much of the report Smythe has made concerning his difficulty in getting New Glarus and my station to line up at one point southwards?"

"Oh, that," drawled Wentworth, frowning. "Don't worry about that little thing. There's no reason for it and I'll speak to Williams about it this afternoon while I'm there."

Then Eloise appeared with several suitcases and hatboxes.

"Hey, you," her father called out. "Where do you think you're going with that truck?"

Eloise flashed him a hurt and surprised glance. "Why, this is only what I need!"

SOMERSET'S hearty laughter rang in my ears long after we had returned to the amphibian and were roaring westward. With an elbow resting on the windowsill I watched the slow march of the countryside below the stub-wing. The sharp, vibrant hum of the Wasp and its supporting spars and wing seemed indescribably fixed in the mid-air while the whole world rose and fell far below us. It was nearing noon, I knew, from the fleeting shadow darting at terrific speed over the farms and the feeling of hunger in my midriff. Eloise and Wentworth sat on the sunny side of the ship; the girl watching the scenery and Wentworth reading a handful of letters he had pulled from his pockets. I was glad when I discovered the third and last projector some three miles northwest of New Glarus, Wisconsin.

A sudden, unexpected, alarming clank and thud announced the extension of the landing wheels and the motors went silent as we slid toward a flat field close to the sharp rise of the considerable height on which stood the projector.

Wentworth drew me aside as we left the plane. "Listen, Mac, don't feel hurt, but the work I have to do here will take four or five hours, and is of such a nature that your presence would be— Oh, well, you get the drift of what I hate to say."

I nodded, understandingly.

"So you and Eloise will have to entertain one another; I'll get you a car if you wish."

When told, the black-eyed Eloise was delighted. I was disappointed, for I saw Wentworth was not yet ready to take me into his confidence by permitting me to see the interior of the projectors. I took the limousine and drove to Madison where the girl and I dined and later watched a dull motion picture and an even duller newsreel. I couldn't get my mind off the greater appeal of the work Wentworth might be doing, and heartily wished myself at his side. This was no reflection on the girl's companionship, however.

AT five-thirty I pulled the car up to the cottage at the New Glarus station and found Wentworth awaiting us. He greeted us, "All set? Now we'll fly home and have dinner at seven with the Kings."

Once more in the air, we were droning southeast.

Now, my impressions were more sedate and reasonable as the shock of discovery was wearing off. The more I dwelt upon the immensity of the work King and Wentworth had accomplished, the greater grew my admiration. They had something more than a mere laboratory experiment, why else this elaborate display of extensive equipment; the power lines, the powerhouse; the three projectors in two states, the number of men (almost two hundred throughout the entire plant), the many cars and trucks, and lastly, but not least, the hangar full of fast planes? If this were the real thing, just what must the rest of the world-known engineers be working on—a lot of pitiful trash?

Television, as Wentworth claimed it to be, must be a marvelous thing—almost beyond imagination in its mechanical wonders. No wonder then that stories written around and about this apparatus were always so indefinite and misty about the engineering problems met with by the inventors! No wonder authors thought best to keep silent about these interesting points, passing up their own inability to picturize their imaginary instruments by claiming deep secrecy of the inventors and the ignorance of the teller of the story!

The part I was to play in this realistic, life and blood story was beginning. And what a beginning it was! Just what responsibilities would be thrust upon my shoulders I did not know, but whatever they were, I hoped they would not put too much demand upon the lines I knew so little of. Still, within the year, when my contract would expire, I would know whether or not I had been of any service to the company. If Wentworth and King would be willing to bother with me further, it would be utter foolishness on my part to leave—especially as there was so much opportunity in this field for future development. However, a year is a long interval of time when it is just beginning and of the many unthought of things that can happen in a year, God only knows.

It wasn't long before we were circling above Television Hill. We slipped sedately down between the banks to the river and surfaced close to the hangar.

"KING in yet?" asked Wentworth of a mechanic, after a glance about the hangar. The pilot tossed Eloise's baggage to me as I stood beside the dripping hull of the Sikorsky.

"No, sir. There was an accident at the field—a collision between a tri-motor and a smaller ship taking off. A bad mess, so I phoned Mr. King."

Therefore we took our way up to the cottage on foot. Wentworth launching into a disgusted series of remarks concerning the danger of the Municipal Airport as a landing field for commercial and student planes.

After removing the traces of the day's jaunt, I returned to the veranda where I found Wentworth smoking his pipe. He said nothing but sat in a listening attitude, his eyes focused to the east.

At exactly six-forty-five there became audible a distant hum. It wasn't from a motor-car speeding on the highway across the river, for it rapidly increased in volume to the crescendo whine of a wide-open plane motor and a moment later, leaping swiftly from the darkening eastern skies, a Lockheed Vega amphibian flashed its black-trimmed orange fuselage over the cottage with a terrific, ear-splitting, blatant snarling, and heading toward the river, banked sharply, dipping directly below the tree line.

Thereupon its roar ceased.

Amazed at the speed in which the plane had come and gone, I stood with craning neck staring incredulously.

Wentworth came to my side, grinning.

"Know who was piloting that ship?"

"Couldn't guess. Might be Lindbergh or Al Williams."

"No such luck. Just our friend…King. I know when he is at the stick. Crazy for speed, he doesn't waste a single move. Takes off and immediately starts in the direction of his destination, gaining altitude as he goes. Although he's over fifty-five years (young) he can fly a lot harder and cleaner than the regular pilot who accompanies him at all times."

CHAPTER FOUR

A FEW minutes later a small green truck poked its stainless steel nose up the drive and the machine came to a skidding stop before the stairs. A helmeted man of average height and of slightly heavier than normal build clambered out of the right seat and assisted a girl to alight. The mechanic-driver reached into the rear compartment and handed out a collection of various sized suitcases and handbags. The older man, who I supposed was King, began to get a handful of suitcases together, but Wentworth and I were upon him instantly, relieving him of his burdens, despite the humorous scowl he gave us. There was joyous, shrill greeting as Eloise dashed from the veranda into the arms of the newcomer. Then the house servants came running and for a few minutes I stood, my arms full of bags, totally forgotten in the handshaking and chatter. Once there was an interruption as the mechanic dropped a bulky trunk on the porch floor. After a semblance of the usual quiet had been restored, King became aware of my presence.

"Why, hello, McManus! When did you get here? Yesterday?"

I nodded, absently, I confess, for my eyes were directed toward the girl. I turned to him, recognizing him instantly, now that he had withdrawn the helmet. His white hair was combed in an attempt to conceal the thinning spot on his crown. Undoubtedly he was not totally immersed in his great work, for his general appearance was neat and well groomed almost to the point of fastidiousness. His brown eyes twinkled. The clear pink of his skin spoke of a rigorous and well-balanced life.

I had seen him many a time in the main offices of the New Era Film Company, and once, without his identity having been mentioned, had answered some very perplexing problems he had presented to my chief, who had referred him to me.

My eyes returned to the girl. King followed my gaze, a slow smile of understanding breaking over his lips. He motioned for her to come over.

"Diane, this is the man I've been telling you about. Mr. Thomas McManus, whom we took from a responsible position at New Era."

I don't know what happened to my tongue, but my agitated brain could not connect with the words I wanted to say; so I just nodded, stammering. "Pleased to meet you…"

Her smile was disarming.

"I think he'll come to like our place a whole lot better than New Era, Dad." She laughed merrily. Eloise then took her into the cottage.

Wentworth was regarding me pensively through narrowed, humorous eyes.

"Oh, ho," he chuckled, winking to King.

I certainly felt foolish when I discovered that unconsciously I had been holding the suitcase during that interval!

WENTWORTH, humanely, changed the subject. "Well, King, how did everything go?"

He eased himself into the swing while I relieved myself of the bags by turning them over to a servant.

"Fine, Bob." King replied, settling on the wide rail. "Everything went okay. Had a little trouble from Elliott at New Era when it came to agreeing that he keep the sources of his films a secret. They will take care of the distributing and furnish us with all leads, swinging in a set of tickers, teletype machines hooked with AP, and radio communications at such times as necessary."

"We will train our own men and women to handle our ends of the lines, instead of importing doubtful help as we had intended doing at first.

"We are to produce a negative and one positive film, and according to the terms of the contract he and I drew up, we must have both reels at the Municipal airport three hours after the news breaks."

HERE he paused, turning to me. "That means, McManus, you will have to swing directly into your work and get your cameras running within the next two months. We have already ordered the equipment we thought necessary and whatever more you need will be put at your disposal immediately.

"How do you like Television Hill? Wentworth show you about yet?"

"Yes, sir. He had me on the move quite a bit today. Gave me my first air ride up to the other two stations and showed me around here. And as to my liking the place—words fail me in conveying the pleasure and *joy* I have experienced since yesterday."

Wentworth grinned. "He's seen a lot of what he expresses as 'wonderful,' and I don't blame him for wanting to stay." He regarded the bowl of his pipe with an assumed attentive stare.

"Where are we bunking him—in the village?"

"That I haven't decided yet," thoughtfully replied Wentworth. "I had him here last night, awaiting your decision."

"The cottage is plenty big enough, so why not keep his room for him here? We can keep our eyes on him the better," King laughed wholeheartedly, giving me a reassuring wink. I had yet to learn of the keen powers of observation he possessed. A wizard in the chemical and mechanical sciences, he could ascertain with uncanny accuracy the actions and character of those with whom he came in contact. Though I could not even suspect it, he knew more about me and my past history at the time than even my closest friends.

"Tonight's the big night, eh?" remarked King suddenly.

"Yes," replied Wentworth, "tonight we run the first of a series of tests to see how the increased power will affect the screening. Our useful range ought to be about five thousand miles, now that we've stepped up the beam range to cut entirely through eight thousand miles. Williams and I went over the entire projector assembly at New Glarus and still we didn't find the reason for the queer skip when the projector is in motion. Still whatever it is, it must be extremely minute at the transmitter when it only becomes apparent at a radius of two thousand miles. And the funny thing about it, King, is that we have that trouble at only one spot on the compass! Matter of fact, it's beyond me and the rest of the men at New Glarus and Lake Geneva. Somerset was telling me today that he caught several curious people sneaking around the fences during the last few weeks. He had one of them arrested and the news printed in the local paper there so he thinks he'll not be troubled anymore."

I HAVE often attended dinners, banquets, and affairs of like pleasantries, but supper that evening was one of the most enjoyable hours I have ever experienced. No mention of shop was made and the two older men joked and told humorous experiences throughout the entire period. King had a rich store of humorous anecdotes, which he related in such a manner that we were convulsed with laughter.

THROUGH many episodes like this my eyes had invariably strayed to Diane who sat directly opposite me. Several times I apprehended her quick glances in my direction. Once Eloise caught my attention; a meaning nod of her head and a slow wink revealed that she had become aware of my actions.

I could scarcely come to believe we were the principals brought together from the various walks of life by the amazing experiment of television. As usual, I began to draw my comparisons with the tales told in fiction, as they would have been depicted in accord with the established canons that those specialized authors seemed to hold to rigidly. King and Wentworth could have been excused if they were found to be one-tracked, super-intelligent, thin-lipped theorem-issuing, physical monstrosities whose predominant thought was the successful completion of their self-appointed tasks to the utter disregard of all else. I thanked the Lord that life was different— that we found a safety valve in laughing at the misfortunes of others, concealing, as it were, our compassion and sympathy.

King and Wentworth, despite the knowledge of all their stupendous accomplishments, were as natural as the average businessman, jeering good-naturedly at the absurdities of the impetuous words and actions of those around them.

Come to think of it, it wouldn't be a bad idea to write a story, or at least a diary, around the experiences here. Surely they would be more amazing and a lot more thrilling than any of those imaginative tales I had read. A year from today I could look back upon these impressions and, perhaps, laugh at them. Then, too, I could work in the entry of Diane in a pleasant little plot. And when King decided to expose his work to the world I would be in position to scoop the world of fiction with the *real story!* I would try it! Though unversed in story writing I would hold the indisputable advantage of actually living my incidents!

So ran my thoughts as we left the dining room and repaired to the veranda. King and Wentworth smoked and commented on the day's news. Then as the moon rose they took leave and strode slowly down the path, heading toward the projector house, I sat comfortably alone in one corner of the porch thinking over the highlights of the day, and wondering quite a bit about Diane. I had to smile when I recalled the sight I must have been when she was introduced to me and I stood speechless and gripping those bags.

"MR. McMANUS." It was Eloise's voice. "Come here, quickly."

I arose and hurried along the west side of the veranda to the extreme north end, where I found the two girls staring uphill toward the unseen projector.

"Look," she directed, pointing to the west and the river. "The projector is in action."

I saw it! A deep lavender glow quivering as though generated by some mighty arc sputtering in a gigantic searchlight, covering a restricted area over the west banks of the river, silhouetting the trees in a bold curtain of exotic purple and black. On the still night air came a distant crackling and a heavy monotone of humming.

"It's always like that—until the tubes have become warm enough to take the terrific shock of millions of volts of plate potential," explained Eloise as the awful grandeur of color faded away slowly.

On Diane's face was mirrored titter amazement.

"You seem quite moved, Miss King," I exclaimed.

"You, too, appear to be slightly wrought up," she returned quickly, seating herself on the wide rail to better watch the flickering spurts of red and violet light flashing over the countryside to the horizon in streaks of horizontal lightning. No wonder a powerhouse was required to feed the projectors!

A phone burred within the hall and Eloise skipped away to answer it.

After a moment Diane took her eyes from the beams and looked at me. She said, "Don't you think my Dad a wonderful man to have brought this wonder to the world?"

I adjusted my glasses with an assumed nonchalant gesture.

"Well, taking things as I've seen them today, your Dad has accomplished some very wonderful things during his whole life."

Eloise ran up then. "Mr. King is down at the projection house and he wants us to come down there, too."

IN daylight the projection house was an unusually plain three-storied structure surmounted by the distinguishing water towers, but in the moonlight, the seven hundred foot building loomed a huge, mysterious block fading into the trees, its square faces broken by the glittering reflections of the moon on its many windows.

At the open door stood King, awaiting us.

"Tickets, please," he smiled leading us through several small rooms fitted out as offices and drafting rooms. He pressed a button on the brick wall in the last room and the heavy fire door was rolled open by an attendant.

We were on the threshold of an unusually plain and business-like theatre some three hundred feet deep. At the far end, almost covering the entire width of the building—approximately sixty feet, and rising thirty feet high above the stage floor was the cyclopean screen! From the manner in which the dome lights were reflected from its surface I was put in doubt as to whether or not it was made up of some curious glass, strangely opaque and yet transparent. It had the defying appearance of being there and not being there!

The floor had the conventional theatre slope, but there were only about a hundred seats grouped near the center. In the rear jutted a balcony. Packing crates and a lot of bulky mechanism littered the entire platform, for such it was, having a level floor instead of the slope generally found. Occupying a position directly below the forward edge of the balcony was a shoulder high circular construction some thirty-five feet in diameter. Above it, suspended from a steel structure, was a great mirror. Filled with wonder and conjecture I took all this in, deciding the projecting mechanism was on the balcony as in the modern theatre.

King led us directly to the last row of seats and left with an apology. I watched him run up the side stairway to the balcony, where Wentworth and several other men were busily engaged in their work. As a pleasant surprise an organ began toning out a vibrant, colorful, futuristic selection.

Slowly the lights faded out and the screen glowed with a steady white light.

It became alive with a whirling, black-lining, streaking, formless display of whites and blacks, reds and blues, the like of which I have never witnessed. It affected the eyes in a curious manner, almost causing one to believe he was sinking into the coma induced by ether. As the dizzying spectacle continued, the organ, apparently frightened, went silent. King's disgusted exclamation cut through the air like an explosion. I closed my eyes momentarily.

A gasp from Diane caused me to open them quickly only to stare in open-mouthed astonishment upon a country scene pictured on the monster screen with such tantalizing depth and definition that I could have sworn we were looking upon the actual scene itself under the reddish glow of some inexpressibly powerful searchlight. The fact that only objects of an apparent distance of a hundred feet deep were shown made it appear the more to be a stage set.

Wentworth's voice cut through the silence. "That scene is from a farm forty miles west of Davenport, Iowa. Now, watch closely—we're going to do a little traveling tonight."

Slowly the scene flowed toward us, coming as though from a distant mist, taking clear definition in close proximity, and fading seemingly at our very feet. Faster it moved, trees and houses dashing toward us as we leaped over the countryside, cutting with a sudden flash here and there through farmhouses, delving into the sudden blackness of the hills and emerging into light as the invisible rays carried us onward.

At length my sorely tried patience gave way and I left the girls and sought the stairway to the balcony. As I threaded my way between the various boxes and other obstructions, I came to the most disappointing discovery I had yet made. I don't know what sort of machines I had expected to find up there, but

I had judged them to compare with the rest of the monster equipment.

King and Wentworth stood beside two men seated before the lengthy console. As I came into the area slightly illuminated by shaded lamps, both of them nodded in welcome. One operator sat in a comfortable chair behind a large steering wheel as you find in an automobile. And like the auto-wheel it had a number of controls clustered at the hub. At his feet were a series of pedals, narrow in width—something like the foot-pedals of the organ. His right foot was pressed on a lever by which he controlled the speed of the motion forward. On his left were many hand-wheels, which he adjusted from time to time, making alterations with the larger wheel slowly. Studying it for a time I saw that the steering wheel caused the scene to shift to the right or left, while the larger of the hand wheels caused the scene to tip up or down.

His vision of the screen was unobstructed save for two red converging lines shining brightly on the mirror surface set so that the lower edge just came even with the top edge of the screen. Right in front of him, in a position similar to that of the dashboard of an automobile, was a series of meters and dials. Some were spinning rapidly while those that moved slowly could be seen to be calibrated in such units as feet, miles, and hundreds of miles. One was a speedometer, which then registered three hundred miles an hour on a scale running up to two thousand miles!

Was it any wonder objects were dashing up to the screen so swiftly that they were indistinct and blurred?

Below this meter was the usual total-meter and beside it the trip meter. On the latter the tenth mile figure returned to zero every twelve seconds!

The operator on the left side watched the screen with intent stare, his restless fingers playing over the five-banked series of toggle switches continually in response to the flashing lights of a hundred or more tiny red lamps.

Wentworth turned to King. "We've got to eliminate that 'mixing panel.' It's only a makeshift at best. I've got Smythe working on an idea of an automatic device that'll catch those little discrepancies in synchronizing and lighting, and right them instantly at their sources."

Here I touched Wentworth's arm.

"Say, how come it's night, yet the images on the screen appear as clear as though they were under a powerful light."

He flashed an amused smile to King.

"McManus, sunlight or moonlight are not necessary to the searching eyes of television! Now, please, do not ask me to explain, for it would take me all evening to do so, and I doubt if you'd understand. But don't worry, you'll find out yet. Take in the show now."

SOMEWHAT rebuffed, I sought my former seat beside Diane, who greeted me brightly, "You disappeared so suddenly I thought you had become frightened. Isn't this too wonderful for words! Just think, we are looking upon sights hundreds of miles from here! How is it done?"

"I'd be much pleased to tell you, Miss King, but you see I know almost nothing about it from a technical and exact standpoint," I had to admit that.

"Jim, my brother, has been telling me in his letters what Dad and Mr. Wentworth have been doing during the time I have been away from home. Before I went to Europe I did not pay much attention to the things going on around here, living as I did with relatives in Chicago. Now, I begin to see some of the marvels they have accomplished."

The expansive screen was alive with a quick changing of scenery as the penetrating eyes of television leaped across the country at amazing speeds. As we sat in those comfortable chairs, there passed startling and revealing views of Omaha, Denver, Salt Lake City, Oakland, San Francisco. Of the hundreds of intermediate towns and villages very little could be distinguished, so great was our speed of passage!

We paused in San Francisco to sweep up and down the main streets to test the equipment under the varying speed conditions met with in motorcars and pedestrians. As one would suspect it was a thrilling and withal an alarming sight to see the steering wheel and dashboard of a machine on the screen, while the far-distant hands of the driver guided his way through traffic, unaware for a single moment that over eighteen hundred or more miles away eight people were watching his every move! We paused once off the Golden Gate to take a look at an Orient-bound freighter. Then up the western coast we raced. Raced is a much-used term for our present day velocities, but I could not think of a more descriptive verb to portray the pace at which the televise rays cut radially as we swept to the north. Starting at a speed of three hundred miles an hour, the operator slowly accelerated the motion until the screen was one continuous stream of horizontal lines. Then he announced. "Three thousand miles an hour!"

The flight from California to Portland, Oregon, was made before we were aware such a distance had been traversed. At Seattle we roved over the sailor-crowded decks of the fleet anchored there. And we saw what the power plants of these mighty sea-fighters looked like, when King sent the closely focused penetrating rays into the very hearts of the ships. It was actually X-raying ships in a land where it was just beginning to take on the darkness of evening and was such an unthought of feat as to be almost incredible! But to see such a thing taking place before my own eyes! What could I say...?

Diane gave her impression in one short expressive exclamation, "Impossible, but true!"

From there we raced even further up the coast. Almost into the Aleutian Island area. Then, retreating now, we swung back through northern Canada, passing Hudson Bay, dropping down through Wisconsin until there was pictured a view of the idle projector at Lake Geneva.

What happened then was one of the most unusual stunts ever attempted, either in actual life or in the world of fiction. A moment of darkness flashed over the screen followed by the black-lining and whirlings. To my surprise I found we were looking upon a scene on the Rock River near Rockford. Following the river, the screen moved along the river road toward the south and in our direction. I almost imagined we were driving over Route No, 2 (The Rock River Road) at a pace close to sixty miles an hour. The machines we passed flowed through the screen slowly with evidence of slight cross sectioning when they were going in our direction and were just a flash when they came from the opposite way. We came to the place where the road turned into a private lane leading to the bridge crossing the river to Television Hill. It is impossible to express the emotions I felt as the scene went from the guardhouse, where the watchman sat, rifle close by, watching the approach of the bridge, across the bridge to the other guardhouse, up the path, and past the cottage toward the projection house. Honestly, my heart was pounding with excitement by the time it was creeping up through the outer rooms and approaching the steel door. Then, breaking through, it screened the theatre lengthways, then the balcony, and crept up to the control system. King waved to his double on the screen. Wentworth laughed his amusement.

"So that's how I look to you people," he said loud enough for us to hear.

The next moment I was in the center of the picture. I arose and stepped into the aisle, drawing Diane after me.

"See," I explained. "You have to face the north if you want to see your face on the screen."

The two girls went into pealing laughter as they saw their actions portrayed instantaneously on the screen, though we were in apparent darkness. Apparent I say, for I sensed rather than saw a faint violet glow throughout the entire theatre. Then, too, my skin felt as though high tension current were flowing over it. Whatever the reason, it wasn't unpleasant.

With that as the climax, the screen went dark as the dome lights flashed on—and the first television performance of the world was over!

Television, now, was a reality! Stark proof had been presented in a manner that silenced all doubts I had held. The bands of interference caused by physical, mechanical, and other natural conditions clearly demonstrated that 'faking' could not have been carried to such extreme care. And seeing myself on the screen had satisfied any questions I might have asked!

There in the space of four short hours we had covered a trip throughout the west that ordinarily would have taken months for the average traveler to traverse. He would see less than we did and would have to undergo the discomforts of long and tedious journeys by rail and motor; would have the concurrent expense of his lengthy trip in lodging and food; and wouldn't be beset at every stop by worry of connections and tickets. We, seated in those comfortable theatre chairs, had looked upon the passage of over sixty-seven hundred miles of the country in less than four hours!

TELEVISION!

It had come!

CHAPTER FIVE

THE days passed quickly as they always do when our time and minds are completely taken up with work that draws every bit of our interest and capacity. The specially designed and built wide-angle cameras were installed on their fixed stands on the balcony front and their shutter-synchronizing devices, necessary for reasons at once apparent to a projection expert, hooked up with the driving shutter mechanism of the television screen projector. The film, Fotophone and Movietone width, was fed into the intake reels by automatic reelers; thus enabling a continuous movement of film through the cameras without a halt being made to reset new stock during a valuable shot.

The exposed film, with recorded sound, either produced by an expert group of sound-artists who had been trained to duplicate every and any sound met with in the usual run of news stuff, or added later from an ever-growing library of phonograph records, was led through a lightproof chute directly down to the basement, where the conventional methods of developing and printing were carried through.

A few hitches were met and conquered in quick order by whole-hearted concentration of efforts on the part of all the various departments involved. Witnessing this, I saw why so much progress had been made; everyone was so intensely interested in producing his best that cooperation came as second nature.

Towards the end of my allotted two months I began to shoot scenes in and about the vicinity of Chicago to make sure the extremely complicated apparatus I had built up was functioning perfectly. As my work became more and more advisory, I had plenty of opportunity to watch the entire television machine in operation—at least, those parts that were in the projection theatre.

King and Wentworth did not make any attempt to inform me of the processes and theories on which their vast machine was based, other than to speak pointedly on those mechanical features closely connected with the "camera-bank."

OUR testing went on. Late one October afternoon there came a sudden clicking of the Teletype machine installed near the control console and I hurried back, hoping it would be something we could film.

"NEW ERA FILMS," pounded out the flying levers, 5:30 P.M. SUNSET SPECIAL, UNION PACIFIC FLYER, DERAILED NEAR FREMONT, NEB. WEST OF OMAHA 30 MILES."

At my call King came on the run, took a look at the typed sheet, and shouted to all, "All right, boys, get set. This will be the first shot we take."

With swift precision the lights were switched out, and the screen, after its usual period of aimless whirlings of black and white, was synchronized in relation with the companion transmitter at New Glarus, on a scene somewhere out west. The two operators were adjusting their instruments with great speed. Glancing upwards toward the overhead mirror I watched the slowly moving red lines reflected there from the circular structure on the main floor.

I hurried to the rail, joining King and Wentworth as they peered into the thirty-five foot opening almost below. At first I had mistaken this for some part of the machine used in the projection of the screen images; but after seeing it in operation once, I had been overcome with appreciative regard for Wentworth's amazing mechanical skill.

It was a deep set, faintly illuminated map of the world! A map so curiously contorted and grotesque that I had spent some time figuring out the contours of the land divisions, detailed. With a spot near the lower western edge of Lake Michigan as a center, the map had been laid out in such a manner that the western hemisphere was depicted in its entirety while the eastern hemisphere was drawn out in such a squat contour that it occupied most of the upper edge of the map. Africa appeared as large as North and South America combined. At length I had to call on King to explain the thing to me.

"You understand, McManus," he had said. "We have to use two transmitters to properly see an object. And that we have to tune both of these projectors on the object by intersecting the televise beams on it. Can you imagine the time it would take if we were to set about to find our object by roving with the screen itself? If we wish to see something a thousand miles away, wouldn't it be simpler to set the projectors to intersect at a thousand mile distance and from there locate?"

"Yes," I had admitted, adding, "that's simple, just figure out the mileage to any city and using it with your other instruments, you would land right on it by pointing in the compass direction from here."

"As easy as that?" He had laughed. "Oh, no! Remember, McManus, you're dealing with something entirely different than a train or an airplane, or even radio! You're reckoning with a beam, a rod of electricity, putting it that way, cutting *deeper* into the Earth's curvature every mile you travel away from here! San Francisco may be two thousand miles away from here figured over the Earth's surface, but you can see it will be some few miles nearer us when figured in a beam line.

"By the way, McManus, didn't you notice anything queer about the pictures of the west coast that first night you were here? Didn't the buildings and the people appear to lean slightly to the upper rear of the screen?"

I shook my head negatively. Maybe I had seen it and had passed it up in the excitement. It was possible.

"Well, watch closely the next time we travel that far and you'll see it. It's a natural condition and the further we travel away, the more noticeable this leaning backward becomes, until directly opposite us on the globe, we will be looking up through the feet of the people. However, that's a minor detail. What I wanted you to see was this: we have to use a more accurate scheme of sighting our projectors than mere findings. To Wentworth we are indebted for the system we are now using. That system called for the making of a new type of map. Therefore, we had to hire a man, highly versed in geometry, to figure out the beam-line distance of all the principal cities of the world with the focus—the equilateral triangle of our stations.

That done, we began to draw the map you see down there. Of course it looks queer, those cities you know are far off, appearing closer than on the usual map. It's called an equilateral zenithal projection map, and means that every city is at the exact beam distance, but their respective distance from one another, figured concentrically, is misleading, for the map is laid out radially. You get the idea in a wagon wheel. The spokes are close together at the hub, but as you approach the rim, they separate."

Then, using the map, he had pointed out to me the astounding fact that it was not such a wonderful feat to hold radio communication between Chicago and Manila or Calcutta, for actually in a radio-distance, these points were only eight thousand miles apart, for the radio waves, in reaching these cities, did not travel southwest to Manila, as supposed by the average radio fan, but shoot directly northwest by north, over the pole!

Then he continued, "On this map we have placed three small but powerful spotlights sending out beams of deep red light. These spots mimic the larger projectors to which they are geared and synchronized in movement. Thus, by watching these red beams and noting the point of intersection, we can determine just about where the larger projectors are focused."

NOW, the narrow light beams struck straight west, finally settling near Omaha. Several shifting sweeps led us to the railroad station in that city and with the rails as a guide, we set down the right of way at a furious pace. As though comparing the speeds of aid of curiosity, we flashed through the length of the swaying wreck-train rushing toward the disaster. At miles a minute we beamed along, jogging from side to side of the track, unable to keep to the rail at our thought of speed. Past Fremont—we slowed to a cautious hundred miles an hour. Suddenly a jumble of cars caused the operators to halt. Even so, we had overrun the wreck. Backing up took a little time on account of readjustment. After the screen had been set up for long shot projection (horizontal view in depth of screen increased from the usual apparent hundred feet to several thousand feet) the bank of cameras began humming, as we crept forward along the torn-up right of way. It was a bad derailment; the engine seemed to have been thrown off the way by a spread rail. It had rolled over, plowing on its side down the low embankment, drawing the tender and the following baggage cars after it in its plunge. The Pullmans, impelled by the sixty-mile inertia, slewed forward, piling up and over the baggage cars, scattering to both sides, in an awful pile of shattered and bent steel.

We worked under a disadvantage, for physical conditions and the acute angle of the projectors only allowed shots along the length of the right of way. So we contented ourselves with several shots taken as to appear filmed from a low flying plane and several stills of the spectacular scenes of the rescue of the injured.   King absolutely would not permit any interior "phantom" views.

Thirty minutes after the screen had closed on this sight, the developed film with its positive was rushed to the river hangar, where one of the speedy Hamiltons was ready to take it to Chicago.

"Talk about getting the news," grinned Wentworth, as we stood watching the roaring plane climb into the air.   This television game has the whole newsreel world scooped."

FROM that day on New Era Newsreel had the rest of the news agencies stumped and guessing.   Springing from an obscure film-distributing firm, it suddenly had blossomed out as the most powerful contender in the fight for supremacy in the filming of events.   Hardly an incident worth covering went by that we did not release through them, over the entire country, startling and thrilling pictures of scenes other companies did not hear of or could not arrive on time to photograph.   No one seemed to be able to get the vantage points enjoyed by New Era.   Then, too, the realistic sound accompaniment was the source of much conjecture, for everything was as natural as life—and timed to the second.   We made shots of everything; covering the entire United States and Canada in a range of twenty-five hundred miles radius.   Our range was much further, but on account of the tilting of the images due to distance, we shunned going beyond this range for the present.

Fires, forest and factory, were thrown upon the screens of the country in life-like roaring.   Once we almost spilled the beans when we followed the firemen through a burning lumber mill in South Carolina.   Ship leavings and wrecks were natural down to the slightest noise.   Some were filmed broadside in storms in the Atlantic.   Notables were filmed on the unaware hundreds of miles out at sea.   The winter maneuvers of the fleet in the Caribbean were viewed with acclaim by the theatre-goers days before the regular companies had broken all records, including a couple of innocent necks, by plane and rail to distribute theirs. The *Los Angeles*, on her cruise down to Panama was our much-heralded scoop, as we secured some really worthwhile shots of her cabins in action.

New Era spread the rumor of a new type camera developed by their engineers, and after this had been firmly established, we recklessly began to astound the wondering public with a series of the most daring films ever taken in news history.

We entered passenger planes while in the air; snapped scenes aboard trains steaming across the western plains; trailed automobile drivers around their racing ovals; followed the heels of football players; taking any imaginable shot the camera and our equipment was capable of registering.

Conventions, gatherings, and speeches in governmental chambers were scooped by having a photographer and sound equipment on hand. The camera was a blind while the sound devices only consisted of an active microphone hooked on the sly to the telephone lines. From the lines that had previously been cleared to Television Hill, we recorded the sound upon the film. Often we did the amusing stunt of stealing the sound by leading the radio transcription directly to the film, thereby seeing and hearing both from a distance at the same instant! Shades of Garret Smith!

Thanks to a very imaginative writer employed by the New Era for the purpose of covering up any slip we might make, the newspapers were filled with impossible stories of how these revealing pictures were made. These stories were taken for their worth until one discerning group made themselves heard on one point: The New Era Company, though enjoying the best shots, was never apparent on the scenes it so wonderfully reproduced! Nothing could be said in answer to that disturbing and often thought of accusation of intrusion of operators. However, from this time on the New Era films had one of the largest and best-equipped groups of photographers in the whole game. They began to make a name for themselves, reaping in a golden harvest—and—incidentally, so were we!

I often paused to wonder what would happen when the news finally leaked out that these newsreels had been filmed by means of television. Without a doubt there would be a short period of astonished silence during which the publications of the country would recount some of the incidents we had filmed, and would fight each other in presenting first page stories painting the possibilities of television in every light and color. There would then be a deluge of half-expressed questions that when answered, would bring solemn thought—and then! Swiftly a rising tide of sudden consternation, of alarm, of fear, and of suspicion from all walks of life—from the whole world!

Television, as I now knew it to be, was a powerful weapon, with more grim possibilities than I had ever before expected it to hold. When the day's work had been done and I retired to the privacy of my own rooms to read or rest, the thoughts besetting my consciousness alarmed and frightened me—at times to the point of frenzy. It's all right to think of television as a novelty; as an experiment with untold promise; as the thrilling revealing mechanism of a story told in fiction; as a dream to look forward to; but when it had been developed to the acme of perfection King had brought it to—when the entire world could be laid bare in all its sordidness and duplicity—X-rayed on a mighty screen before one's eyes—then it did not seem to be such a marvelous and inspiring mechanism. It was in such moments that I came to the vague conclusion that he had brought into existence a machine the world was not ready to receive. Truly, our present civilization, with its uncertain reactions to the swift progress being made, was not in position to take to television for centuries to come. And the thought of hundreds of these machines, scattered throughout the world sweeping and peering into the homes and lives of millions, caused me to sigh with heart-troubled perplexity.

Once I spoke to King about these ideas and his answer only augmented my fears.

"Yes, I know, McManus—all about those things. That's the real reason why we've made such a fight to keep this monster a secret as long as we can. Once television is commercialized, the entire social life of man will have to undergo a decided and sudden change. No longer will he be secure in his secret actions; no longer will he be able to enter his home with the relieved feeling that here is his domain, and here he can do as he pleases; no longer will thievery, murder, and the kindred lawless acts thrive, because the protecting cover of opaque walls will have been removed and the criminal will be living in a world, whose substances, whose constructions, manmade and natural, will be as clear glass. There is no insulator to televise rays! There is no metal or composition capable of deflecting or absorbing these powerful rays, *generated with the intention of penetrating eight thousand miles of the solid earth itself!* Yes, man will have to undergo a change."

CHAPTER SIX

A LITTLE over six months had passed since the day I had entered Television Hill. All my equipment was running perfectly. Our planes were leaving on schedule three times a day, and oftener as news broke. The work was exacting and interesting to the extreme, and time sped along unregretted. All through these months of worry, of disturbing thoughts, I had come to think more and more of Diane. Despite my earnest efforts I was unable to break down the tantalizing and charming aloof barrier she had set against me. And against me alone!

She was forever asking questions about the marvel of television and could be seen at any time strolling with one of the engineers or workmen, talking about his special work. Of course, knowing this, I spent much of my own time studying and learning about the machine, so as to be able to converse with her. When my conversation drifted toward personalities she became an attentive listener—nothing else.

"Tom," she exclaimed one January evening as I was reading the paper and half-listening to what she was playing on the piano. She arose from the stool with a little spin and seated herself on the sofa beside me. With a pert smile and a light in her violet eyes that challenged argument, she withdrew the paper from my hands and tossed it to the table. I had to smile at her actions.

"Tom, I asked Dad today about the projectors. He said you knew all there was to be known about them, and that you could give me better information than he could."

"What!" I exclaimed with some surprise. "Well, Diane, I believe your father is putting too much faith in my powers of observation. Your father and Wentworth have never told me much of the mechanism in and about the projectors or back of the projection screen. Besides, if they did, I wouldn't be able to tell anyone what I knew. That's my promise to them."

She narrowed her eyes and her voice expressed her disappointment, "Why, Tom, you have never said that before; you used to tell me everything!"

"Yes," I nodded solemnly, inwardly gratified at the display of emotion my assumed refusal was causing. "I did, but now, when you want me to tell you of the inside workings of the projectors, I'm afraid I must refuse, out of respect to your Dad's request."

She bit her lip, studying me. She smiled. "Isn't Dad funny that way?"

For a moment I held her gaze—then she looked away.

"No, not funny, Diane—just playing safe," I stated softly. To my amazement she turned frightened eyes in my direction. Her face had paled and she fidgeted with a corner of a cushion.

"Why, what do you mean by that?" she stammered.

"Oh, nothing to alarm you, Diane. It's just a little trick I've sprung on you to have a little fun at your expense. You know that story I've been writing—the one based on my experiences while here?"

Once more her usual poised self, she replied, "Yes, I know, and some day I'm going to get angry at you for bringing me into your silly story. Don't make excuses. Almost every word I say finds its way into that story. Everything I do, the clothes I wear are explained in vivid description, which I am forced to read— But, Tom, just how are you going to end it? By bringing in the happy ending so well known of heroes and heroines? Oh, I know you." She laughed merrily.

"That's just what I'm trying to figure out now," I told her. "You see, I'm trying to abide by the popular custom of this type of story—in order to sell it—and destroy the machines, doing away with the inventor and all others associated with the invention, so the world will be safe for Democracy and men again. But I have exploited the hero and heroine to such an extent that I'll not be able to dispose of them in a manner to suit Mr. Average Reader. I've made her appear with that delightful and haughty air so heart-rending to the hero and so pleasing to the reader, who alone knows she is only playing until the last paragraph, when she will confess to her love."

Diane drew back to the opposite side of the sofa, regarding me with a glance calculated to show haughty disgust.

"She's a strange little thing all the same," I went on, noting the ghost of a smile doing the best to make itself evident," and I've been trying to work her in, as in the employ of a foreign government, spying on the machine, carting off the plans and in the end destroying the entire plant, when she learns she is sealing the doom of the world's peace."

There was a thoughtful frown on her forehead as she retorted. "But, Tom, how are you going to explain the girl is the *daughter* of the inventor of the machine?"

"Oh, that's simple—if I can get away with it. Wilder things than that have been told in this type of story. I make her confess to be a clever substitution, and that the real daughter is imprisoned in this foreign land."

She gave it some thought; then laughed. "But even then, it's such an impossible ending! Isn't it too fantastic to be true to the wonderful story you have written so far?"

"Perhaps, Diane, you can suggest a better one?" I returned, catching her eyes meaningly.

"I could, but it's likely I'd commit myself!" she returned, flashing one of her rare smiles that, I declare, made me feel like going forth to conquer the world.

"BUT, really, Tom won't you tell me about the projectors?" revealing she was determined to learn what she could from me.

"Aw," I frowned. "Oh, well. It sure has me stumped as to why you should be so interested in this stuff. However, I'm going to punish you this evening with a detailed story of all I know about it, so that you will never bother me about it again."

"Is that nice? Maybe, if it were told in the right way, I wouldn't ask so many silly questions," she declared quietly, interested in the nail of her forefinger.

"Well so be it," I warned settling deeper into the sofa, while Diane assumed a forced attentive attitude, which brought a spontaneous laugh from both of us.

"IT seemed as though your Dad had all the seven devils of luck working at his elbow when he started out to investigate the possibilities of the original liquid films. His search led him into the field of electrical rays in the effort to find a carrier beam for the theory he had built up. He found one that must be closely allied to the Coolidge ray but it is so extremely powerful that it approaches the so-called cosmic ray, besides being able to penetrate through the sphere of the Earth. Just what kind of a ray it really is I don't know—neither does anyone else around here except King and Wentworth and two or three others. I don't blame him for wanting to be close-mouthed about it, especially when there's so much danger involved in it.

"The transmitting tube—I've seen one being repaired in the powerhouse—is a monster; being almost thirty feet long and easily ten feet in diameter, a massive cylinder of pure quartz, with a removable section allowing a man to enter and replace defective parts and to renew filaments and arc-carbons. Inside it is a perfect maze of construction, having in dead center a hollow cylinder of platinum alloy in which is suspended the anode and cathode and other elements found in the ordinary high-frequency generator. Around this assembly is a fine meshed grid-work and outside that a concentric tube of platinum—the plate on which is impressed about two hundred amperes at seven million volts. Then there is an impossible-to-describe assemblage of rods, balls, connections, and other projections all over the inside of the tube, suspended, for the most part, from flat copper straps adhering to the inside of the quartz walls. There are many valve openings through which are fed helium and other similar gases by a system of pumps. For cooling purposes liquid air is pumped through the high voltage electrode, which is made of two separated plates.

"When this projector-tube is in operation, the hiss and spit of hundreds of amperes leaping across the six-inch space in the rear arc causes a deafening roar inside the projector housing. The rush of gases through the lead pipes makes up a heavier beating monotone pounding on one's ears, while the awe-inspiring blaze issuing from the unshielded openings in the thick lead walls makes one feel all the more the exhilarating aura of high-tension electricity surrounding the entire projector assembly. Why, one comes to believe he's dead and is in an eternity of thunder and pleasant tingling!"

"But, Tom, why all this power?"

"You may have heard, Diane, of scientists taking pictures concealed by an inch or more of lead. You know it takes considerable power and equipment to accomplish that successfully. Then how much power would you require were you to photograph an object hidden by three thousand miles of the earth's soil and minerals? Your brother Jim wrote recently to your Dad that he was present at some experiments conducted at the G. E. plant where a giant Roentgen generator has been built. They have been able to photograph composite views of objects and houses two and three hundred feet away from the tube itself. An X-ray tube of this size is necessarily a powerful one and requires much power to operate it!"

"Out of King's projector tube there issues a beam—just what you would call it I do not know, except that it is capable of penetrating the Earth's body; it may be a tunnel of rays through space itself, perhaps ether, traversing all matter as water through a sieve, kerosene through cast iron, infra-red rays through hard rubber. However, it has one property, a most curious property, in that it is a conductor of ordinary electrical impulses! A radio transmitter could be hooked up in the path of this beam and become what our present radio engineers are earnestly working toward—a perfect radio beam transmitter. A beam transmitter that could only be picked up in an area less than a hundred feet wide and two hundred feet high at a distance of a thousand miles—the extreme limit to which the minimum divergence of the rays can be held.

"And then there is the much-desired advantage not enjoyed by modern radio transmission—that of being focused directly upon the distant receiver once the beam-line dips below the curvature of the earth. In like manner, with ordinary equipment, electro-photographic television and pictures could be sent to a picked receiver, thereby clearing up the crowded condition felt today in the established practices of widespread aerial broadcast. I don't know whether you are interested or not, Diane, but a noted radio engineer who is striving toward wired radio, is proving his contention that radio transmission belongs underground; King holds the key for this latest development.

"I'm going to try to draw a comparison between the principles used in Movietone and Photophone sound systems and the theory King has proved possible. The former systems transform sound vibrations to electrical impulses that actuate a kino-lamp whose fluctuations are registered on the narrow band of film seen to the left of the screen when projected. In projection the sound is taken off either a few feet before or after the frame containing the expressed audible action is shuttered through the lens compartment. Behind the narrowband is a powerful light and the light passing through the film is impressed on the sensitive photoelectric cell in exactly the same flickering as the original kinolamp. This flickering controls the current passing through a photoelectric cell, breaking it up into surges of electricity, which when properly amplified and sent to the speaker hidden behind the screen, produces the words and music we hear so clearly and so perfectly timed.

"Your Dad played with a system similar to this back in 1925 while he was testing and developing a series of new tubes and amplifiers. Not satisfied with this cheap success, which he knew would come into general use within a year or two, he had carried on his intensive research work along into the discovery of these telesight rays, as he sometimes terms them. He had found that electric currents of various wavelengths sent along this beam were reflected by objects in the path of the rays and *returned* with appreciable strength to the transmitter *via* the beam! His further search revealed he would get ghost pictures of everything in and between the ranges of his instruments. Then, after much thought, he decided to make two projectors, separated by miles, and focus them on the object, figuring he'd get additional reflection and delineation from the object. He figured rightly. His receivers, something on the order of thirty to fifty stages of fixed-tuned radio-frequency, caught the reflected electrical impulses and converted them, by proper scanning mechanisms into light frequencies again."

"Pardon me. Tom," broke in Diane laying her hand on my arm. "Where are those receivers located?"

"They are mounted in the nose of the projectors and are tuned and focused in conjunction with the projector each serves."

"But I don't understand how they can pick up the extremely weak reflections from distant objects. I know ordinary radio waves can be turned aside and absorbed by steel constructions, but I imagine they are scattered pretty well over the surrounding vicinity and therefore must be exceedingly weak."

"Clever little mind. Here is how that can be explained: those impulses strike *all* objects in their onward rush and there are many and untold reflections in all directions, but the greater percentage would naturally come from the point or place where two projectors would be focused. The receivers are also focused automatically on this point and so they register to these stronger reflections riding back over the weaker ones. Edison proved it possible to run two-way communication over the same wire, and King has proved it possible to send and receive the same electrical or radio impulse over a beam that, actually, is a better conductor than silver! Now, if you have been following me, you ought to ask how it is that these delicate receivers can pick up these minute reflections when they return right in the path of the outgoing powerful impulses."

"That question would be logical," she replied.

"Diane, much as your Dad has done in the research and development of the electrical and chemical end of television, he would have been handicapped was it not for the rare mechanical genius residing in Wentworth. It was Wentworth who first saw the need of positive and precise control of the projectors, and it was his brain that first conceived those mighty machines in their present state. Yet, compared to the work he did there, and the system he developed to control these monsters by means of a single manual control board, the marvelous piece of engineering found in the nose of the projector assembly transcends all his previous accomplishments.

"From now on, Diane, my lecture is going to become more or less indefinite as to details, because I'm speaking of something I really know very little about, having gained my information from remarks of the men and from one or two chance glances at the machinery.

"We know that the main oscillator tube projects a beam no metal can absorb. Directly in front of this tube (speaking of the front as the place where the rays are emitted) is a series of scanning discs about ten and a half feet in diameter. The rear disc, that is the one closest to the tube, is about ten inches thick and is composed of an alloy of lead and copper, and has a steel band sweated to its circumference to keep the disc from flying apart at the high speed at which it is revolved. In it, in conventional scanning disc manner, are the two hundred or more slots arranged in a spiral, each slot being approximately two inches apart centerline to centerline. Then, in front of this scanning disc (known as the 'transmitter disc') is mounted the receptor dissimilar in size and whose axle runs as a sleeve over the transmitter disc axle. The receptor disc in reality is made of two plates of bakelite an inch or so thick, separated by a space of twelve inches. It is between these latter supporting discs that the receptor antenna, two hundred little cylindrical objects, each as big as a tomato can, are arranged in the same positions and center lines as the slots on the transmitting disc. Both of these wheels, the transmitter, and the receiver can be driven at the same speed, but since the axles are sleeved the receptor disc can be retarded or advanced. The reason for this I will explain in detail. In my opinion, it is the most marvelous piece of work in the entire television machine.

"Once more, the carrier beam is a continuous emission, understand? The electrical, or rather the radio-frequency impulse riding this beam is not! It is an oscillating current breaking abruptly on and off about five hundred thousand times a second! Since no physical means can be found whereby the transmitting scanner can be made to cut off the penetrating beam, as does the scanning disc in a light-governed television machine, King had to resort to breaking the secondary wave so as to scan distant objects. This oscillating impulse is timed with the speed of the transmitting disc so that the shots, stronger where they have passed through the open slots, dash out and are away across the ether. Objects in the path of the beam reflect this secondary wave, which reflections ride back to the transmitter, if they happen to be returned—most do, because of a law that states: the angle of reflection is equal to the angle of incidence. Naturally, the reflections returned by the object on which two transmitters are focused will be stronger and so they will register that much clearer. These reflections, upon their arrival back at the projector some minute fraction of a second after they had left, will find the receptor disc with its antenna coils right in line to pick it up. The transmitter disc has moved onward and is then engaged in projecting other shots. The movement of the solid part of the wheel slightly screens the returning impulse from colliding head on with an outgoing impulse.

"Now, Diane, for the interesting part of the whole affair; and that is the reason for the independent movement of the two scanning wheels. This calls for an example.

"Let's say that the transmitters were tuned on a spot in New York City, which, we'll say, is nine hundred and thirty miles from Television Hill. It would take just one one-hundredth of a second for an electrical or radio impulse to travel that distance and *return*. That means by the time that impulse leaves the transmitting slot, and before it returns, a hundredth of a second later, both discs must revolve enough to bring the receptor antenna into position to receive it! Just think of that for a few moments.

"For every mile you approach nearer to the transmitter; the discs will have to spin faster, for you are cutting down the elapsed time of going and return of the impulse traveling, roughly, one hundred and eighty thousand miles a second! Can you imagine the unthought-of speed those ten-foot wheels would be spinning if we came as close as Chicago, one hundred miles away? Why, they would burst into a million pieces and wreck the entire projector, on account of the terrific centrifugal force generated!

"No, Diane. Wentworth knew his engineering. Those discs revolve only sixteen times a second and the difference in the elapsed time elements are made by simply retarding or advancing the position of the receptor disc in relation to the slots in the transmitter by means of a most ingenious method of gearing, automatic in action and which is synchronized with the diverging or converging of the beams of *both* active projectors. Then, the thing that sounds impossible! Both scanning discs are so timed that the impulse from, let's say number one slot on Television Hill's transmitter, leaves at the same instant as the impulse of number one slot at Lake Geneva, and *both* these impulses strike the object on almost the same spot, being reflected back as one strengthened impulse, which is picked up by the receptor antenna amplified by the receivers, transmitted over seventy-five miles transformed into vibrations in range of sight, and thrown on a screen-perfect images of the original scene. All this is done in the space of a fraction of a second. When you realize that over thirty thousand impulses ride out of the transmitting slots in the sixteenth of a second that each has to go through the story I've tried to tell you, you will come to think as I do—your Dad and Wentworth are centuries ahead of the times.

"All this equipment—the great powerhouse, the monster projectors, the delicate scanning mechanism, the wonderful control system, almost wholly automatic—all is required to obtain a weak, pulsating current of a few milliamperes at seven hundred volts. Scarcely enough juice to shock the average person."

Diane stirred and settled into a more comfortable position.

"Enough?" I smiled.

"No, please go on. For one who stated he only looked at the machine, you certainly absorbed quite a lot of information!" she laughed—those violet eyes twinkling merrily.

"Diane! Now, you did it. You made me forget my line of thought."

There was a mischievous narrowing of her lips as she said, "The received current is carried from the projector housing down into the little shack under the projector, where it is stepped up to sufficient strength to carry it through the tunnel, to the transformer-house, to the towers, where it is conveyed to the projection house, passed through a series of filter-condenser-resistance amplifiers, cascade type, to the Kino-lamp."

For a moment I gasped at her breath-taking detailing.

"Say, what's the idea? I thought you wanted me to tell you the story? I'm beginning to think you know a lot more about this subject than I do. I am willing to wager you are only using this means as an excuse to talk to me." It was a bold assertion and I anxiously awaited the expected explosion.

Instead, she fought back a smile, averting her eyes for an instant. Then she dared a glance in my direction and in those violet depths I read the answer that words can never convey. She did care!

"Please, Tom, go on," she begged a slow flush creeping into her cheeks. Our eyes met.

"Aw rats," I muttered after a moment. "Here I am with the most wonderful girl in the world and all she wants to talk about is machinery. Bah!"

She smiled at me flirtatiously.

"The projecting house," I began half-heartedly," is divided into two parts. The projection theatre and the screening tunnel. The amplified current is led to the immense Kino-lamp your father has developed. Its fluctuations, about five hundred thousand a second, are scanned by a miniature disc of two hundred apertures driven in direct shaft speed conjunction with the shaft of the transmitter shaft. (Another miracle of engineering science.) These light shots are impressed on King's liquid film, which, as you probably know, retains in its chemicals the image of the object scanned upon it until an electrical current sent through it breaks down the state of exposure. Sixteen times a second images are built up and destroyed. At the point when the Kino-lamp scanner is about to begin anew its covering of the liquid plate, and while it still retains the black and white image in the liquid, a shutter, with a plane mirror set in its interior face at an angle to reflect the light from a powerful lamp off to one side, comes around, shuts off the light from the Kinolamp, opens the shutter to the side arc light whose beam strikes the mirror and is reflected upon the liquid plate. This flash is only momentary—a hundredth of a second in duration, but it projects a sharp image upon the next plate—our positive, from which, by means of a system of shutters and the required synchronism, an extremely powerful light is shuttered through the positive, thus projecting a perfect image on the last and final screen. That is all there is to it. Although it sounds rather intricate and almost impossible, it's exactly how it operates and the result is perfect reproduction of images hundreds of miles away from here.

"And with all this delicate synchronism of the whole affair, there are vexing periods when the various parts get out of time, and then it is one herculean task to retime everything. Everything has been studied to the nth degree and the mechanics in charge during operation can tell by their instruments the instant and place of fault.

"Looking at it, Diane, one must admit that your father and Wentworth have exploded the established opinion that we of today do not build as carefully and thoughtfully as our fathers did. They have accomplished one of the greatest feats of precise, scientific engineering ever attempted. Their names will go down into history along with Edison, DeForest, Bell, and will, without a doubt transcend even the names of Michelson and Einstein."

"Not only to Dad goes all the credit, Tom," asserted Diane, "but to all those intelligent men who are giving their every effort toward the fulfillment of my Dad's dream."

"Yes, it started as a dream—and has developed into the marvel of the twentieth century. Just think of what it really means, Diane…

"Television!

"Television breaks through the last barrier to man's intimate knowledge of his world! Truly the mountains will be leveled and the valleys filled under the revealing sweep of television. Why, haven't we made pictures of Dick Byrd in the Antarctic? Films we had to destroy for fear of revealing how we had taken them? What about the amazing newsreels we have scooped the photographic world with? What about the interesting news-travel films we have made of the unexplored regions in South America, Alaska, Arabia, and Africa?

"What about the furor we raised when we exposed that secret Monorail system operating along the western coast of Canada and traversing Alaska? Just pause to think what this machine will do once it is released to mankind.

"What will become of travel; of the average man's curiosity for looking upon scenes in other lands? Why travel thousands of miles when with a flip of the wrist you can see and chat with distant relatives and business associates? You could drive over the entire country in an evening, seeing the wonders of the land right in your own parlor!

"And then give solemn thought to the strange effect it will have on the social life of the race, on mankind.

"Once seclusion is removed from our private lives by the penetrating eyes of commercial television, what will we do and think? Will we act as we do now; will we be calm and reserved in company with strangers and throw aside all restraint when in our own intimate circle? What will the reaction be? Frankly, Diane that is a question I cannot answer. Only time will tell...

"Will the standards of education undergo a similar change? Education today is based on knowledge gained through the medium of books, because books are the convenient and ready source to facts gleaned from widely scattered sources. Even today educators are leaning toward the talkie-motion picture as a means to illustrate and convey to the young sights and customs of people far distant. With the front of the schoolroom, a screen opening upon the whole wide world, there is no telling what the children of the future will learn.

"There would be no need for the movie theatre or the drama, the newspapers and periodicals, or the present methods of bringing the life and blood romance and tragedy to our attention—we will be able to see these as they actually occur.

"As a class, the type of human who cares little or nothing for the conventional limits of law and order will have a hard life, for when police and Federal stations are put in operation, there will be no such thing as concealment! Publicity and secretiveness would be a humorous farce, with the whole world watching!

"Wars would become impossible, for each side would be watching the frantic attempts to surprise the other and a successful war, we know, depends on one adversary conquering the other by surprise moves.

"And then what of the commercial value of television? Imagine the release of thousands of workers from monotonous tasks at machinery requiring only intermittent attention. Of how the transportation companies, especially air lines, could send Television watched—robot controlled machines across the country, through all kinds of weather, with no risk to a pilot's or driver's life. How quickly it would be put to work aboard ships and planes, giving them eyes to peer miles ahead through the thickest fog. The Weather Bureau will increase its scope by permitting the department to watch the movement of storms and hurricanes hundreds of miles away.

"Then into industrial life! Geological surveying from thousands of miles away in search of oil, coal, and gold deposits. Mapping and exploration as never before attempted or thought possible! Why, Diane, you cannot begin to realize what a stupendous marvel television really is! There is one possibility it holds that is going to bring universal acclaim from builders of machinery. Suppose, for example, a customer reports to a manufacturer that a certain machine he had bought is out of commission due to a broken part. The manufacturer puts in a call to a television exchange and requests an investigation be made of that certain machine for broken parts; he might even send a service man to the television station. The part being found, it is dispatched by airmail to the nearest service station, saving time and expense for both customer and manufacturer.

"That, Diane, is what Television holds for mankind; it tears virtual blindness from man's eyes."

Diane had listened to my outbreak with a soft smile and now she murmured, "And to think my brother and Dad started it all! Oh I realized what it means! It thrills me with joy and pride." She clasped her hands tightly and her glittering eyes reflected the pleasure animating her being.

Suddenly in a serious turn she inquired. "But withal, Tom, don't you honestly believe it came too soon? That the world has not yet developed to a point where it can stand the shock of its presence?"

"Well," I drawled for a moment, studying her beautiful, questioning face. Here was the chance I had been waiting for! "Whatever the world may do and think about it, I for one am most thankful that it was the work of your Dad, for it has brought *you*..."

For a moment her lips twitched, almost forming a smile. "Silly," she declared, jumping to her feet. "I might have known you couldn't stay serious very long."

"I am serious, Diane," I said, catching both her hands and drawing her to the sofa beside me.

CHAPTER SEVEN

ONE afternoon in late January, after we had run off some particularly good news-shots of an airplane wreck in Ohio, I found King and a few of the engineers in a huddle on the balcony over the projection map. I joined them.

"—and we have not been able to solve the problem of synchronizing New Glarus and Lake Geneva in the direction of New Orleans and points past. In every other point of the compass we have been able to cover a radius of seven thousand surface miles."

"I'm sure it isn't in the control system or the driving mechanism at either place," stated the lean-jawed, sharp-eyed chief engineer.

King turned to him, a frown on his forehead.

"Now," he said softly, "the entire assembly is driven from the rack— Say, I wonder if any of the teeth might have been crushed in some way? They were all right when I was up there two months ago. I paid special attention to that point."

"Perhaps," murmured Smythe, looking about with a foolish grin, "that's it."

"Well," said King, "you take the Lockheed and take a run up there and look at them. While you're up there, hop over to New Glarus and see what kind of a job Williams has done in the installation of the new receptor scanner. He expects to be finished about three this afternoon."

TWO hours later the phone call came in for King and as he placed the receiver on the hook, he appeared agitated and alarmed. He motioned for me to follow him. He paused over the projection map.

"McManus, you have seen this map in operation so many times; you know it is the only check we have, outside of the visual screen, of where the intersecting televise beams come together.

"For months we have not been able to get the two northern stations to bear on a line south by west—the direction of New Orleans. Now Smythe has made an investigation of the rack in this particular place and finds that the teeth on the driving racks of both stations have been mutilated to such an extent that it is actually impossible to bear in that direction. There's something mighty funny about it, for Smythe says the teeth were *milled* so as to cause the slip or leap when the driving gear meshes."

"Perhaps it was in that condition when first laid—and it's pure luck that they line up as they do," I hazarded.

He shook his head. "No, McManus, it isn't a coincidence that this trouble lines up in one direction. Smythe is the one who personally inspected each rack section when it was being milled and he says the two faulty sections are not of our manufacture…"

"What!" I ejaculated.

"There's something back of this—"

"What do you mean?" I ventured, when his brooding silence had become unbearable.

He glanced about, then said quietly, "I've got a hunch that someone inside our organization is trying to put us out of action. I've said nothing of this before, because I wanted to be sure. Plans and calculations have been disappearing at regular intervals during the last few months."

Astounded, I stared at him. Despite their precautions, was someone actually stealing their plans?

"What steps have you taken to—to apprehend this person," I asked.

"I did all I could do under the circumstances. I have had a search made of everyone I suspected and fingerprint tests made of everyone in the plant—excluding you. Whoever the fellow is, he certainly is working cleverly. But I have my eyes open. And, McManus, please keep this quiet—I don't want it to get out."

I was more amazed to learn of this news than to feel surprise at someone working against us. And I had thought I knew of everything going on about the plant!

King started downstairs, but recalling something, returned. "We will replace the sections of rack in the spoiled spots and then—get this—we're going to make a sharp survey of everything in that particular projection line!"

FROM that January day I lived with the subconscious sensation of being on the top of a volcano that might, without warning, blow us all into eternity. It was an impression gathered when Wentworth informed me that under each projector assembly was mined over ten tons of dynamite! Switching arrangements made it possible to set off anyone projector from any station. And the reason: safety to the interests of King and the world!

As I ran my bank of cameras, viewing the spectacular sights, now becoming more and more familiar, I felt, at times, as though other eyes were constantly watching our every move. I drew King's attention to this fancy and he admitted that he, too, had felt something decidedly strange was in the air.

"I can't fathom the reason of those curious electrical interferences that disturb our screenings when we run toward New Orleans," he continued. "I am almost tempted to say it is similar to the parallelogram of disturbance our projectors cause when they are in focus of an object. But I am more than sure that there isn't another Television machine in the whole world—at least not down that way," He laughed at that supposition.

"Has anything else disappeared since last time?" I asked.

"Yes, even though I've posted Diane to watch my room and installed a capacity alarm system, I'm telling you, Mac, it's so deep I can't see the light."

FOR a time he was silent, beating a thoughtful tattoo on the guardrail. At length he spoke.

"We have beamed the entire length of the line through New Orleans, down past the Federated Republic of Central America; we discovered nothing of any note."

"I wonder," I mused, "why you didn't try further?"

"What for? All the rest is water. The Pacific—one of the least traveled sea stretches in the whole world, once you get past the Canal Sea-tracks."

"All the more reason to try it," I announced.

He smiled. "Well, if you expect us to find some uncharted island down that way with a bunch of crooks trying to put us out of commission, you're going further than that fantastic fiction Wentworth likes to read and laugh at. Seriously, I think we'll try it tonight."

"Tonight, gosh!" I spoke with dismay. "Diane and I had a date this evening."

"For the love of mud," he said. "Some picture show?"

I nodded.

"Well, you've got me! You're like the sailor who takes his best girl out motor boating. However…" He stroked his cheek in a thoughtful manner, gazing at me with a humorous twinkle in his brown eyes. "...it won't be long now until you will come stuttering and hot under the collar—wondering if I'd care if you and... Go ahead, Tom. I've been watching you two since that first day and I can see the inevitable end." He took me by the upper arm and inflicted a comradely slap across my shoulders as he turned and retreated down the stairs.

IT was well after one in the morning when I guided my coupe across the guarded bridge to the eastern shore, and after admission, took up the steep climb to the garage. Diane and I had spent a wonderful evening attending a lengthy drama in Rockford and had stayed twice to listen to the startled exclamations of the audience when the New Era Newsreel was thrown on the screen. Returning, we had loafed along the moonlit highway. The projector was dark and some premonition warned me of impending evil. I drove the machine into the garage and Diane and I paused to take one last look at the waning moon, just peeping over the western tree lines.

The lights were on in the parlor and as we entered, we came upon King and Wentworth sitting at opposite ends of the room; Wentworth smoking his pipe with steady contemplative puffs; King with drawn lips, staring into the widespread leaves of an atlas. Both looked up at the same moment and in their eyes was mirrored such startled amazement that Diane gasped in fear.

"What's the matter? What happened?" I asked glancing from one to the other.

King closed his book slowly while a slight forced smile twisted his lips. "Shall we tell them, Bob?" he asked Wentworth.

Wentworth still seated, nodded. "Tom, yes, Diane, no..."

"Diane," King went to his daughter and placed his arm about her shoulders. "Listen, dear, don't be alarmed, but something happened here tonight that I think you ought not to know—for the present at least. No—no one was hurt or anything like that. Please go now. We wish to talk to Tom."

Diane's arms went about her father. She pulled his ears. "All right, Dad—see you in the morning." She waved to me and tripped from the room. In the meantime I had removed my overcoat and seated myself on the sofa.

King took his stand beside the library table, one hand on the huge atlas.

"Well, we did it," he announced, his voice strangely vibrant with a temper that sent queer chills into my being.

"We swept along the line of trouble, increasing our range, until I felt we were at the limits of our power. Then," he paused to open the atlas, "we found—an island, a big one too, in direct line with the damaged teeth in the rack..."

"An island not on the maps!" broke in Wentworth. "Yes, an unknown island some fifty or more miles in length and easily thirty in width, mountains in character—and, most astonishing of all—inhabited!" he looked to Wentworth for verification.

"Amazing and impossible as it may seem, there were indisputable evidences of a people whose cities and artificial constructions were of the types found in highly civilized countries!"

"We can't begin to tell you, McManus, of some of the things we saw. We actually are afraid to speak of it after what we came upon. Why, it goes into the realm of fiction, into those wild fantastic tales of no particular value other than to amuse. We spent close to three hours wandering about over this island and probably would be still exploring if we didn't bump into a construction housing a Television apparatus similar to ours! It happened to be the screen room and—" King choked, overcome by his emotion and with a futile motion of his hand signaled Wentworth to go on.

"It's almost impossible to believe, but it checks up with the sensations we've been subject to for the last month or so—that we felt as though we were being watched. We *are*! On that television screen was mirrored our projection theatre! It covered the balcony on which King and I were operating the machine. I'm telling you, it was some shock! It seemed incredible!

"And as soon as those watchers down there became aware that we had found them, there was a flurry, much running to and fro, and there came a wave of interference, a counteractive wave, that broke into our secondary radio wave, rendering it inactive to that region. Just listen to the radio."

Wentworth turned the switch and there was dead silence until the tubes had warmed up. From the reproducer came a steady, heavy, snapping crackle and pound that increased and decreased in volume.

"There it is. There is the reason for that curious rat-a-tat static radio fans so often complain of. Do you know what that means, McManus?" demanded Wentworth, knocking his ashes into the smoking stand.

"It means that those fellows have had Television just as long as we have, if not longer!" He declared.

King had reseated himself and was staring into the atlas he had propped on his knees. "I'd say this island is located somewhere around 130 degrees west longitude and 60 degrees south latitude. About one thousand miles southwest of Cape Horn; out of the regular steamship lanes; in a region temperate in climate, foggy in summer due to the northward drift of icebergs, and extremely cold in winter. Withal it seems ideally situated for seclusion."

I just sat there listening to these remarks, thoughts running rampant, trying to picture the fantasies that they told me. An unknown land to the south of us inhabited by progressive scientists! Never! Impossible!

I gave vent to my unbelief. "Mr. King, this is too much. It's too wild for me to believe. To even imagine a large island undiscovered and unknown lying at any place on this earth is going beyond common sense. It smacks of sensational fiction, but not of hard, convincing fact."

Wentworth shook his head slowly. "I understand, lad. We have spent a half-hour debating on that very question and have come to the same conclusion. Our friends to the south have a reason for wishing not to be found out..."

I could stand no more of this nonsense.

"Bosh!" I laughed, jumping to my feet. "Wait until the sun rises and then think this thing over in daylight—sanely," With that I gathered up my coat and hat and hurried from the room, followed by their solemn gaze. As I swung around the doorway, I discovered Diane making every effort to gain the top of the stairway without attracting my attention. I was after her in swift silent leaps. At the top she grasped my arm with a little smile of understanding. Her finger to her lips cautioned me to silence.

"Tom, what was it they were talking about?" she whispered. "Poor Dad acts as though he's seen something terrible."

"Oh, it's nothing, Diane. They are excited over some discovery which they think is of grave importance. In the morning they'll have forgotten all about it. Goodnight, dear."

In the quiet of my own room I sat thinking over the stories of King and Wentworth. Though it was all very indefinite, that they had undoubtedly seen such a place. Now the fun would start around Television Hill!

At breakfast in the morning little was mentioned about last night's episode other than a remark by King that the heavy static interference had ceased. In silence they finished their coffee and immediately set out toward the projection house. I followed at a distance. I did not feel like going into any retrospective ruminations concerning the likelihood of another secretive people sharing this globe unknown to the world. I would hold back all thoughts and ideas until I was certain that this discovery was not some freak of the televise rays or a practical joke devised by one of the engineers. Once before we had been fooled by Smythe who had hooked up a movie projector in the light tunnel and took us, apparently, into a little known region in South America, showing us amazing scenes of animal life we knew to be of the long past ages.

In the early morning the projection theatre always held an air of hollow vastness and promise of future life and action. Today there was a suppressed current of excitement throughout the entire plant—that electric and unspoken communication of trouble ahead, which every man feels unconsciously, but is unable to tell from where it is coming, or what its nature is. The mechanics hurried about their duties, touching up the delicate mechanisms with their usual silence.

King leaned over the balcony rail, staring at the projection map. He switched on the duplicating spots and their beams intersected on a point about a thousand miles southwest of the tip of South America.

"See," he said and pointed, "an isolated region to be sure," He rubbed his chin reflectively. Turning he called to Wentworth, "Bob, let's have another trial this morning. But clear the building first."

It was almost nine-thirty before the attendants had completed their work. Wentworth settled into the driving console with King at his side, while I took my elevated position near the camera banks. The many-toned buzzers rattled out their calls as the warning went to the powerhouse and the two northern stations. The screen began its wavering flow of flashes and lines as the dome lights dimmed.

Gradually, on the screen was built up a scene, faint and hazy, of a rough and awe-inspiring cliff. From its upside down appearance I needed no second thought to tell me we were looking upon something at a great distance; that we were cutting pretty deep into the depths of the earth due to the curvature of the globe. Under Wentworth's control we ascended the cliff— the impression was one of flying downwards. Reaching the top, we started to travel in a curious distorted fashion, on account of the acute and unnatural angle of vision, across the countryside. One had the sensation of sliding just under a film over the surface of the ground, comparable to a submarine skimming under the surface of a river, looking upward at the trees and objects on the shore. Once we passed a lake of considerable size, which proved upon investigation to be artificial, being impounded by a small, well-built concrete dam!

On and on we went, I gasping my amazement and utter surprise in shouts and exclamations pardonable under the emotions sweeping over me. Power lines, towers, steel constructions of sizes and shapes new and puzzling, swept by; paved roads, over which dashed swift-moving two-wheeled vehicles, were sighted at times; and the astounding discovery of a monorail system exactly similar to that we had uncovered in Canada!

"Hold," commanded King when we had picked up the monorail train. "Just look at that, Wentworth! No wonder Alaskan Monorail officials tried their best to silence all our newsreels by discontinuing service immediately after our exposure! I'm wagering there is something *big* back of all this!"

But we continued on, looking into homes and buildings of architecture wholly new, all the time climbing the rise of land toward the northwest. At length, dropping down the ridge of mountains we came upon more and more evidences of a highly civilized people—homes were more frequent, people more numerous. We approached a city, which, as it flowed upon our screen excited in us a desire of seeing it in person. It was apparently the most beautiful metropolis in the world; efficiency and beauty seeming to have been welded in the formation of those appealing three-storied structures, homes, and business palaces, which rolled on unbroken for almost four miles down the tree-lined, extremely wide avenues.

The people, those whom we were able to glimpse with momentary clearness, were of the white race, apparently of average height, possessing figures speaking of athletic tendencies, clear-featured, and almost without exception light haired. Apparently we had little to fear from them, for they were obviously a sociable lot. The street clothing of both men and women was simple—a two-piece suit with leather puttees and stout shoes.

At the central section of the city the buildings seemed to have cast aside all restraint, all their somberness and humility, rising with utter abandon to great heights. To be sure, there were only a few of them, but their futuristic beauty and towering sweep were impressive in the extreme.

King and Wentworth went into raptures of verbal delight.

Grouped about this central section were many other structures not quite so high, but more sedate, leaning heavily to early Grecian designs. The predominant feature over all was landscaping; trees and grass plots being laid out with mathematical preciseness over open courts and other superstructures such as viaducts and bridges.

Beyond this section, to the northwest, was a vast sheet of water that we took for the ocean. On its surface we found several ships as we roved about like a submarine. We came upon a few rusty tramps conveying cargoes of machinery—thus the penetrating televise rays revealed. Once we had the good fortune of finding the ship in position so that we could read its name. It was *Winterboro* of New York City, and the flag it displayed was that of the Comet Shipping Lines of that city!

Again we moved on, speeding through the water until we came to a wide range of docks, at which were moored steamers from all over the world! Quite a few under foreign registry were rusty, decrepit tramps, but almost every one bearing the American Flag was a well-painted, trim steamer of the combination type. To convey the thoughts that beset our minds is impossible—we just stared with uncomprehending eyes, silently wondering in dazed stupor. Their cargoes were mostly foodstuffs, wheat, corn, barley, rye, sugar, meats, and fruits, with quite a bit of machinery interspersed. Steel plating, nitrates, coal, cotton, oil, were transferred to the dock monotrain system with amazing rapidity by giant cranes that seemingly gored into the very hollows of the hulls. This disclosed what their cargoes were.

Suddenly across the screen moved a shadow. Wentworth sighted and focused on the shadow, until there appeared the hull of a flying boat, of a size comparable to the mighty German DX-O, scudding toward the water. It connected with scarcely a splash and, turning about, headed toward the docks. A tug, a fast motor launch to be correct, picked it up and towed it into a slip. Many passengers disembarked, some hurriedly evidently knowing where they were, others having to be led, giving signs of confusion and alarm.

A close-up was even more surprising. These latter arrivals were undoubtedly Americans, judging from their dress and actions. They were of all types, ragged derelicts, leather coated aviators, one policeman, and several well-dressed men of wealth and leisure. One we saw was a newspaper photographer, and he was busy snapping pictures, until a guard came over and politely took the camera from his hands.

After a time Wentworth shifted the scene, following a fast motor launch over the water straight west—and so we thought—out to sea. After about ten miles of travel we were amazed to see another shoreline rise abruptly a hundred feet or more. The speedboat made for the wall of rock and disappeared into a channel. We followed it.

Another of the never-ending surprises leaped upon us!

Stepping down into the very depths of the earth, or so it seemed, were a series of locks, walled in on both sides by the sheer cliffs which were of such enormous size that the Panama Canal locks were put to shame by comparison. We descended these watery stairs, commenting on the completeness of the entire work. Finally, after traversing five miles and dropping over four hundred feet, we came into a great circular basin in which several hundred wrecked ships were beached. Some of the early-modeled craft, now just wooden hulks rotted away until only their sturdy ribs remained, must have been old when the United States was born! Among the later arrivals there was one beautiful seventeen-thousand-ton combination freighter, lying stern-first on the beach, its prow sunk in fifty feet of water. Evidently some sort of work was being done on it, because several squat barges were moored alongside her lean flanks. Wentworth let loose a gasp of utter incredulity when closer investigation proved it to be the *Ramsday,* the lost flagship of the Pacific Mail and Transport Lines. She had been lost to man's knowledge, since the day she had fearlessly plunged into a typhoon off China in August 1927.

"THERE," pointed out Wentworth, "lies the solution of many a mystery of the sea! There lies many a ship that left port and never was heard of again! Pirates!" For my part I was now so steeped in wonderment, I took what came into view with a puzzled chuckle and exclamation.

Television was without a doubt the revealing light of the world—but what was it revealing?

Continuing on (there was no stopping us now) we scouted until we found the channel leading away from the locks. It was a narrow canal, hemmed in by vertical walls rising upwards of six hundred feet! A mere crack, extremely tortuous, in which the seas boiled and whirled in terrifying violence, speaking eloquently of instant destruction to any querulous ship daring to come up that passage, leading as we discovered, from the broad Pacific!

After a moment we began to retrace our way up the channel when there came a muffled explosion from someplace in the theatre. Soon after, to our startled ears, came the sound of a great hissing and almost Immediately a cloud of brownish smoke broke from the stairway leading to the developing rooms below.

CHAPTER EIGHT

"THE film racks in the basement—they're afire," I shouted, dashing down the stairs intending to close the fireproof door. As I struggled with the release catch, Wentworth threw off the Television machine and turned on the lights. Already the lower part of the theatre was filling with the choking fumes of the released bromine, and after the door slammed shut, I was glad to dash up the balcony stairs. We opened the exit door leading to the fire escape just as the fire-whistle began screaming at the powerhouse, giving the location of the blaze by three short blasts.

Plunging down the steel stairs we raced around the building until we came to the ramp-way leading into the basement.

"McManus," directed King, as he unlocked the doors, "run to the powerhouse and intercept those men coming here. Tell them to get the masks. There's no great danger of the fire spreading, but it's certain death to enter the building now without protection."

I turned and dashed along the narrow path, meeting the men before they were half, way to the scene of the fire. Three of us took the Ford chemical engine, while the rest ran back to get the masks.

The fire had gained headway by the time they had returned and heavy clouds of smoke were pouring from the shattered basement windows, while the roar of burning celluloid could be heard a hundred feet away. Protected by the masks and carrying the chemical extinguishers between them, the men dived into the doorway.

As the minutes passed, additional reinforcements came into action and soon fifty men were in the basement. The sound of the streams from their hoses, and of their battering and tearing, came dully to our anxious ears. I made several attempts to don one of the masks and plunge into the doorway, but King's curt command to stay out of that hellhole and the two husky guards, made it impossible.

The womenfolk gathered at a respectful distance, awe-struck and fearful.

Half an hour later the fire was under control. When the last of the smoldering debris of a once complete developing department had been dragged out into the open and the excitement had somewhat relaxed, it was almost suppertime!

IT was well into the evening before King, Wentworth, and I were together again. Diane had been sent down to the village to visit those unfortunate men who had been injured fighting the fire. Doctor Howard, the company physician, had accompanied her.

To lead off the impending discussion, I asked, "Did you find out the reason for the fire?"

"No," said King. "It must have been spontaneous combustion."

"Nothing doing," I dissented. "Do you know what I found in the, bottom of the film vault? I mean the big one that had its door blown off? The shattered remains of an alarm clock and something attached to the case that apparently was one of those pyrophore-cigar lighters. There was a piece of sheet steel still bolted to the lighter and it's my guess this steel plate might have come from a cylinder originally. I've got it in my room."

"An incendiary bomb!" ejaculated Wentworth, leaning forward.

"McManus, are we going crazy?" asked King after a moment of quiet. "Or is that damned machine playing a trick on us?"

"Neither, Mr. King," I declared. "It's real. We have stumbled into something so wonderful, so fantastic and yet so real, that we ought to shout out our discovery to the world without a second's hesitation. Why, from all appearances I'd say that island is the domineering power of the Earth, operating secretively toward its goal, whatever it may be. At any rate, we ought to let the various governments know of the new rival."

"I think I'm beginning to see things your way, Tom," agreed Wentworth. "But I'm afraid we won't be able to go through with it—first because of our own desire for secrecy on account of television, and secondly, if they, whoever they are, seem to have kept their presence entirely unsuspected all these years, what would happen if the world actually found them out? It would probably mean a sudden change in their plans, a sudden wild fear from the nations upon learning of this cancerous growth, and probably a war, the like of which the world has never witnessed before. I think I have an idea of the scope of their operations but I just can't get up the courage to tell you without drawing some doubt as to my sanity. Another thing is worth considering. If they have been following our actions by means of their television machine, it is no guess to state they have progressed far in the sciences, and the fact that they have placed operatives, spies, in our midst shows they are well aware of what we are doing. Then what chances would we have of telling the world? That bomb was nothing but a warning to keep away from that region and to keep our mouths shut as to what we have seen."

IT was no use to try to keep anything from Diane. After a sort of an effort on my part I gave in and told her of the things we had seen in the theatre previous to the fire. She listened with rapt attention until I concluded. "Now, if your Dad learns that I've told you, he'll never trust my word again."

She clasped her hands. A pensive smile was on her lips as she exclaimed, "Isn't it thrilling? It's just like a story."

"Yes, Diane, and believe me, there are going to be some *real* thrilling incidents happening around Television Hill in the near future—or I miss my guess by a mile. This latest affair has broken your Dad's spirit; he's terribly worried lest something disastrous occur. Wentworth says little, but you can see he's doing a lot of thinking. Both of them are undecided as to the right course to take in this most unusual condition of things. Put it up to me, I'd call in the War Department and give them a look at this mysterious island."

"Might not that start a war?" she asked, a troubled light in those violet depths.

"War? It's strange your Dad and Wentworth think the same thing! I don't think there's the slightest chance of a conflict arising out of this revelation."

"What if these people of the south do not wish their identity to become known for reasons of their own? Might not they become enraged if we were to intrude upon their rights, and retaliate in the same temper as does a total stranger when we become so bold as to ask him his personal plans?"

"Even so," I returned, laughing at her serious demeanor, "it's our right to ask such a question when we and our interests are involved in apparent danger. Besides, what could one little island do against the combined world, if it came to that?"

There was a petulant smile on her lips as she returned. "A man can choke himself to death, but unless his brain desired death, his hands could not kill him by their own volition..."

FOR the next few months things went on as usual around Television Hill. We kept away from the region surrounding our interesting island, finding enough work to do in the usual run of newsreel stuff. Now, however, our eyes were opened for incidents we could trace back to our silent friends of the south. We kept a check on ship arrivals and were not in the least surprised to find the *Winterboro* making her appearance in San Francisco with a cargo of fruit she had picked up at Honolulu. How we wished we could safely question the master of that ship!

Although our guards had been doubled about the entire plant, we were troubled more and more by determined persons who tried to gain entrance under various pretexts. Somehow, word was being passed about that we were experimenting with a new system of television, and newspapers and magazines stormed us with interviewers and telephone calls for the rights to publish accounts of our work. King denied all rumors, calling on the War Department to back his statements. After they had made a report to the newspapers telling of the immatureness of the equipment, and the poor exhibition we had presented, we were left alone. Of course, it was understood, between King and the officials, as a scheme planned long before, to quiet just such rumors as were flying about the country.

One morning while engaged in filming a dizzy spectacle of a flag-raising on the almost completed Merchant's Mart in Chicago, the screen unexpectedly went dark. Shortly after there came a phone call from the powerhouse telling of the breakdown of two of the Diesel engines.

Hurried investigation revealed the center left Diesel had burnt out three connecting-rod bearings through the sudden clogging of oil feed lines. The other five units were in bad shape, for we had been driving all at their maximum limits for the last six months. Despite the tremendous output generated, it was not enough to satisfy the insatiable demands of the giant projectors. Accordingly, King ordered a general shutdown for the period of two weeks until the necessary repairs could be made. The period of inactivity allowed Wentworth time to increase the defenses of the plant and to carry forth new additions and refinements to the various mechanisms.

Meanwhile I took advantage of the opportunity, having quickly completed the changes in the bank of cameras, and the final installation of the new developing machinery to replace that damaged in the fire, and drove to Auburn, Indiana, paying a weekend visit with my parents. While there I saw and purchased a wonderful passenger sport sedan—a powerful appearing, low hung, sleek, chrome-trimmed, front wheel drive beauty, complete in every detail, even to a compact radio set built into a wide ledge behind the front seat.

I drove this sparkling creation back to Television Hill, impatiently watching the miles purr swiftly under the almost dream-like motion of the car. It was late afternoon when I finally did reach for the parking brake on the gravel drive before the cottage stairs. With an expectant smile I pressed the two-tone trumpet salute and its not unmusical blast reverberated over the hill.

From within the cottage came a commotion and Diane appeared at the door. Under the lowered brim of my hat I watched her as she stared with open-mouthed surprise at the machine.

Frowning, she descended from the porch and came alongside. Then she saw!

"Why, Tom!" she gasped, throwing her arms into the open window and taking my caress mutually. She stood back appraisingly. "Oh, it's wonderful!"

"What is?" I asked, feigning innocence.

"Why, the car, of course! Silly—did you think I meant—" the flush appearing on her cheeks and throat conveyed the rest of her sentence.

CHAPTER NINE

AS the bank of cameras went on clicking their record of the unusual scenes on the mighty screen, Diane became daily more and more interested in the camera balcony, claiming, without even so much as a quiver of her level eyes, that the view was better there than any other place. Needless to say, I did not dispute with her. Her questions concerning the operation of the machine were becoming exceedingly technical, as she became acquainted with the principles involved in the system.

"See here, Diane," I expostulated once. "I'm sorry to say I cannot go on. You have me stumped. At present you have outdistanced me in your knowledge of the theories and machinery around this plant. Why in the world does this stuff appeal to you?"

"There now, Tom, don't fly off the handle. Possibly you are under the impression that I'm not aware of the things going on about here, since that January night Dad stumbled into the mysterious island? I know Dad is worried almost to a frenzy over those strange fires breaking out over the place, the breakdown of the Diesels, and the disappearance of his plans. Then, you know, some of our best men are leaving and that constant electrical interference is daily becoming stronger. All this seems to point to one thing—that these unknown island people are earnestly striving to put us out of commission. Daddy has been beset with several appealing offers for the outright disposal of the entire system by tall, wonderfully educated men, supposedly representing the War Department. More than ever now, Dad does not wish the plant to get out of his hands, claiming it to be too great a risk—since he is afraid of what might happen should others uncover that—that 'Terra

Incognita.' So it is that he, himself, has begun to teach me and acquaint me with the details of everything, saying that if the worst came…" Here she paused to stare with compressed lips at the screen. "If the worst came, I could help to carry on from where he leaves off." Her hand lying under mine on the guardrail clenched the pipe tightly.

I think I began to see the seriousness of the whole affair from that moment. Before, I had merely dwelled upon the thrills revolving about the announcement of our exposure; but now I became cognizant of what that selfsame knowledge meant to our own safety. If King thought the danger great enough to teach his daughter how to carry on—well, it was high time that I, too, looked at it in a different light.

THAT we were not alone in our knowledge of a foreign power resting quietly on the Earth's surface was a chance discovery I made one May day immediately after dinner. I had settled myself on the veranda for the purpose of glancing over the morning *Tribune,* which had been brought from Chicago by one of the returning planes. As I was basking in the pleasant spring sunlight, my eyes swept swiftly ever the various articles, noting that nothing of any importance had happened in the city beyond the average run of news. However, on the last sheet I came across a story that made me call King and Diane to my side.

"Say," I said as I spread the sheet before me, "here's a real find! Listen!"

McDOWELL SAILS INTO THE SOUTH SEAS
Transport Chief and Party aboard Private Yacht
"Astra"
Silent on Details of Mysterious Quest

San Francisco, May 23—Enshrouded in a cloak of mystery, the four hundred foot palatial sea-going yacht *Astra* set sail early last evening bearing J. C. McDowell, sole owner and president of the Pacific Mail and Transport Lines, and a large party of guests.

From various sources it was learned McDowell had been preparing for this voyage for the last two months, equipping the *Astra* with a rapid-firing gun on the fore deck and making provisions for launching an amphibian plane from the boat deck. The plane was absent at the time of departure last evening.

The party includes such well known figures in the scientific world as Mr. H. Sommers, late head physicist at University of California, Mr. E. M. Sollett, assistant astronomer from Mount Wilson; Mr. John J. Anderson, well known in political circles as an international investigator; and Mr. A. Rogers an agent of Lloyds, who lends the air of substantiation to the rumor of McDowell's reputed search for his lost freighter, the *Ramsday*.

It is recalled throughout shipping circles that McDowell once made a statement declaring the seventeen thousand ton freighter never sank, but disappeared in some strange fashion unknown even to him. The *Ramsday*, burdened with a hold full of heavy machinery, ran into a typhoon several hundred miles off the coast of China three years ago and the fate of her and her crew of 110 men remains a mystery.

Perhaps it is to follow up the sea trail of the ill-fated vessel that this present voyage is planned.

"YOU see!" I exclaimed, with the joy of having come upon something important, "McDowell suspects something about his ship, the *Ramsday!* Somewhere, someone has slipped and he's hot on the trail of our island friends! And he means business, for he's carrying the planes. I know the *Astra*. She's a real boat; not one of those fragile eggshells millionaires dress up with paint and brass-work. She's a rebuilt cruiser, one the Navy rejected immediately after the war, an experimental ship capable of turning up thirty knots an hour! And she looks it, too."

King was watching me through narrowed eyes during this outbreak. "You know McDowell?"

"You bet I do," I returned.

"How much—to what extent?" he demanded. I knew what was in his mind. He thought I had passed the word along, did he?

"I met him several years ago while working on the coast; we were shooting a movie and used his yacht as part of the setting of the story."

"Of course, I know you better than to suspect you might have let something slip about what you saw of the *Ramsday* down south." There was more of a question than a statement in the tone of his voice.

I could not control the rush of anger sweeping through me. "You have had my word of honor!"

He raised both hands in a complacent manner. "Please, Tom, don't take it that way. I know you didn't; only it—it's funny." He stood for a moment, a worried frown on his forehead as he stared off into the distance. After a long sigh, he turned and went in the cottage, where I heard him call Wentworth on the phone. Wentworth was at Lake Geneva.

"Daddy surely did get a shock from that," murmured Diane, sitting down beside me and taking up the paper.

"It's great, Diane, old girl! Don't you get the real significance of this little bit of apparent ordinary news? The denouement supreme is on the way! I know Scotty McDowell and his tenacious frame of mind, once he sets out to do anything. He'll find that island, if no one else ever will, and then... Boy!"

I don't know how long I might have gone on in this wild state, if it hadn't been for the interrupting hum of a plane. It couldn't have been Wentworth, for King was just then talking to him over the phone. Curious, I descended to the walk, craning my neck about until I espied it, high in the air overhead and slowly circling. Though it was at a great height, in fact so high that its details could not be distinguished, the throbbing, resounding vibrance of its roaring gave me the idea that it was a multi-motored ship. As the minutes passed and it continued circling immediately above us, my interest changed to perplexity.

There was something strange going on up there! At length it appeared to be getting larger and gradually I could make out the lines of the craft. Closer it dropped until it thundered barely a hundred feet above the trees on the highest part of the hill, seemingly interested in the projector.

In size and build it bore resemblance to a Boeing thirty-passenger liner, with the exception that it was equipped with pontoons instead of wheels. There was no mistaking its intention of alighting in the river close by, and with a shout to Diane I dashed down the path toward the hangar. Arrived there, gasping from our run, we were just in time to see the mighty aircraft settle on the surface. Motors booming, it swept swiftly to the ramp way, a man making his way across the lower left wing with a rope in his hand. This he tossed to the mechanics, instructing them to payout the rope at his signal, but to keep it taut. Then the left wing motors roared and it appeared as though the plane were trying to pull the mechanics into the river. However, the dozen odd men gathered in the building rushed to their aid and to our amazement the plane swung about until its tail section overhung the dry portion of the ramp. It was the neatest bit of maneuvering I had ever witnessed.

A doorway opened near the tail section and a ladder swung out and down. One by one four leather-coated, helmeted men climbed down, their keen eyes taking in everyone and everything in swift discerning glances.

Our men drew apart from them. Somehow it seemed they brought with them a chilling atmosphere of antagonism. I felt a strong desire to ask their business and order them from the place.

"Pardon our unexpected intrusion," began the evident commander of the plane with a disarming smile as he looked over our party for one with whom he could speak. "I'm looking for a Mr. C. King."

I stepped forward. "Mr. King is up at the cottage. Shall I call him?"

He shook his head. "No don't bother; we'll have to see him at the cottage anyway."

"I see," I said. To Diane I whispered, "I don't like the looks of this. You take them up to the house, and I'll stay here, and make sure nothing happens—you know what I mean."

After a brief introduction, Diane led the four mysterious men from the hangar, while I called our men together and told them to be ready to return any suspicious overtures our self-invited guests might make. What had strengthened my feeling that all was not well was the fact that the ship's motors had not been shut off, but were idling. Their sharp, steady, liquid pulsations brought exclamations of delight from the pilots and mechanics who stood in groups scanning the lines of the strange ship. I heard one fellow shout to another, "Hi, Jim, just take a listen to some real motors!"

There was continual movement of several men still within the plane. Now and then one would stop to stare out of a porthole.

With a wink to the group nearest the plane I ambled over to the ladder and cautiously made my way up the rungs. One fellow came to the door and with a smile filled with amusement and welcome invited me to come right in.

The plane was divided into two compartments, the rear being fitted up with comfortable seats while the middle section was occupied by a square construction with many gear racks and hand wheels. It took me just one glance to recognize it as a powerful telescopic camera! Two men were busily engaged about a portable motion picture film-developing tank.

I moved into the forward end of the ship. This was no ordinary plane. One look at the unique system of framing and construction assured me of that. It was too well built, too staunch, and bore too much evidence of careful design and refinement to be an American or Continental craft. It had a new, fresh, foreign atmosphere about it. At a word from one of the men at the developing tank the rest of the four men gathered about him, holding up to the light several glass negative plates. Their comments were low spoken and serious.

"TOM, oh, Tom." It was Diane. I hurried to the door and found her at the bottom of the ladder.

"Dad—he wants you to come to the cottage—immediately," she gasped. Her face was deathly pale, even though she must have run the entire distance from the cottage.

"Keep your eyes on that plane, boys," I instructed as we departed.

"What's up, Diane?" I asked as we strode swiftly up the path.

"Oh I don't know, only Dad has called Wentworth from Lake Geneva, and has sent for Chalmers and Smythe. Those men seem to know everyone about our place and asked where you were."

THE parlor was filled with men. The four men occupied vantage positions at the four corners of the room, facing each other. King stood at the table, his narrowed eyes anxiously darting from one to the other. There was no welcoming smile on his lips as Diane and I entered, only a firmer drawing of the muscles of his jaw. Chalmers, a puzzled and mystified frown on his features, was nervously twirling his greasy cap; apparently he had been called from some repair work at the powerhouse. After a glance in my direction he returned to his intent study of the design on the rug. Smythe was the least concerned of the lot—he had a slight smile on his lips as he sat smoking a cigar, with long satisfied puffs. Diane slipped her arm into mine as I stood aimlessly near the door.

"Mr. Thomas McManus?" inquired the leader, arising to his feet.

I nodded, scrutinizing the fellow. He was of average height, with an athletic figure and a poise that told of military training. He was clear featured, and had the keenest, discerning gray eyes I ever looked into. He turned to King.

"Mr. King, I understand it will take half an hour for your partner, Mr. Wentworth, to come from Lake Geneva?"

King nodded in assent.

"Well, in that case we will have to do without him. You can inform him when he arrives of what I am about to say," The fellow glanced at his mates. "You, Mr. King, are a man of precise speech and are not wont to quibble or to beat about the bush when it comes to direct talk. So am I.

"You have developed a successful and proven system of television and by doing so you have few equals in mental skill and patience. You have accomplished an unequaled feat in mechanical design of a higher order than the world of today thinks possible. And, as we suspected, you discovered traces of our work, found our island home, and thereby placed us in a precarious position. We have kept watch on you through all these years and partly in respect to you, and partly because we planned to let your research work go on unmolested, we have made no serious efforts to hinder you until several months ago. You have proved a foe of such resourcefulness as to be worthy of our admiration. But you have gone too far. We are now ready to strip all evidences of secrecy from our presence and put before you a proposition that you may take or leave. Either way it means the dismantlement of all the machinery here at Television Hill and the loss of your system of television to the world for a few centuries."

If a bomb had been thrown into the parlor of the cottage, the shock would not have been any greater. I was stunned into complete stupefaction. Chalmers had risen, with anger contorting his face. I expected him to hurl himself at the speaker at any moment. Smythe's cigar hung from his gaping mouth. This certainly must be a shock to Chalmers and Smythe, for they were not aware of our previous television exploration down south.

King placed both hands on the tabletop to steady himself. "I don't know who you are, or what you represent," he began in a low composed voice, "but, if you have an idea that you can scare me into turning my plant over to you, or even stopping my experiments, on account of my knowledge of your presence here on Earth, you're absolutely insane!"

The leader gave a little resigned motion with his hands.

"I understand perfectly, Mr. King, your righteous attitude toward a proposition calling for such a complete disposal of the marvelous result of the labors of both you and Wentworth. But I don't believe you know just what you are opposing! I'm not making this demand. I'm just an envoy, sent here in the interest of seven million people who are directly involved; indirectly the entire human race is in—well, danger! If you take the foolish choice of trying to fight back at us, I warn you, you have not the slightest conception of how effectively we can strike back at you. The odds against you are greater than you know. We are too well established in world affairs to let anyone man disrupt our plans. Come, now—what is the answer I am to carry back— Are you willing to turn over Television Hill for fifty million dollars and forget you ever built a television machine, or must we take it away from you and put you and your associates out of the way, and thus safeguard your secrets?"

"If what you say is the truth," snapped King, now thoroughly aroused, "you can go back to your people, those damned parasites of the earth, and tell them I will never concede to such a demand!"

"So be it," agreed the man, nodding.

"Go now," blazed King. "This is final."

"Presently, Mr. King," drawled the leader with a complacent motion of his arm. "But first, permit me to say a few things which might give you food for thought."

"Please do not think you will be able to bring our presence into the light of the world, if I may put it that way, we want you to remember this: If this is going to be a fight, and it's very likely to, if you do not concede to our pardonable demand, we can force you into silence far more easily and more quickly than you suspect; with such indisputable evidence on your side as motion picture newsreels!

"You have looked on some of the sights about our island home and you know just what kind of people, what class of intelligence, resides there—but you don't know of the origin nor the power of these selfsame people. I'm sorry I cannot relate to you a few instances that have happened recently, just to give you an idea of what you are standing against."

King laughed, a cold, disdainful laugh. "What are you trying to do; scare us by such insane threats?"

"Whether they are insane or not, the future will reveal. However, I'm sorry to see that your present state of mind cannot be won over. You know what that means? Virtual war!"

"War!" King turned the word over as though he had never heard of it. "Between whom? Between your bunch and the United States?"

"Mr. King, I regret our meeting has turned out as it has. May I wish you the best of luck in your fight?" The leader drew on his helmet. The three other men arose to their feet and drew together at the door. The commander went to King and thrust out his hand in a friendly gesture. King, after a moment of indecision, slowly grasped the man's hand, regarding him in bewildered perplexity. At the door, the leader paused beside Diane and murmured, "We beg pardon, Miss King, for being so—so rude and inconsiderate to your father and his work, but some day you might understand the great good we are doing," With that, and a nod to me, they tramped down the hall and out on the veranda.

CHAPTER TEN

JULY came. Swiftly. It was on the morning of the tenth, the dawn of a hot, sultry day, when scarcely a breath of air stirred in the clear, steel-hot skies that the first murmurings of danger came. It was in the form of a radio weather report from an eastern Missouri station bearing the mutterings of disaster in the form of a widespread storm sweeping northeast at alarming speed...

The arms of the teletype machines seemed strangely silent as the stifling morning hours dragged on. At about eleven o'clock the house phone took King away from the projection house. Some ten minutes passed before he returned. There were serious lines on his face as he trudged up the stairway.

"Well, I guess the fun is to begin—shortly," he said. "New Era just connected with our pay phone in the cottage hall, saying they have been sending half-hourly reports via our regular lines since seven this morning, following the path of a twister in Missouri. Somehow the messages have been intercepted or the lines cut. I have reasons to believe it's the latter. Anyhow, they gave us some interesting news. The Weather Bureau has plotted the path of the storm and they believe it will pass close, if not through the Rock River Valley. So, if it comes this way, New Era wants some good pictures of the twister in action."

"If one doesn't get us before we see it," I laughed.

"This isn't a laughing matter, McManus. Wentworth and I have feared such storms ever since we came out here. We had a narrow escape in the fall of 1928 when the twister or tornado tore through Rockford. If one heads this way all we can do is to take to our heels. We have a storm cellar down near the hangars, but that is filled—" He checked himself suddenly when Wentworth gave a warning motion with his hands. "Yes, all we can do is skip," he repeated.

We sat on the balcony for another half hour, telling each other of experiences we had during storms. At length Wentworth rose and said he was going to the cottage.

After he had gone, King sat for a long time staring toward the screen.

"McManus," he said softly, "I've got a feeling something's going to happen here today and that it isn't going to be pleasant. Do you know that one of the twisters is already as far north as Galesburg, only eighty miles away?"

"Already," I queried, wondering why he had kept that news to himself. Yet the reason was as plain as day. He did not wish to needlessly alarm the plant. Wentworth would probably warn the men to be ready to move.

"Yes, one is that close. What do you say to our getting a look at it?"

I could see by his expression that he wished no one else in the theatre and with a few commands I sent the attendants and film men on their way, telling them to be ready for instant recall.

King seated himself at the controls and shortly had the screen on the region round and about Galesburg.

It wasn't long before we found the twister and by expert maneuvering he followed the swift erratic movements of the swaying lash of destruction. Then, drawing back on the vertical wheels (on the screen, of course) we began to climb up the whirling thing. Up we went, seemingly flying into the very teeth of the gale, as we pitched and rolled in the effort to keep in advance of it. We drew toward a bank of clouds, which King made clear and distinct by a sudden leap from the controls to the mixing panel. At the top of the spout a veritable fountain of shattered, wind-torn debris sprayed.

"Look at that," commanded King as something black, huge, and utterly strange, appeared on the screen. He made quick adjustments to the controls, grabbed the telephone, dialing the cottage. He pushed it to one side, while he made further corrections at the console.

"That you, Wentworth?" I had picked up the phone after finally overcoming my stupor.

"Yes, Tom, what, is it?"

"Come to the projection house immediately. Hurry!"

"Thanks, Tom," grunted King frantically working the controls in the attempt to get a comprehensive view of the whole blur. It was not natural, we saw at once. Monstrous, it was—a great triangular-shaped construction of cylindrical sides and bulging corners apparently caught in the head of the twister. But as we followed it, the incredible truth dawned upon us.

Instead of being helplessly enmeshed in the cone of the twister, this ghastly thing was—the GENERATOR of the twister! It was, without

the slightest doubt, a man-made creation of stupendous size, whose three sides gave evidences of thousands of shifting and whirling beams of light or rays.

At this moment Wentworth rushed in, followed closely by Diane. Their sudden gasps of amazement were amplified in the silence. We all stood there awestruck and dumbfounded—all except King, who was tuning the focus so as to get a view of the interior.

"What's the idea of that thing?" burst out Wentworth, his common sense overriding his surprise.

"That's just what I'm trying to find out," replied King.

The screen seemed to halt and slowly one of the corners of the triangle drifted toward us. The penetrating beam of the Televise rays cut through the metal covering and there flowed over the screen a cross-section of the whole construction—long corridors filled with intricate machinery, whirling and spitting flame. Nowhere did we find an operator, although the entire interior was combed as diligently as only television rays can comb. We did find one room, which we thought was carefully insulated, because of the extreme difficulty we had in getting a clear reproduction. This room enclosed a switchboard filled with a great number of automatic switches that were opening and closing at regular intervals.

"Remote control," decided Wentworth, "being run from another place. But what's the damn thing making a twister for?"

"I think," declared King, beads of perspiration rolling down his face, "I've got an idea. That thing is heading this way for the express purpose of wiping us out for good."

"Not while I'm here," returned Wentworth. "Come on, King, we're not going to let them scare us away." He grabbed the phone, dialing the powerhouse. "Chalmers? Say, Alex, open the Diesels wide and give us every watt you can kick out of the generators. Slam the storage cells into full amperage for a shock. Get the twin high frequency generators going immediately. Chalmers, listen, get this, stand by—this is no test, this is the actual thing!"

At that he slammed the phone down and tore down the stairway. At the bottom he pulled open a side door revealing, with the spotlight he carried a shallow switchboard. He was busy for some minutes making deliberate and studied connections with a number of flexible cables. Closing the door, he raced back up again, a dancing circle of light fleeting over the floor from his spotlight. At the mixing panel he drew a deep breath as he flipped over a number of switches.

"All set, King, old man. Just keep your controls following it—and we'll blast it from the skies."

"But isn't it too far?" queried Diane anxiously.

"Eighty miles or eight thousand," snapped King. "It's going to go!"

Wentworth rolled over a row of toggles with one sweep of his hand and the screen went dark! Instantly I felt as though some titanic force had seized upon every muscle in my body, contracting the sinews until they seemed about to snap with the tension, while in the darkness of the theatre I almost fancied a million stars were blazing in blinding splendor. Almost as quickly, the sensation had passed and the screen was alight. Diane's face was white—even in the semidarkness I noted that she shook with fright.

King was sweeping the skies for the strange machine, but when a half hour had elapsed without our finding a trace of it he gave it up.

"We seem to have won that move this time," smiled Wentworth, after he had returned from disengaging connections from down below. "Do you know what we did?" he asked me.

"Not exactly, but I've got an idea," I returned.

"We only beamed, or rather intersected, twenty-five million volts into the control room of that mysterious machine. No wonder it ran away, eh?"

CHAPTER ELEVEN

AFTER a short time the men were recalled and we began to take our usual shots of the wind-torn sections of Missouri. Diane and I stood near the console and watched the regular operator as he picked his way through and between the shattered buildings and homes.

Then, without warning, the screen again went dark; but not black as before, for it retained a misty image that might have been construed to be anything.

Wentworth was in action immediately at the panel. "New Glarus is dead. We're running on Lake Geneva alone."

The dome lights were thrown on and we stood around silent, the attendants staring wide-eyed at our group on the balcony. They all knew something out of ordinary was occurring. As the phone buzzed, I reached for it. The voice was incoherent and hurried.

"This is Williams at New Glarus. Lightning just struck the projector, killing the guard in the tower, and fusing the left tower legs. The high wind struck the projector and we are afraid the whole thing will collapse at any moment. Will call again in a few minutes."

King and Wentworth were aghast at the news.

"We'll take a look up there," declared King, ordering the man once more from the theatre and setting the machinery in operation again.

It was all as Williams had said. The Television screen pictured the scene at New Glarus with its usual faithfulness. A terrific bolt of lightning (only we had very good reason for the suspicion of its not being of natural origin) had struck the lower end of the outer tower leg, weakening the entire supporting members. The high wind was bearing with force against the wide surface of the projector housing and it was swaying slightly. The men and Williams were working like demons trying to turn the projector so as to relieve the strain. Even as they struggled with the driving mechanism another shaft of this strange lightning tore into the upper part of the projector. It hit somewhere near the pivots. The projector leaned further. Already the three-foot thick shafts were tugging at their foundations, bending slowly as their retaining bolts held. Age-long minutes later they majestically dropped the seventy-ton housing to the ground. We almost imagined we could hear the tearing and snapping of steel members and popping rivets as the entire construction collapsed into a meaningless wreck Williams and his men then retreated across the field after entering the watchtower and bringing forth the inert watchman.

Disaster—mysterious and diabolic—was upon us!

WE needed no second thought to come to that conclusion. It was enough. The television machine was closed down and the lights turned on. King and Wentworth stood staring in downright stupefaction at each other. King, after a shrug of his shoulders, shivered. Perhaps I stood, mouth agape, like some senseless lout. I don't know, one never knows how he looks or acts in such moments of stress.

"Come on, let's get out of this place," commanded King suddenly, grasping Diane's arm and propelling her ahead of him down the stairs. Once outside I drank in the sultry air with relief. The sky to the west and south had become heavily black with the storm sweeping upon us.

"Say, McManus, did you ever see or, hear of a storm that's reported to be coming from Missouri, taking a leap up into Wisconsin before it strikes here? Funny, isn't it, that it should put one of the bearing projectors out of commission, just at the right time so that we cannot interfere with the plans of our friends down south?" King's laugh was forced and filled with suppressed nervousness.

Wentworth answered, "Sure is. It looks as though Television Hill is going to be a hot place when the storm hits it."

Diane and I kept silent. I for one was trying to calm the wild thoughts their words and past incidents brought up. We arrived at the cottage. King and Wentworth went inside while I seated myself on the porch stairs. Diane stood nearby, leaning against the doorframe, watching with fearful eyes the sullen approach of the storm.

Everything was dead quiet—the quiet that heralds the storm. The trees along the river were standing in expectant attention, awaiting the impending outburst of nature's titanic forces. A poplar leaf came sailing down in a whirling spin, while afar off came the dry chirp of a robin, and faintly, from the shallows of the river, the deep croak of bullfrogs. I stared up into the soft, beautifully molded features of the girl, until she became aware of my gaze. There was a momentary flicker of a doubtful smile as she settled down beside me.

I rose to my feet and started down the stairs. A light restraining hand was laid upon my shoulder and I turned to her questioning eyes.

"I'm going down to the garage, Diane. This silence is getting unbearable. I need action," I did not wish to let her know of the fear creeping into my heart.

She stood where I had left her and as I turned the curve in the drive I glanced back and saw she was watching my movements. Down at the garage I busied myself about my sedan, changing the oil, greasing the steering wheel quadrant and helix and the front universals. Long before I completed my work I became aware of the distant rumbling of thunder. When done, I took a look at the other machines. The Ford roadster was completely out of commission, for someone had forgotten to put in oil the last time it was used. The limousine was at Dixon, being overhauled. Diane's smart roadster had a flat tire. I could not withhold a grim laugh, when I found the spare tire flat also. If we had to leave this Hill in a hurry, my sedan would be the only machine in condition to move. I expected rather than suspected foul play and rather than think more about it I climbed into the front-drive and headed for the cottage. It was safer there.

Diane came down and seated herself beside me. There were tears in her eyes which I laughingly wiped away telling her we had not, as yet, seen any signs of danger involving us directly. I did not tell her of the things I had discovered in the garage.

"Oh, Tom, I just know we're going to get into terrible trouble; something tells me to flee, to run away, to hide, to get away from here. I don't know what to do." She gave herself over to hysterical sobbing.

"Here, listen to this," I turned on the radio and the speaker pounded out a sprightly orchestral selection. The ether was filled with interrupting, shattering static. I turned the set off.

The cloud formation had drawn nearer and now we could see the leading band of white cloud rolling in the vanguard. Soon the skies grew darker, while closer came the deep booming roll of thunder. The grey storm-leaders came up and passed over with the distant sound of rising winds. It grew so dark I turned on the parking lights. Diane shivered when the first heavy drops came plopping on the taut roof of the sedan. As usual, there was a let-up, and we took advantage of the break to leave the car and hurry to the veranda. King and Wentworth were there, with calculating eyes on the rolling clouds overhead.

A moaning sigh arose and the trees on the west side of the river leaned in our direction.

"Here she comes," I warned, setting to and turning the porch chairs upside down. A newspaper eluded my grasp and distributed itself with much slatting over the veranda floor and against the side of the house. Under the steady blast the trees fought to retain their vertical positions, while their loose leaves and torn branches flew through the air on horizontal paths. The hollow roar of the wind whipping about the porch and sending spray sheets of rain slanting inwards, forced us into the cottage where we settled in chairs, closing our eyes as the lightning seared the storm-tossed world outside. Bolt after bolt came and the thunder crashed in stunning splendor. Diane quivering, as though she expected every moment to be her last. The cottage shook at each reverberation of thunder…

Between crashes, King tried to speak to me.

"New Era just sent in word that the twister at Galesburg petered out just about the time we sent our paralyzing beam into it. Reports are that everyone in the district was stunned by a terrific thunderbolt." He grinned.

"Maybe you blew the thing into atoms," I suggested.

"Maybe. We don't know what might have been in there you know. Williams also phoned in saying the guard he thought was killed was only stunned, and outside of being injured during the fall of the towers, is feeling all right. The storm is raging pretty badly up there—sweeping east," Now that the excitement had been dampened by the rain outside, he was his old collected self again.

"Say, do you realize we're late for dinner? The cook's been raving about for the last hour and a half."

Dinner, nevertheless, was a period of strained silence. I could not help noticing Diane's nervous actions. She would gasp at each searing flash, biting her quivering lips when she became aware of my stare. She did not eat, but toyed with her fork.

At length even King became aware of her fright and threw his arms about her shoulders, laughingly telling her to quiet her fears. Thereupon she began sobbing and without further ado she left the dining room, going upstairs to her room.

FOUR o'clock came, tolled off by the Telechron. The storm was breaking all precedents by increasing in intensity as the hours passed. Phone calls, via the pay phone, came inconstantly from New Era, informing us of news of the storm, which was becoming widespread over entire northern Illinois.

The lightning display was awe-inspiring. Television Hill, being the highest point of land in the vicinity, seemed a lodestone for the heavy discharges crashing everywhere. These flashes were not of the usual jabbing streak, but more in the order of sheet lightning, dropping with deliberate speed to the ground and holding there for periods, almost as long as several seconds at times.

Once more the library phone rang and Wentworth answered it. He reported to King, "Several of the cottages down at the village have been struck by lightning, and someone has spread the report of a twister heading this way. The men want to know if we'll allow them to take their families out of the valley. They're all ready to go."

"Surely, let them go," agreed King after a moment of deliberation. "It's better and safer. This storm might get worse, and to tell the truth, I think we're in for a real cyclone or something like that. Tell the bunch to head northwest; they'll clear the storm path sooner."

King then went into the rear quarters of the cottage and told the house servants to join the party leaving Television Hill. They, thoroughly frightened by the storm and the whispered stories of danger, were only too glad to dive out into the rain and await the long string of private cars and trucks that shortly appeared on the bridge.

A PHONE roll call of the plant found that Chalmers and several, of his assistants had elected to stay at the powerhouse, while in the village several strong-hearted families made light of the storm, laughing at the fears of the others who had fled. In our cottage were King, Wentworth, Diane, and myself. Diane had not appeared since she had taken to her room. Another age-long hour passed, while I tried to concentrate my thoughts on a novel I had picked up in the library. However, the predominating sensation of disaster intruded constantly.

There was a scream from upstairs. Diane! I was on my feet instantly. There came the rapid clatter of her feet down the stairs and she burst into the room, wild fear in her eyes.

"Fire!" she cried. "The hill is on fire! Upstairs, you can see it!"

Upstairs in her room we crowded about the windows facing the powerhouse and watching the leaping flames coming from a point half way up the hill on the east side.

"The oil storage reservoir!" was my exclamation, while Wentworth nodded, with a pained drawing of muscles about his eyes.

"Sixty thousand gallons of crude up there; the powerhouse is going to get the worst of it, if those tanks have burst wide open," cried Wentworth. He clenched his hands tightly.

To the north we could see the fragile looking towers of the projector, which still stood unscathed atop the hill, although it must have been the target of countless thrusts of lightning all that afternoon. A blinding flash illuminated the entire countryside and in the short interval the hot pencil electricity played about the water towers of the projection house. For a moment later darkness descended and the glow of the oil fire could be seen again.

I saw a moving light, red and ominous, flickering in the windows of the projection house, just about where the lightning had struck.

"Look! The projection house is afire, too!" I pointed, when my doubting senses had made certain is wasn't a fantasy.

"My goodness," murmured Wentworth. "What next?"

"Come, let's get down stairs before a bolt hits the cottage," cried Diane, drawing me out of the room.

I was for donning raincoats and dashing over to the projection house and fighting the fire, but fate or some other force was planning otherwise.

There came a running of many feet up the porch and Chalmers and his two assistants dashed into the parlor.

Chalmers drew off his rain-soaked hat. His wrinkled face looked older and strained. "Well, they got us! It's all over! I don't know how it happened but the oil tanks up the hill blew up and the oil has seeped into the battery rooms below the powerhouse. A regular hell is blazing away down there and the gases—Whew!"

"What about the projector house," I cut in.

"You saw it— It's too late now. We ran in there thinking it only a little blaze, but we found the upper floors soaked with gasoline. Man! But there certainly is dirty work being done around here. It's terrible, King, all the work of eight years going up in smoke."

The lights flickered and began to dim. "Guess the fire is getting at the batteries now," explained Chalmers. The bulbs dimmed until just a faint line of glowing filament stood out in the darkness during the intermittent blazes of light outside.

"WHAT are your plans? Going to stay here?" asked Chalmers.

"I've not decided what we're going to do," returned King, out of the darkness.

"Well, we're not going to stay here and risk our lives. How about it, boys?"

"Nothing doing," they agreed. There was a sudden movement and they ranged near the door.

"So long, Mr. King and you Mr. Wentworth; hope things come out all right. Au revoir!" sang out Chalmers with a hollow rasping laugh entirely out of place in the present state of affairs. It was almost mocking I thought, as I leaped to the window to see where they were going. The three paused a moment beside my sedan and then climbed into Chalmers' powerful coupe which stood nearby.

There was a hollow tube-like whine as the fast machine started and sped down the drive. "King," I said suddenly as a suspicion dawned upon me. I turned from the window.

"What is it?" he asked in a curious tone of voice, as though he already knew what I was going to tell him.

"I'm ready to stake my life on the supposition that we'll never see Chalmers and his assistants again! Chalmers may be connected with those people of the south," I declared.

As I expected, a silent agreement met my words. "I've got it," I exclaimed. "We'll get them at the bridge." I leaped toward the phone and lifted the receiver. There was no answering buzz. Of course, the power was gone!

"Come on," broke in Wentworth. "We've had enough of this. Let's be going, too. We don't know what may come next. Let's get out of here."

I guess we all must have had the same idea but didn't have the nerve to express it, for at his suggestion, we dashed about getting into raincoats and locating flashlights. I went to my room, and scattered my belongings about, stuffing only those valuable things I wanted into a suitcase. We gathered in the parlor where Diane had lit a candle. A sorry group of humans, we were, too.

King, in his leather flying jacket and helmet, appeared a stocky gnome. Wentworth, tall and perfectly fitted in his light coat and black hat, was a duplicate of the stock movie detective—even to the unlighted black cigar he held in his teeth. Diane. She was a picture! Her close-fitting hat was pressed over her blond hair and her trim figure lent an air of romance to the scene we presented. At my appearance they selected the various burdens piled near the door and we filed out of the door.

The projector house was already ablaze, long licking tongues of flame leaping high above the dark silhouette of the nearer water tower. Back on the east side of the hill rose another roll of flame; clouds of black smoke by lightning flashes and crimson glowing in the darkness ensuing.

I splashed out to the car and opened the doors. They piled in quickly. The motor, though well protected from such water immersions as occur in wet weather, at first refused to start, and when it did, coughing and spitting, we moved down the gravel drive. I kept in second gear so as to get the engine warmed up quickly and to keep the sliding machine under better control.

"Head for the hanger," directed King tapping me on the shoulder. I ran the car close up to the door on the concrete shoulders. By the time we had gained access to the interior, we were wretchedly wet, despite the raincoats.

Our searching beams of light traveled over the hangar, disclosing it to be deserted with evidences of hasty departure everywhere present. The crimson Lockheed airplane, which had been kept ready for instant use early that morning, stood on its landing wheels, awaiting its call for duty. The giant Sikorsky plane, standing over the Lockheed and the other two seaplanes, looked like some mighty bird guarding her brood from the tumultuous rage of the storm, which shook the steel building.

King drew us together. "You know, it would be safer for all of us to split up? They might be watching us with their television apparatus, and it would be a simple matter for them to keep tab on us if we stayed together. Although it may be of no use to try to get away from them, we can try it. Wentworth and I will take the Lockheed, and you and Diane will take the safer route by your machine, which, thank goodness, can make real speed. Diane, I know, will be in good care, safer in fact, than if she were with me. Head northwest for this storm is moving northeast."

He opened the cabin door and made his way into the pilot's compartment. There was a sob from Diane as the battery-operated inertia starter engaged. The ringing whine of gears rose to a high pitch as the flywheel was spun. Suddenly the singing whine changed to a labored grind as the five hundred horsepower Hornet chugged over easily. After one or two false explosions, its bull throated roar thundered in the closed hangar. Wentworth and I tugged at the cables opening the immense overhead doors, straining every ounce of our strength to get it into motion. As the hinged sections rattled upward, the wind tore into the opening, sending a spray of rain over the planes, rocking them in its cyclone blast. The river, already high, was rolling and splashing on the ramp way. At best, the bright fuselaged plane seemed a frail construction in which to fight that storm and I said so to King.

"I know it," he shouted as he climbed out of the cabin, "but I've an idea we'll have a better chance this way." He gave me a hard, determined glance that would brook no opposition.

He drew Diane to him, embracing her, looking over her shoulder at me, mute appeal in his eyes—if anything went wrong while she was in my care!

"Tom," he said as he was about to enter the plane again, "we're going to hop up to Lake Geneva and await further developments up there. If, at the end of two hours, you have a chance to get to a phone, get in touch with the municipal airport at Chicago and we'll let you know where to meet us. Okay? Now close the doors after we leave—and beat it. God have mercy on you."

Without another word he climbed into the plane, followed by Wentworth, who shook hands solemnly. I tossed in the pile of bags and suitcases they had brought with them.

At Diane's side I watched the plane taxi across the floor and slip into the water. King was forced to give the ship full throttle to keep the wind from sweeping them against the northern wall of the hangar windbreak. It seemed to be making very little progress as it rolled and tossed in its fight for the center of the wind torn river. King was driving it on by sheer determination. Struggling praiseworthily into the gale, it gradually worked up speed.

Suddenly it lifted its pontoons from the water and rose sharply, zooming upward with a blatant snarling heard even above the thundering, as the powerful engine pulled the ship from its immediate stall. King courageously banked, losing much of his precious altitude as he swung with the wind. At terrific speed he was hurled into the north, barely clearing the treetops, the whine of his motor dying into the distance instantly. They were gone!

Diane aided me in drawing down the doors and as the long horizontal sections clanked over the ways, I felt as though the curtains were being drawn on our fantastic drama. As yet I could not reasonably convey to my consciousness the indisputable fact of the impending total destruction of Television Hill and the scatterings of its peoples. It was too much like a dream, a horrible nightmare from which I hoped to awake before witnessing the inevitable climax. One did not know of the temper of these resourceful people of the south!

That they were intent on crushing the revealing presence of Television, could be envisioned in their unprecedented use of a machine to create a cyclone. If they had succeeded in reaching Television Hill, the world would have had only a few crumbled ruins to gaze upon, representing what had been the King-Wentworth experimental radio plant! Perhaps the two other transmitters might have been wiped out of existence in the same manner. But King's sudden electrical thrust must have brought an unlooked for change in their plans. Once their work of removing this point of danger had begun, there was no chance of withdrawing—they must carry through, despite the resultant cost.

King and Wentworth might escape by taking the unexpected course through the air, while the safety of Diane and me depended wholly upon my retaining presence of mind.

To escape! It was not natural or sensible to go rushing wildly across the country with the blind fear of an unknown enemy following; an enemy whose intentions seemed of no greater evil than to destroy inanimate machinery. However, since the present situation called for such procedure, I had better call off these ruminations and start moving.

In the dimness of the flashlight-illuminated hangar I led Diane toward the door. She had given herself up to hysterical sobbing, which my consoling words seemed to augment rather than alleviate.

I helped her into the sedan and ran around to the other side. The motor, idling the while, was now at normal temperature and anxious for action. Into reverse I jerked, cutting a short circle on the concrete shoulder. Then a wrist-snap into low speed; a slap into second as the forward gears whined—the spinning front wheels gradually taking traction on the flying gravel. A quick jab at the brakes and we were rolling easily across the rain-swept bridge. At the opposite postern we were forced to halt until the guard opened the heavy steel gate. As we slipped past, he waved his shotgun suggestively and set about securing the barrier again.

We set forth up the slight grade toward the highway, lights blazing their way through and among the close growths of foliage. Near the entrance I experienced a start. Set in position so as to halt any machine coming from the bridge, was the huge bulk of Chalmers' coupe. All my suspicions as to his connections with our present state returned in a single convinced flash of thought. He meant to stop us, to hold us, thinking King and Wentworth were in the car! I acted upon impulse, instantly. Snapping the car into second, my whole weight went on the accelerator pedal. With but one choke the powerful motor breathed in the sudden influx of gas an emitting and ever rising stuttering bellow from the exhaust, leaped up the rise toward the blockading coupe. Within ten yards of his machine I spun the wheel to the left, lurching down into the shallow rain-filled ditch behind the car and after a series of skidding jerks brought it back again to the road surface. Still in second, I gunned the respondent machine all the way up the lane until we were skimming along on the hard concrete, heading north. The perfectly balanced motor under the polished bonnet settled down to a steady whining murmur.

I glanced at Diane with a satisfied smile hovering on my lips. The incident had evidently frightened her out of her hysterical mood, for she reclined against the seat, holding her handkerchief against her mouth. She closed her eyes in a shuddering gesture, signifying she did not countenance such reckless maneuvering.

The slanting rain pelted against the windshield so hard that the fast swinging arms of the wipers failed utterly to keep it clear. There came to our ears the intermittent sound likened to escaping steam as the balloon tires sucked at the watery pavement, sending a splattering spray over the entire width of the roadway.

For several minutes we sped along at a reasonable speed. The wheel bracket mirror reflected the dazzling beams of a car fast creeping upon us. I permitted it to come up close so as to identify it. A flash of lightning revealed the black coupe.

Chalmers was after us!

He came up and began to swing to the left side to pass. For a moment I thought of stopping and confronting him with a demand for an explanation of his actions, figuring he'd have little chance for hostile actions on a public highway, even though it was almost deserted, but a glance at Diane decided me.

Well anyway, Chalmers would have a chance to prove his long held argument that his coupe was the better car when it came to sustained speed!

I rested my foot on the accelerator and the quivering speedometer rolled steadily around. The road swept up to us illumined at close intervals by the daylight flashes, of lightning and the reddish glare of the headlights. The machine took every bit of my attention, for the high wind and the wet pavement created a hazard not to be disregarded. For a while Chalmers hung doggedly to our rear, the fingering beams of his driving lights playing on my mirror, told me that, but as the miles tore past, the pace began to tell upon him. His machine, old in design though not old in years, could not, with safety, hold the increasing rate of mileage on the sharp turns and curves. He dropped back little by little, striving to make up his lost distance on the straight stretches.

We flew through the town of Oregon at sixty miles an hour.

Holding the center of the black line, we roared along at reckless speed and thirty minutes later we were gliding easily through the residential section of Rockford.

As I slipped into second gear, preparatory to awaiting the change of lights at the junction of Route U.S. 20, my eyes lighted upon two huge sedans drawn close by on the opposite side of the street. As several rain-coated men were grouping near the machines, evidently looking in our direction, I didn't feel any too great reassurance.

As the light changed, I was off with a leap, but instead of continuing on, I cut a sharp left turn. Then, throwing all caution to the winds, I stepped on the gas and sped out of Rockford, clearing the way with every forward light blazing and the trumpet salute shattering the unusual quiet of the streets.

Soon we were far out in the country, spinning along undeterred at seventy miles an hour. Now I felt more secure— we had something more tangible than wild fear to drive us on. The storm gave no indication of abating, the rain still falling with the same sullen relentlessness, giving me the impression that it would continue indefinitely.

Diane, to my sidelong glances, seemed resigned, her hands clasped in her lap, closing her eyes in fear as we careened around turns and twists of the road. Once when the rear wheels left the road during the blinding period following a dazzling burst of lightning, I felt her hand fall lightly on my shoulder as I spun the wheel. Straightening out, I glanced into her face and found a mute appeal in those deep eyes.

The liquid slap of the tires, the howl of the air through the radiator webbing rose in a crescendo over the vibrating beat note of the motor. In my mind I tried to picture the sight of those eight pistons reciprocating fifty times a second—second after second, minute after minute. The sound and the resultant mental impression seemed to thrust me into another universe, another wet, dripping world, in which a thin wheel in my hands guided a rectangle of raindrop-studded transparency along a hard-to-follow, slick, blackened ribbon. I stole many a sidelong glance at the girl's face until she noticed and warned me to watch the road. I was trying to fathom the set appearance of her lips and jaw.

"Diane," I said at length, breaking the silence that had held for the last sixty miles, "I'll have to stop for gas pretty soon— The way we have burned up the sixty odd miles since we left Television Hill over an hour ago is telling on the car. I'm going to stop at the next station—I'll get some sandwiches, too."

"I wish you would," she smiled faintly, "but do you think we can do it safely?"

"I think so. I think we've outdistanced anyone pursuing us enough to warrant our taking a brief halt. At that, I wonder how your Dad and Wentworth made out."

"Please. Tom, don't, please! As it is, it's almost driving me mad. Why couldn't they have come with us, so we would be together?" Once more she began to cry—softly this time.

"Well, your Dad seemed to know what he was doing—he wouldn't pull such a foolhardy stunt as flying in a cyclone without some good reason. Even we haven't done so badly."

"I hope so," she murmured.

CHAPTER TWELVE

THERE appeared the far-off glow of many lights and easing up on the throttle; the machine rolled gently into the cindered esplanade surrounded on three sides by gaudy-painted shacks. It was essentially a gas station, around which had grown a repair shop, a small garage, a now deserted roadhouse, and a lunch stand of inviting appearance. I braked at the roadside filling pump. A toot on the salute brought the attendant on the run through the puddles.

He grinned pleasantly. "Some night, eh? What'll it be, sir?"

"Whatever she'll take. High tests. And see how the water and oil are."

The hose clanked hollowly in the tank. I opened my billfold, extracting a crumbled piece of currency. "Diane, you pay the fellow. I'll run into the lunch stand and get a few sandwiches." I struggled out of the car and sprinted to the house.

As the door slammed, the woman at the counter came forward.

"Fix up a half dozen assorted sandwiches," I directed my eyes lighting on several thermos bottles, fetchingly arrayed in their paper cartons. "And fill up two of those bottles with coffee," I added.

The door opened and the attendant entered. His face was a study as he scrutinized me. My glance fell to the bill he held in his hand.

"What's the matter, can't you change the ten?" I queried, puzzled by his strange action.

He came closer, biting his cheek, nervously, I thought.

"I didn't get a chance to change it," he exploded.

"Why, what happened?"

"What happened? Why, that girl you had with you pushed it into my hand and told me to keep the change."

"What do you mean," I demanded, *"had* with me?"

"Yes, *had.* She's gone!"

I stared at him—uncomprehending, yet alarmed. I pushed out of the way and dashed to the door.

He had told the truth—the car was gone!

A choking welled in my throat, my knees went weak, and for the moment the floor seemed to rock under my feet.

I turned to his stare. "I think she's just turning the car around," I muttered, although knowing full well she would never dare to do such a thing.

"Nothing doing," he explained. "She handed me the bill and then sliding into the driver's seat started the motor. Before I knew what was happening, she was moving out of the driveway."

"I didn't hear anything."

"She went slowly at first, sneaking, I thought. I was tempted to leap onto the running board and stop her, but I didn't know what was up and I didn't like the idea of getting mixed up in any trouble. Fact is, I had the idea it was a trick to get me away from the station so's you could hold up the wife," concluded the man.

"I don't blame you," I began, staring out into the downpour of rain. Then I lapsed into silence. What did it all mean? Why in the wide world had she deserted me in this lonely spot? No one, to my knowledge, had forced her to drive on. We had at least ten minutes or more clearance before the fastest of the pursuing machines would reach this station. That meant I must get away from here as quickly as possible, for they might stop and ask questions I dared not warn the attendant to evade. I must get away and get in touch with King and Wentworth, informing them of what had happened. Really, I ought to give chase to Diane.

"Say," I paused in my wild pacings before the attendant, whose eyes followed me tirelessly. "Have you a machine here capable of overtaking her?"

His face broke into a suspicious smile. "No, I haven't." He signaled his wife to silence when she broke in with. "The Lincoln, Jim—"

"But if you can wait a few minutes I'll call a young lad, the son of the local sheriff, who lives just a half mile off the road. The kid's a bug on speed and has the fastest little car you ever laid eyes on." There was a meaning wink to his wife as he said sheriff.

"Well, get hold of him!" I exploded.

"Take it easy. I'll phone." He took his way leisurely to the wall phone, cranked the generator, and sent in his call, his eyes never leaving my person. He certainly did not trust me!

He spoke for quite a time. He asked, "What are you willing to pay the lad?"

"Anything he wants—a hundred dollars, if he gets here within five minutes," I almost snarled—at my wit's end at the vexing deliberateness of the man.

I strode to the door, noting the sandwiches were ready. I paid for them and motioned for the woman to take them away.

One westbound car hummed past as I stood near the partly opened door. At length there came a far-off whine of an unmuffled motor. Two intensely brilliant lights came leaping from the east and a machine came to a sliding halt close to the filling tanks.

A young fellow, water dripping from his short leather coat and helmet, dashed into the door that I held open. He pushed his goggles up on his head and wiped his wind-reddened cheeks with a piece of cotton waste. "You the man who called for me?" After a sort of introduction and a recounting of what had happened he grinned slightly and said, "Pretty bad night for you to walk home, eh?"

"Not that," I thought quickly, "she's run off with a lot of valuable notes and plans of a new invention of mine," I lied.

"Oh, that's it. Well, come on, I'll get her or burn out Lizzie in the attempt."

WITH his aid I managed to squeeze myself into the tiny cockpit of the machine. It apparently was the product of a home workshop, the chassis being originally a model A Ford. The body had been replaced with a slim, streamline racing shell, scarcely wide enough for two to draw a deep breath in its narrow confines. There was no top, only a diminutive, slanting windshield to protect the rider. I could tell of the extreme care and perfect timing by the sharp, even murmur of the exhaust. Ray, (his surname had sounded like Heinen, but I wasn't sure) had to take on gas and I fretted at the loss of every second, for those in pursuit might be nearing the station any moment now. At last I gave a relieved sigh as he climbed in. Amid a shower of cinders and water raised by the fenderless wheels, we skidded out of the drive onto the concrete.

Man! How that machine climbed into mileage! It was a racing car and the willing way it took to high speed and held it without a quiver of complaint was amazing. Ray was an expert and the speedometer clicked off the miles to the deafening tune of a rocketing roar from the unmuffled motor. Withal it was making an impression on my memory that would stay with me until my dying day.

The car was much too light for the pace it was maintaining, and it slipped and skidded around the curves at unslackened speed. I no longer blamed Diane for becoming frightened, when I was driving at almost the same speed and with the same degree of carelessness. The fenderless wheels whipped a disc of water high into the air, from where it was thrown into our faces when the front wheels deviated from the straight path. Muddy water was trickling down into the corners of my mouth, mixing there with the salty tears of my wind-irritated eyes. My spectacles were poor protection.

At intervals the wet concrete was hurled under our car at eighty miles an hour and we overtook the machine I had seen pass the gas station. Ray gave just one short blast of his exhaust whistle and we flashed past as though it were at a standstill.

I began to wonder how far Diane was ahead of us; how fast she was traveling; if she had turned off on some side road; or if she would in some manner return to the gas station and find me gone.

"You'll know the car by the tail lights on each mudguard and the leather trunk," I shouted into Ray's ear as he restlessly juggled the wheel.

We zoomed up a steep grade, the speed dropping quickly. "Cross Roads" warned the yellow sign. A car stood on the road and a man with a flashlight signaled us to stop.

"What's the matter," demanded Ray. Our headlamps revealed the other machine, a ramshackle touring car, to have the left rear completely battered in and torn, while the wheel was nowhere in evidence. The hub was riding the concrete over which it had slewed in a wide, grooving path.

"Oly yurnpin' yiminy," exclaimed the farmer. "Here I come up the hill thinkin' I'm the only one on the road in this storm. I slow down to make my turn. Suddenly, right out of the sky comes bright lights and from behind me I hear a *Twat Twaa*. I get frightened, and before I can think—*Wham!* The whole car sails into the air. I look for the locomotive or whatever it might have been and I find it's one of those new, long cars. I could look right into it and I saw a young girl driving. She looked back and before I could lay hold of her she'd scooted down the side road."

"Which way?" I interrupted. Great joy overcame me. "She went south, toward Baalton. She was making a lot of noise; must have had a flat tire."

"Thanks, old man. We're after her. We'll send a tow truck," Ray said pulling into reverse. Off we were then. We didn't travel as fast on this road for it was gravel—rough and pitty—and very likely to throw us into the ditches. The rain still fell in a steady drizzle and the encompassing blackness was torn into confined brilliancy by the headlights. Up and down those choppy graveled hills we sped, the lights white hot and concentrated as we fairly leaped down the slopes, illuminating dimly the distant country-side as we poised briefly on the crests of the elevations. Afar off we sighted the lights of a town and a minute later we thundered into it, heading for the first group of lights marking a garage.

A commanding blast brought the heavy-set mechanic on the run. He nodded, with a grin, at our questions concerning a girl driving a front drive.

"You bet. She left here about five minutes ago. Don't know how she did it but she came in here with a flat that was no more—the inner tube was in ribbons. I switched one of the fender wheels and pulled the mudguard out of the way. She said she "was in a hurry—had slid into a fence up the road.""

"Enough," I declared. "Which way did she go?"

"Toward Adeline—south."

Off again. The chase was getting hotter!

As we sped over the gravel Ray commented, "Boy...she must be some girl! A little daredevil. I'd like to meet her!"

The thought must have pleased him, for he fed more gas to the leaping racer. Protecting my face the best I could from the wind, I wondered if the whole night was destined to continue this way. It seemed ages since the blithe moment I had stepped from the sedan. Diane!

Whatever was the cause of her sudden and unexpected action, it had evidently steeled her nerves to reckless abandon. Perhaps, the thought paralyzed me, the terrible strain and the racking experiences of the day had unbalanced her! I must get to her.

I doubt if anyone in the whole world had ever gone through what I had experienced since morning; witness the destruction of the only Television machine ever built, destruction wrought by some totally unknown enemies, escape, danger of capture, imprisonment, or even perhaps of death, by fleeing wildly across the state in company with the dearest companion in the world— and the climax to have her desert me. And for what reason? I could not fathom it and gave it up. Now I was pounding over shocking gravel in company with a youth I had never thought of existing an hour previous. Strange, indeed, are the tricks of fate!

Many were the times that the rear wheels would ride on the rubber bumpers, rebounding to the road with a swinging slide. Turns were but chilling skids of the rear wheels, which the driver corrected, with a reverse turn of the wheel and a vicious jam on the accelerator. He was driving hard, fast, and clean!

Stones, picked up by the tread of the tires, were thrown into the air, snapping sharply against the car body and close-by trees. The swishing grind of the larger ones was interrupted at intervals by the hollow *phlock* sound as the rubber impelled them, with considerable force, across the road. All the time trumpeted the barking exhaust, rising and falling in cadence.

"Those your lights?" shouted Ray suddenly.

Far in the distance two points of red twinkled for an instant. Yes, there she was! We drew nearer slowly, losing, for a time, the red dots as we dashed without caution around a series of curves. My heart now was filled with apprehension lest Diane crash into the deep ditches, for it was evident she was aware of a car following her and she was striving to stay as far ahead as possible.

However, when it came to driving, Ray was the more skillful, and the space lessened until our lights were playing about the rear trunk of the careening sedan. Our speeds were well in the fifties and I could not help but imagine the sight we must present to any of those farmer folk who might happen to see us pass.

First a far-off whining, blending into a rising roaring, increasing in volume as brightening, leaping lights on trees and road grew more intense. Then two cars, one long and black, slinking along, the other, white and small, thundering and screaming out a blasting exhaust whistle. A blatant disturbance in the stormy evening, fading abruptly with the lowering, pulsating cadence into a distant hollow hum, as red taillights dipped into the next declivity.

Seizing an opportunity, Ray tore alongside the sedan and after a brief radiator to radiator struggle, worked ahead just in time to clear a deep, water-filled rut. I believe luck smiled upon us that one time, for had Diane held her pace, we might have had to run her into the ditch to prevent a serious crash.

Once in the lead, Ray began to slacken his speed regardless of Diane's threatening efforts to slip past us. Watching her every move, he cut down the pace slowly.

Then, without the slightest of warnings, her lights swung away to the left and for a moment I thought she had crashed into the ditch. But when I saw the darker bulk of the sedan flashing through the trees down a narrow lane, my chilling fear passed, to be replaced by utter admiration. Diane, though we had been traveling close to thirty-five miles an hour, had spotted a lane, which we had passed without seeing, and made an abrupt swerve into it. Only the fact that the machine she was driving was low hung and pulled instead of pushed had made the feat possible. Otherwise, she would have turned turtle.

The stones ground as the speedster's locked tires bit into a quick halt. In reverse we roared back to the entrance of the lane. Rocketing in second gear, the light car sped in pursuit. Half a mile later we came to the lane's end. A farmyard littered with the usual farm implements met our questing light beams. Our cursory investigation convinced us Diane had not gotten this far; that she was somewhere between here and the other road. Perhaps, even now she was retracing her way down the lane. As a querulous door opened in the house we sped out of the yard.

Working on an idea that had suddenly struck me, I told Ray to drop me off and to continue up the road and that I would meet him at the crossroads in a short time.

Silence, except for the patter of rain on the road and the rustle of wet leaves returned as the putter of the racer's exhaust died away. When my eyes became accustomed to the grayish darkness I began following him, stopping numerous times to peer into thick masses of foliage growing close to the roadside. Barbed fences bordered the road and it was the hardly indistinguishable wires that I scrutinized. I had covered about a quarter of a mile when I became aware of a groaning whine to my right. I halted. There was no mistaking it! The low growl of gears rising in pitch to a shrill grind was too well known to me to make a mistake. It was my car off the road, and stuck in the mud! With a chuckle of satisfaction I turned off the road, plowed through the mucky gumbo of the ditch, and felt along the brush lined barbed wire fence, until I came to the break I expected. Behind a copse almost a hundred feet distant from the lane I heard the whining again. How in the world had she succeeded in plowing through so much mud! I descried the dim glow of the dash light illuminating the squares of the windows.

Creeping closer, crouching beside the bushes, I stole up behind the machine. Steadying myself by gripping the trunk, I chanced a momentary look into the sedan.

Diane, both hands on the upper part of the wheel, was intent in her work of loosening the car from the tenacious hold the mud had got on the wheels. The car lurched backwards unexpectedly and I leaped out of the way. With one hand on the running board I moved forward on the right side of the machine. One hand on the knob, I raised my head until my eyes were on the level with the lower panel. Then I stood upright and opened the door.

Instantly the girl's head jerked in my direction and the gasp she uttered came almost as a choke. Her eyes dilated with unknown fear and she made a movement as though she were going to flee through the other door.

"Well, Miss King," I heard my voice, harsh and strange, "just what do you mean by such unwonted actions? What was your idea running off like that? Deserting me?"

In answer her lips thinned to a narrow dark line. The lines of her chin became sharply defined.

I splashed around to the other side. Sullenly she opened the door lock and moved over to the other seat. I climbed in, switched on the dome light. She avoided my questioning gaze. Yet, as I studied her I saw it was a mask, a forced shell covering deeper emotion within her. Her whole attitude held a listless despair that was reflected in those deep violet eyes, reddened by crying.

"Diane," I said softly, "what happened; did someone frighten you?"

After a moment she shook her head. Her voice was colorless.

"No—and yes. Oh, Tom," her sobbed, "I can't—I can't tell you. Please don't ask me. I knew what I was doing, but please, don't ask me now."

CHAPTER THIRTEEN

THOUGH mystified and anxious to have her explanation, I turned my attention to the freeing of the car. With a great deal of quick shifting from forward to reverse and spinning of the wheels, I finally had it grinding its way across the field toward the lane. Another stubborn fight was necessary to get it through the ditch and up the steep shoulder to the gravel.

Nearing the crossroads I came upon Ray's speedster standing to one side, lights out, and motor idling. He started at once to roll alongside, but slackened when I signaled my intention to stop. He certainly took no chance of letting the sedan escape.

"Come inside," I invited as he came to the window. He entered the rear compartment, his wondering eyes settled on Diane, while something like a faint smile twitched in the corners of his lips.

Diane did not even glance in his direction, keeping a rigid stare out of the window.

"Where did you find her?" he queried, sensing the awkward atmosphere.

I recounted my experience since he had dropped me, concluding with my puzzled supposition as to why she had fled, though still laying much stress on my former statements concerning the plans of my fictitious invention.

He laughed when I had finished. "Well, whatever she did it for, she only knows," he agreed, adding, "there's one thing about blondes you have to watch out for—you can't depend on them—they're sly and tricky."

Thereat Diane turned quickly, regarding me through narrowed, tear-red lids.

"Cut it, Ray," I commanded, quietly, wishing him to be off as quickly as possible. "I am certainly glad to have met you." Reaching in my billfold, I gave him the sum I had promised.

AFTER the roar of his car had dwindled into the night, Diane and I sat gazing at each other; I awaited her explanation. She crouched in the corner of the seat, one arm resting on the seat-back. Her eyes became puzzled as the minutes dragged, swelled though they were by long weeping.

"Tom," she murmured at length in a low appealing voice, "I'm—happy that you followed and found me. Why did you do it?"

"Why? You ask me—why? Diane! Do you think I'd let you leave me without any reason or warning? At first it was a shock—an appalling climax to the series of disasters at Television Hill. But all those thoughts, everything, was wiped away by the thought of you, of your safety? Why, I don't know what I might have done had you managed to elude me."

"Goodness only knows what you've risked in following and overtaking me!"

"I'd follow you a million miles, if necessary."

A shadow of a smile flickered in her eyes at that. A solemn light came into her face.

"You really do love me," she stated rather than asked.

I could not refuse that admission! "Enough to forgive you for running away from me." I told her.

"To whom are you referring—to me or Diane King?" she murmured, her hand touching my shoulder.

"You or—Diane King," I repeated in amazement, for suddenly I grasped a fleeting idea of what she was striving to make me understand. "Say, just what are you driving at? Surely…?"

"Tom," she began, "I am going to tell you the reasons for my unexpected behavior tonight. First, I want you to believe me, when I say my love for you is as great as yours is for me.

"I—know I can't—oh—Tom, I'm not Diane King," came her startling words, uttered with pleading light from her eyes. "The real Diane King is far away from here—down on that island that Dad—Mr. King found so unfortunately. I am just as the heroine is in your novel. I'm an agent—a spy, in simple, damning words—I'm a spy, who, on the verge of being discovered, tried to escape.

"My story, Tom, I know you would never believe it but for the indisputable facts and incidents you were witness to during the year you were at Television Hill with me. Why, even you unconsciously hit upon the real cause of trouble when you told me of the scheme you were using to get rid of your fictitious Television machine at the end of your story. When you first told me of it, I thought you had guessed my identity. It seemed too much of a striking coincidence that you should devise such a parallel sequence of characterization, to base it on fiction. You frightened me at first and I planned to draw your confession, your admission, or your knowledge, by pretending to reciprocate your attentions. That is where the change began. I found that you didn't even dream of such an affair ever being possible in life and that you even doubted it could be successfully undertaken in fiction. And that," she broke off to turn her attention to a car coming up the road, "—that is how I came to know and to love you."

"Diane!"

"Please, Tom, please hear me through," she begged. "Tom, you saw that island; you saw the civilization that has grown up there; you saw the great engineering feats they have accomplished. I have seen them, Tom. Not through the distorted eyes of Television, but with my own! I am native—that is my land—my country—my home, and the thought of what my people are working toward in their secretive, yet compelling way, fills me with pride. Tom, you know what patriotism is! You may have felt it during the last war period—that enlivening, thrilling, soul tingling joy to put your hand, your life, if necessary, behind your cause, your home, and your ideals. If you only could realize what boundless joy it is for those of my country and race to aid in the continuance of the greatest plan, the most amazing policy, ever attempted for the sole purpose of saving the world from the impending chaos that daily is growing nearer and more evident. But, Tom, you don't know—you couldn't understand, even if I were to tell you everything I know. You would be filled with apprehension—if not horror.

"I dare not tell you more than you have seen. That island is not of late appearance; it has been there for untold centuries, and its people have mingled among the races of the world since forgotten ages—working, scheming, and planning for the great day!

"Just to give you an example of how we work, I'm going to tell you of my part in Television Hill. It was in 1920 that word was first sent to us through our Intelligence Bureau warning our leaders of a possible danger in the research being conducted by one Mr. King of Chicago. Promptly an investigation was made and King was spotted. That is, he was kept under surveillance by operatives we caused to be placed in his employ. You know, Tom, Mr. King is very susceptible to men who are intelligent, and who are filled with ambition, and so there was no difficulty experienced in having such well recommended persons as Alexander Chalmers, John Somerset, and Ralph Smythe placed in responsible positions where they could aid and yet hinder King, should he become a hazard. But we underestimated the combined knowledge of King and Wentworth. Together, they tore down the barriers these hardworking operatives built up and in the end they were successful in their quest. They had built up an actual Television machine.

"Now, Tom, this is where I entered. When Television had become an actuality, it was necessary to work along with King in his desire to keep it a secret. Diane, the real daughter of King, was induced to go to Europe by a girl acquaintance, and there occurred the substitution! Diane and I have but slight physical differences, and as five years would elapse between the time she had left home, these differences would go unnoticed. I had plenty of opportunity to study the girl whose life I was to live, mimicking her in action and speech until, when the day came and I returned, Mr. King never suspected for a single second that a total stranger—an enemy in truth, was posing as his own child. Protected by this knowledge, I could act as I pleased—going where I wished—asking what I desired to know—and taking into concealment those plans and models Chalmers and Smythe wished to smuggle from the plant.

"Do you understand now, Tom, my reasons for being so interested in the machinery? You often would go into wild conjecture as to the cause of my open-mouthed wonder. You see, now?"

I had sat there, one hand clenched on the steering wheel, staring incredulously into her comely face the while she was speaking. Her eyes had never wavered once; she was telling the truth. The awful, impossible truth!

"Yes, Diane," I commented. "I understand. I see everything. I was going to ask you how it was you and Eloise got along so nicely, speaking so intimately of affairs and incidents since you had met at high school, thinking I'd trip your story there. But I see now how widespread is the influence of your people. Yet, Diane, there is one question I'd like to have you answer. What are you going to do if Jim, Diane's brother, ever comes to see you?"

For a moment I detected a laughing light in her eyes. "What will happen?" she countered. "Why, nothing."

"You mean you'll carry the deception through as you have before?"

"That won't be necessary. Do you know the G.E. people have been considering sending him and his wife to live in the Argentine, to take command of their interests there? Right now Jim must be somewhere off the coast of South America," she concluded.

"So that puts him out of the way?"

She nodded.

For another period I studied her.

"What would you do if I were to tell King about the things you have just related—tell him of your identity?"

"You see, Tom," she said, seemingly ignoring my question, "King did not have the least conception of the tremendous powers he was so rashly resisting, when he hurled his defiance at our envoy, who had been prepared to complete the whole negotiations involving the transference of the television plant peacefully and satisfactorily to both parties. He brought destruction upon himself—just after he had been warned. It is through him only that superior forces were forced to step in and carry through a series of maneuvers, which would crush into oblivion the one real danger point on the face of the globe. These same superior forces will take care of King and Wentworth, even though the latter manage to escape the welcome Somerset and his men are going to extend to them at Lake Geneva.

"And…" She paused, while a quiet smile broke over those lips which had been twisted in tears so shortly before. "…and as for you, I can take care of you! I took advantage of the chance at the gas station and intended to leave you stranded there with memories only—and a story you would not dare to tell the authorities for fear of being branded as insane. I drove like mad, knowing you would attempt to follow me, and would have disappeared altogether, if I hadn't crashed into the rear of an ancient touring car. After that, well, I did my best to elude you."

OF ALL the incredible tales I had ever heard of or read this was the climax of impossibility! Yet, stunned and sick in mind though I was, I knew it was the truth. Yes, this was the reason for her unique interest in things mechanical! And, too, this explained all her other strange actions; why she had always managed to be present at the various meetings and conferences held either among the men or personally between King and Wentworth.

And King had been so confiding to her! She, an enemy artfully concealed in a cloak of resemblance, playing as his daughter, leeching him of his secrets, his plans, his knowledge, which he would not even trust to Wentworth! Overcome with anguish and a wave of sudden despondency, I turned away from her.

As I gazed unseeing through the windshield, an electrifying chill swept over me. If everything was as she depicted, what was to be my fate!

I flashed a glance at her and saw she was watching me with steady contemplative eyes. With a deep breath I tugged at the starter button. Driving slowly, I stared dumbly ahead at the wet gravel, dodging the ruts only by mechanical impulse. I could not think. The world was one madhouse of plotting and intrigue, and it mattered not what I thought; others could do that for me!

Shortly, we passed through Adeline, and making a left turn we rolled toward Mt. Morris. Meaningless miles of splashing, slipping gravel grinding under the tires slipped through the tunnel of night, while the right mudguard clanked and rattled in a steady shimmy.

Oregon appeared and I sought and found a drug store close by the railroad crossing.

"What are you going to do?" queried Diane, grasping my arm as I made to climb out of the car.

"I'm going to call up the Municipal airport at Chicago and find out if there is any word yet from your Dad—from Mr. King," I corrected myself, adding, as I removed the keys from the lock, "And you're coming in with me this time."

Together we entered the door. The clerk, after a start, stood gaping at us. We did appear rather strange. My hat was soggy and battered from the elements and my raincoat sticky with half-dried mud, as was my face where my handkerchief had failed to remove all of the evidence of the wild ride in the speedster. My shoes were enlarged lumps of mud. Altogether, I was as much of a wreck in appearance as I was mentally.

Diane, on the other hand, was a picture by contrast. Her clothing bore no signs of disturbance but were spotless and trim. Even the curling fluff of hair stealing out beneath the edge of her close fitting hat gave no indication of our recent thrilling chase. A few expert touches of a powder puff had camouflaged all traces of redness about her eyes.

She took command of the situation instantly.

"Isn't he a sight," she laughed making an attempt to cut away some of the mud from my features with her handkerchief. "We should have waited until someone came along."

"Right after the worst of the storm," she explained to the Clerk, "we skidded into the ditch and Tom—he went out in all the rain and worked in the water and mud until we were back on the road. Why, he must have built a solid pavement of rails he pulled off some farmer's fence."

The clerk laughed with her and showed me the way to a washroom. Returning to the store proper, I found her perched on a lunch counter stool, sipping coffee.

"Hungry?" I inquired in a strange, husky voice.

"I'm famished," she nodded, closing one eye in a slow mischievous wink, which brought a responsive scowl from me. I retreated to the phone booth and put in a call to Chicago. The operator informed me it would be some time before connections could be completed.

While waiting I seated myself beside Diane and ordered sandwiches and coffee. The clerk was interested in us and imparted some information.

"We certainly did have one whopper of a storm here this afternoon. For a time I thought the roof was going to be blown off this store."

"Much damage done?" I asked.

"Well, we don't know yet. Practically all the phone lines are down in the vicinity. The storm seemed concentrated east of the river, where it's said to have come close to being a cyclone. But talk about lightning! Why, it just rained from the clouds! Several motorists came in here about six o'clock and said that the big radio plant between Grand Detour and Dixon was completely in flames."

"Anyone hurt?" Asked Diane with concern.

"I really don't know. Must have been, Miss, as there were over a hundred men employed there. They lived with their families in a little industrial village close to the plant. Still, I remember a sudden rush of motor cars and trucks this afternoon when the storm first began; maybe they fled fearing a cyclone was on the way. We thought so, too, for a while."

The phone interrupted and I hastened to the booth.

"Municipal airport—Chicago, speaking," came the metallic reproduction of a heavy voice in my ear. Diane stood near the partly opened door.

"A plane—a crimson Lockheed Amphibian. Commercial 4956 was supposedly headed in your direction. Can you tell me if it has arrived?"

"Wait a moment..." I heard the voice fade away into a murmur with, "Say, Roberts, what was the number of that crate?"

I listened closely, trying vainly to make out the distant murmur of voices, sensing unpleasant news. A moment later came the inquiry, "Who is speaking?"

"Thomas McManus, an employee of Mr. King and Mr. Wentworth who were in the plane."

"I see," There was silence. Then, "I'm afraid we have sorrowful news, Mr. McManus; a ship of the type you describe and bearing those identification numbers has been reported to have crashed and burned near Roselle, Illinois. The two occupants did not escape."

The receiver dropped from my hand and I turned a blanched face to Diane. She recoiled from the expression of utter anguish that must have aged my features in the space of a second. With a shuddering gasp I drew my senses together and picked up the receiver. My voice, dead and colorless, brought sympathy from the man at the other end. He told me to go to Roselle to complete the identification of the remains.

Leaving the booth, I moved in an unseeing sea of bewilderment over to Diane. Grasping her by the arm I led her to the door. On the step I paused, and gazed long into the comely, frightened face of the girl. "Diane," I mumbled thickly. "Your Dad—King and Wentworth crashed to their deaths—near Roselle."

For a moment she returned my gaze, then, with a little cry she drew away from me. Taking her again by the arm I led her to the car. Under the street light the once beautiful sedan presented an aged appearance. The entire right side was battered and dented, while the mudguards, once so sparkling and perfectly curved, were crumpled and torn. A deep gash compressed the panels of both doors.

Everything about me was going down in destruction!

And the perpetrator of destruction was this trim, lovable slip of a girl who stood beside me, her arm entwined about mine. I now was ready to resign myself to the fate that seemed to be the only logical end of this day's horrible experiences.

CHAPTER FOURTEEN

THE memory of that night will ever be imprinted in my mind. Diane drove south from Oregon, and we started the circling swing to the west around the bend in the river. Afar off we saw a glow in the murky skies and as we drew nearer, we came upon the smoldering ruins of the various structures on Television Hill. There were quite a number of machines parked about the entrance to the private lane. We paused for a while.

In the dripping silence we could hear a puttering of motor boats and I looked to Diane. What did that mean? The Bridge? We stole away then and took up the trail toward Chicago.

The following days were a hectic confusion, in which grief and joy were mingled in an intolerable mixture. Diane and I were subjected to a continuous round of questioning by newspapermen and state officials, who wanted an explanation of the strange affairs that had taken place before and during the storm. Diane held the center of the stage, representing herself as the daughter of King, which she was to all appearances, and carried on practically all the conversations. I only agreed with her when it was absolutely necessary. The latter part of the investigation had been held at Television Hill where only responsible men in the state's employ were permitted to enter the portals. When they had finally gone, Diane and I started out on a trip of exploration over the whole Hill.

The bridge still stood. What had happened that horrible night of destruction was that the inquisitive mobs were unable to force their way by the watchman, who guarded the barred gate at the bridge entrance. Therefore, a few had brought motor launches up the river to gain the other shore. But there, as we expected, the high fence had halted them.

Pausing beside the ruin of the projection house I studied it, wondering if it would be necessary to rebuild the flame-seared walls from the foundation up. The fire had gutted the entire structure with the exception of the reinforced concrete first floor upon which all the charred debris of the two upper floors had collapsed. The projection theatre, the projection tunnel and its secrets, and the well-equipped developing department were gone. Gone beyond recognition.

Turning aside, she and I passed through the trees to the powerhouse. With extreme care we picked our way over the burned timbers, through the control rooms to the generator room. Tears came to my eyes as I gazed upon the destruction that had been wrought here. It was as though a huge shell had torn into the north end of the building, crumbling a section of the wall. The wood sheathing of the entire roof had burned away, leaving only the latticework of steel arches silhouetted against the sky. The rain and burning embers had fallen on the generator assemblies; they were covered with rust where the flames had licked the paint away. Cautiously we made our way forward over the three-inch deep layer of ashes, hesitating a moment to regard the blackened windings of the two northern generators. It appeared as though oil had seeped into the wells below and the ensuing cauldrons of flame had done their worst. Although the transformer section was directly over the battery sub-basement, wherein the burning oil had seeped, it had withstood the terrific heat better than expected, and blackened by a thick layer of oil smoke, which adhered to everything, little other damage seemed to have been done to the huge transformers. Nevertheless, much of the lighter supporting grillwork had bent under its heavy burdens and all of the glass-floored balconies were only steel tracings—the glass having melted and dropped to the concrete floor from which all the rubber mattings had disappeared. It took me just one glance to see the utter shambles of mixed rubber-encrusting, melted glass, fallen wires, and oil residue that lay in the evil-smelling sub-basement. I wondered, vaguely, if it ever would be possible to clear that mess out.

Sick at heart, I took Diane's hand and led her out and away from the place. Together we plodded up the hill. The oil storage tanks next underwent our investigation. Diane supplied the information of how they had been set afire.

"Tommy," she said, anxious eyes peering into my drawn face, "I'm a horrible wretch. I'm sorry I ever agreed to work against Mr. King. He was such a pleasant and lovable man, never once did he suspect my duplicity. After looking upon those ruins, I could almost wish myself dead. To think that I was responsible for the entire destruction. Oh, it's horrible."

"You? What part did you take in the burning of the plant?"

"I became frightened by those heavy sheets of lightning. You see, Tommy, that wasn't natural lightning—at least some of it. It came from—from above," she stammered indefinitely. "I was afraid they would hit the cottage, would kill someone; so I signaled Chalmers to go ahead and aid those above."

"Signaled Chalmers? How and when?"

"When I went to my room during dinner. There's a secret telephone concealed in my room connected up with Chalmers' line. It was put in when the cottage was built.'

"When the cottage was built! Why that was over five years ago!"

"Yes," she asserted defiantly, "five years ago that phone was placed in that room, while Dictaphone apparatus was installed in all the rooms of the cottage. All the wires led to Chalmers' office. There he could listen in to anything King and Wentworth might try to conceal from him. Similarly, the rest of the plant was wired."

"And-" I commented when she paused.

"Why, can't you see it? Can't you see that Chalmers and Smythe had as much to do with the designing of the plant as Wentworth, who in actuality was the adviser? Everything here was laid out just as they wished. The reservoir was an important part in the plan and by means of proper handling, Wentworth was prevented from taking the logical step of running a spur track here to transport the crude oil. The tanks were built with a double bottom, in which benzene was placed with a valving arrangement to permit its being withdrawn quickly into an underground pit. Should its need ever be dispensed with, all that was necessary to send the tanks into flames was an electric spark, which was applied at my command that afternoon. The shattered tanks permitted the oil to flow down the hill toward the powerhouse—as planned."

"Diane! That isn't true! Such a thing couldn't be done!"

"No?" she queried, narrowing her eyes. "Well, take a look at those tanks."

I looked over the torn sheeting and saw that she had spoken the truth; the tanks had had a double bottom. There could be no doubt about that.

"I see," I said weakly, overcome by the intrigue of the whole affair. After a long moment, I started to walk up the hill. Diane falling in step beside me.

The projector loomed ahead of us. It had survived the crush of destruction without a trace of damage, and was still pointing toward the north, where last we had looked upon New Glarus. I unlocked the man-gate and we entered the enclosure.

I gazed about me contemplatively as we silently walked across the suspended bridge-way to the massive foundation flooring of the tripod towers. How I wished Wentworth was again beside me, showing me the wonder of television as he had done a short year ago! Espying the ladder ascending the tower leg. I told Diane I was going to go up and take a look about.

Hand over hand I climbed up the rusty steel rungs. Hearing a rustle below me, I glanced down into the upturned features of Diane just a few feet below me.

"Watch your step, Diane," I warned. "The top is sixty feet above the flooring." Anxiously, I climbed the rest of the way and awaited her. At length she stood in safety beside me on the level, guard-railed platform.

About twenty feet away was the companion platform and between both was slung the great bulk of the projector housing. I fully appreciated the weird appearance of the projector assembly now from my elevated position. Thick circular legs dropping down to the spreading mass of the flooring, a bridge-like extension running off to the encircling rack-rail track was the impression presented.

After a long interval I turned to the girl. The breeze was whipping her blonde hair about her fine features and a rare smile played about her lips as she stared, unaware of my gaze, off into the south. I could scarcely believe her to be the same cold, calculating, creature she tried to make me believe she was.

"Diane."

She turned with the same smile. "Why do you persist in calling me Diane?"

I frowned. "Why—because that's all I know you by."

"I'll make a bargain with you, Tommy. You tell me what you intend to do with Television Hill now that you are the remaining official and I'll tell you my real name. Remember, no secrets!"

"Who could keep a secret from you—you violet-eyed fay!" I laughed. "Since the moment you gave me the reassuring news that it wasn't King and Wentworth who crashed in the Lockheed, but two other men of your people who were to lure me to Chicago and take me prisoner there. I've lost a lot of my fear of them. I've been thinking of calling upon the Government to aid me in rebuilding the entire plant."

She laughed merrily. "Oh, no, you're not! What do you suppose I'll be doing while you're trying to carry out those rash plans?"

"Why," I declared drawing her into my arms, "you'll be doing just what you vowed to do before a justice of the peace and two witnesses just two days ago! 'To love—and obey!'"

"To love? Yes, Tom. But to obey…? That is another question." Her lips held a ravishing, inviting bow, which faded away quickly as we heard the sound of someone coming across the plank walk of the truss below. She darted to the rail, gazed for a moment, then turned with her hand compressed to her mouth.

"Tommy," she pleaded, pushing me to the opposite side of the platform. "Please, turn around and don't look until I tell you. I want to surprise you."

Somewhat fearful, for I did not know what sort of tricks this resourceful bit of femininity might yet play on me, I did as she requested. I heard the scrape of feet as someone clambered through the opening in the platform.

"Dad," cried Diane. A man's gruff voice answered. Instantly I turned. Amazement, utter and surprising, shocked me into silence.

There was no mistaking the wrinkled, squint-eyed features of the man who stood beside the smiling Diane.

"Chalmers!" broke the exclamation from my lips. "You! What are you doing here?"

"Business, Tom, business," he grinned in his usual humorous manner, winking to the girl, who watched his every move with adoring eyes.

"First, Tom, I'm returning to take my former position so as to be able to prevent you from making any attempts to rebuild Television Hill, or cause it to be rebuilt; secondly, to do as much as I can in the silencing of those rumors which may later circulate as to the destruction of the plant being done by a foreign power; and lastly, to see how my little girl was getting along since she has become Mrs. McManus."

Diane, arm about his thin shoulders, smiled happily at me.

"She—Diane—your daughter?"

I stammered as I spoke, and everything began to take on more clarity.

He nodded, chuckling. "Where else did you suspect she'd got that devilish spirit of adventure? King's daughter, Diane, may look like my Ruth, but she's got to step some to keep up with my girl. What Ruth says—goes. Eh?"

"Sometimes, Dad," she dissented.

"Well, anyway, if Ruth says Television Hill stays ruined— ruined it stays, then.

There was no trace of humor in his voice as he uttered the last statement.

I turned aside, gazing toward the north and the wide bend of the river. Would it be worthwhile to attempt anything in the line of rebuilding this much-wanted marvel of the age? A marvel which our unknown friendly enemies of the south seemed to hold a great peril to their plans, and who were, therefore, determined to keep its revealing presence away from the unsuspecting world. I knew I could restore every bit of Television Hill even to the smallest tube with the aid of the complete set of plans King had hidden in a well-concealed storm cellar close by the hangar. The remark he had made previous to the storm had caused me to make an investigation of the grounds during a free period immediately after we had returned to Television Hill, the day after the disaster, and I had found it. But even with this aid I would need financial backing, a backing that would be willing to furnish ten, twenty, or even thirty million dollars. That is why I thought of the Government. As another associated idea struck me, I confronted Chalmers, "Say, Chalmers, what about those duplicate blue prints King sent to the War Department? What if Uncle Sam should decide to build a Television machine after hearing of the wrecking of this plant?"

"Don't worry about that, McManus—that was taken care of months ago. Some of the plans still are in the Governmental vaults, but the essential and important details are missing! Did you think we'd 'slip' there?" He laughed in downright amusement.

"And say, Tom," he chuckled. "I might as well be frank with you and tell you that Smythe is right at this moment digging out the contents of the vault near the hangar!"

THE END